The Gone Man

The Gone Man

Brad Solomon

Random House: New York

Library of Congress Cataloging in Publication Data

Solomon, Brad.
    The gone man.

    I. Title.
PZ4.S68832 Go [PS3569.0595]   813'.5'4
ISBN 0-394-41274-5   77-5992

Manufactured in the United States of America
9 8 7 6 5 4 3 2
First Edition

The Gone Man

For
My Parents
Jacqui
Steve Haberman

1

Nine-thirty in the morning. The phone's ringing. I'm nervous already. I'm afraid to answer it.

A goddamn ball of courage. That's me. Don't even have the guts to answer the phone.

It's still ringing.

I know what I want it to be. I want it to be a case. I need a case.

If it starts off simple, that'll be okay. As long as it doesn't end up simple. I don't want something that ends up simple.

Please, Charlie! Answer the phone!

But what'll I do if it isn't a case?

"Hello," I say.

Settle down, Charlie. It *has* to be a case.

"Hello," I say.

"I want to speak Mr. Charles Quinlan, please . . ."

A stiff, measured voice. I don't recognize it.

"This's Charlie Quinlan," I say.

"Yes . . . Good . . . I am Mr. Simson speaking . . ."

Simson. Means nothing to me. I hope it's something good.

"I am speaking on behalf Mr. Ethan Stockton . . ."

Stockton. Damn. Why am I so nervous? You'd think I never had a case before. Settle down, Charlie.

". . . regarding arrangement of interview this morning if such is possible . . ."

Did I get it right? Ethan Stockton?

"All must be kept very quiet . . . Very confidential, please . . ."

Yeah. This'll be good. I feel a little better now.

"Very confidential ... You must understand that ..."

No problem, friend. I don't understand much, but I understand confidential. Everybody wants things kept confidential. I understand Ethan Stockton, too.

"You please meet Mr. Ethan Stockton at offices Sunset Boulevard ..."

I know where those offices are. I can make money on this one, all right.

"Please to arrive eleven o'clock exact if would be convenient ..."

It's convenient. I've been waiting for something like this.

"Mr. Quinlan? ... You there, please? ... You understand, please?"

"I got you," I say. "Confidential and quiet. You want me to bring one gun or two?"

He doesn't say anything. It gets very quiet.

Nice going, Charlie. You blew it already. Better do better.

"Just joking, Mr. Simson. Eleven o'clock? That's when you want me there?"

"Yes, Mr. Quinlan ... Eleven o'clock exact, please ... Thank you."

He hangs up.

Short and sweet, just like that.

Sounds simple, huh?

We'll see.

Oh boy.

I hope I can keep it cool.

2

Earlier in the summer things were slow. I was going out of my mind. I'd come in in the morning, stare at the phone and think: Things're getting to you, Charlie. Watch it.

But I didn't do anything about it and things only got worse.

They began shooting the new TV season. Danny, a friend

who's an assistant director out at Universal, called me every couple of days to come out there and work as an extra. I usually went out when he called. Danny's a good guy. He'd try to get me some lines to say so they'd have to pay me more. So money wasn't a problem.

Still, I needed something. I needed some action.

You know how it gets? When all you do is sit around and wait for things to get popping? And nothing pops? You get restless, don't you?

One night I found out how bad off I was.

Carolyn and I were at a bar in Hollywood. A guy started to get fresh with her. I saw my chance and tried to pick a fight with him. He wasn't dumb enough or drunk enough. He backed off. I let it go, but it was close.

I felt like hell about the whole thing. I like to think I'm not that kind of guy.

Carolyn didn't like it, either. She told me I was nuts. I told her she was right. She told me to do something about it. I told her I didn't know what to do. She said she saw that. Then she shut up for the rest of the night.

I'll tell you the truth. I was getting worried.

3

In August, I got a call from a friend with a summer theater in Northern California. I went up and did a small part for him. A production of *Damn Yankees*. I wanted to get out of town, so I went.

It worked. It was the first time I'd been on a stage in over two years. I got to say a couple funny lines and sing some songs and smile while the audience applauded. It felt good. Damn it, it felt too good, but I'm not going back to that.

Anyway, it gave me back my sanity, or whatever sanity I've got left these days.

I did three weeks of that, counting rehearsal time. Then a

5

week's freedom in San Francisco. I didn't call my mother while I was up there. I didn't want to deal with that.

Then back to the city of rubber walls. I thought: You're okay, Charlie. You're ready to go up against Los Angeles again.

I aired out the apartment, called some people to tell them I was back in town, checked my answering service and reopened my office. I was back in business.

Nothing happened for a week.

But something's happening now. I've got the call from Mr. Simson, whose name doesn't mean a thing to me.

On behalf Mr. Ethan Stockton, whose name means plenty.

You know what it means?

It means money.

4

Brother, does it mean money.

If you can tell anything from names, it sounds solid enough. If you can tell anything from names, which you can't.

But I've heard some things about Ethan Stockton. They say he's slightly older than the century and probably one of the fifty richest men in California. I don't know exactly how much money that means, so it must mean lots.

He wants to see a private detective. Maybe he has some trouble. Or maybe he just wants to see a guy played for a fool and almost killed, which has happened on occasion. If that's it, I'm available and he's a client who can pay. Not all my clients can.

Still, I do okay.

I drive down Sunset and park on a side street. The offices are *STOCKTON FILM, INC.*, a solid brick building which takes up the entire block. There's an elevator attached to the outside of the building. One of those glass-walled jobs which start on the sidewalk and go straight up the wall.

The thing takes me all the way up to the fifth floor, where I find myself in a spacious reception room. California contemporary.

6

Lots of furniture you can see through. A plexiglass standing clock near the far wall says 10:45.

A receptionist sits at an oversized glass-and-chrome table. This is fine with me, since she's got a very short dress and the kind of legs some men write songs about.

So far, everything looks just dandy. It's Monday morning and I'm ready to start a new case. I feel good.

5

"I don't mean to interrupt," the receptionist says. "I'm just getting curious. You going to stare at me that way all day?"

I'll give it a shot.

"I'd like to," I say. "You mind?"

"A little. Your mother should've taught you better manners."

"She tried. I was a poor student. It didn't take."

Why is it when I smile and try my best to make like Warren Beatty it still comes out Charlie Quinlan?

"Got an appointment with someone?" she says.

"What do you think about Indonesian food?" That line usually throws them.

"To tell the truth, I don't really think about it."

"They got this thing they call a *rijsttafel*. Means rice table. They give you a big thing of rice and a lot of different courses. You put a little rice on your plate and then have one of the courses. You take a little more rice with each course. It's good. But you got to like hot stuff. Some of it's sort of hot."

"Sounds interesting. Where do you go for this kind of food?"

I'm going to make it. Indonesian food usually does the trick.

"Westwood Boulevard. A block or two down from Wilshire."

"Okay. I'll give it a try sometime."

I'm not going to make it. Guess I'm not her type.

I say, "You didn't get the message, huh?"

"I got the message. You got my answer. Now you got an appointment?"

"I'm really striking out."

"I'd say you are."

"White flag. I give up. You win."

"Hey! Hold on! I'm thinking it over!"

"I still got a chance?"

"Let me think about it. This could be a lot of fun, seeing you make a fool out of yourself. But first I got to know something."

"Have I got an appointment."

"Right. If you're just here to fool around, I might get to saying some things I wouldn't want to say to someone who's got business here. You wouldn't want me to do that and get in trouble, right?"

"Don't worry. Nobody gets in trouble with me." She looks great. Maybe she wants me to be more aggressive. "I'm never much on Monday mornings. That's the problem. Would you go for something traditional?"

"I might."

"You ought to be in pictures."

"I keep telling my agent the same thing."

An actress! Come on, Charlie. You can handle an actress.

"Your agent doesn't listen?"

"Sure. That's why I'm sitting here answering phones."

"Get a new agent."

"Yeah, I figured you're in the business. I figured actor or agent. Agent, huh?"

"Nope."

"You're an actor?"

Am I an actor?

"Not exactly an actor, either."

"You sure? You say it like you're not sure."

"I'm not in the business. I was, but I'm not. I'm in another business now. One that pays."

"Uh huh. Look, I like guys trying to pick me up, even if I figure I'm not going to let 'em get very far, but you still got to tell me something—you got an appointment?"

"I been trying to get one for five minutes."

"I know. You shouldn't come on so strong."

"It's awful, isn't it?"

8

Sometimes they like it when you agree with them.

"Let me try and help," she says. "Back off a little. Maybe it'll work better."

"I'm always open for suggestions."

"With the lines you got, you better be."

A thin, efficient-looking woman appears in the doorway. The kind of secretary who usually gets hired by the boss's wife.

"Got to hold on a minute," the receptionist says. "Looks like the fun's over."

6

The thin woman marches across the carpet, looks down at the receptionist and says, "It's almost eleven. I told you to have those release forms prepared and ready by eleven."

"I finished them half an hour ago," the receptionist says. "I put them on Mr. Stockton's desk."

The two women look each other over, with little love lost in their looks.

"I didn't tell you to put them on Mr. Stockton's desk," the thin woman says. "I told you to put them on *my* desk."

"*Mr. Stockton* told me to put them on *his* desk."

They do some more looking at each other. The thin woman was all set to chew the girl into little bits, but now she's lost her opening. She doesn't like it. I've seen what's happened, so she doesn't like me, either.

"Are you Mr. Quinlan?" she says.

"That's me."

"Mr. Stockton called in from his car telephone and said he'd be a few minutes late. He hoped you wouldn't mind the wait."

"No problem."

"You're sure?"

"I'm sure. Things're getting interesting around here."

"Very well." She looks at the receptionist. Back at me. Around the room. Back at me. Then she gives up.

She turns and goes out through the doorway.

"Who's the ice maiden?"

"Miss Blitman."

"She always so sweet?"

"A little worse, lately. We been having problems around here."

"Yeah? Like what?"

"Like it's none of your business, Mr. Quinlan. So you got an appointment with the boss. I'm impressed."

Impressed? Time to move in.

"If I'd known it'd impress you, I'd've brought it up myself."

"No you wouldn't. You would've been cute and played around it."

"You got me pegged. Why're you impressed?"

"Mr. Stockton doesn't make appointments to see people. He just talks to people on the phone. You important?"

"I don't know. All I know, I was trying to make it with a sexy receptionist. I wasn't getting anywhere."

"You really don't give up."

"If I really thought you wanted me to give up, I'd probably give up."

"What're you going to do now? Hand me another line?"

This one is almost as cautious as I am.

"You always so defensive?"

"This's a film company. I meet a lot of weirdos here."

"Don't take it all out on me. You from Los Angeles?"

"Are you kidding? Is anyone?"

"I am."

"You must be the only one. You know what they say. Somebody turned the country on its side and everything that wasn't tied down ended up in California."

"Lady, this's dream city. People came here chasing dreams. They still do. Sometimes it works, but dreams're a tricky business. Where'd you come from?"

"Seattle. I worked with a theater company up there. I started getting good parts, I thought maybe I was ready to come down

10

here. So I came down here. That was two years ago. Now I answer phones and put up with Miss Blitman. And guys like you."

"Two years ain't so long. You got the looks. Maybe you'll make it if you stick to it."

"You're a man who knows?"

"I'm a man who doesn't know much of anything. I know this. This's a tough town. And it's a tough business. It destroys people."

"Come on."

"I mean it. I was in the business. Till I found something else I could make a buck with. But I know something about this town. And I know a couple guys who used to be in the business. And now they're dead." Charlie! Don't go into it! "And if they hadn't been in the business, maybe they wouldn't be dead now."

"You really tell nice stories, don't you?"

"Don't get me wrong. I love the business. But I got out 'cause it scares the hell out of me. If you're going to stick with it, you got to know what you're up against."

"Mister, I'm going to make it. Sooner or later, I'm going to make it."

"If someone told you the only way you could make it in the business, you'd have to kill to make it—could you kill to make it?"

"What? I don't know. How'd I know? That's crazy."

"That's not a bad answer."

"Huh?"

"If you said yes, you *could* kill, I'd be scared to death. And if you came right out and said no, you couldn't, I'd figure you'd never make it. But if you got to stop to think it over, even for a second, then maybe you got a chance."

"You're nuts."

"Yeah. I know. But that's the business, lady. You got to want it so bad, you're not sure *what* you'd be willing to do to make it. It's that kind of business."

"You make it sound lousy."

"It *is* lousy. But if you're really hot for it, you got to stick with it. I understand that part of it, too."

11

7

Miss Blitman's in the doorway again.

"Mr. Quinlan," she says, "Mr. Stockton will see you now."

I'm not finished with the receptionist yet. I lean toward her and say, "Got any pictures and résumés?"

"Sure. I always have some with me."

"Give me a couple. I know some people, I'll give them your résumé."

"What'll it cost me?"

She's been in Los Angeles for a while, all right.

"Nothing," I say. "It's my gift. Free of charge."

"I heard that one before, too. If I give you my résumé, what else I got to do for you?"

"Lady, you don't have to do anything for me. You don't have to eat Indonesian food, you don't even have to see me again. Look, you want me to give out some résumés for you or you want to forget about it?"

Believe me, lady. I really mean it. Strange experience, but I'm telling you the truth.

The receptionist pulls open a drawer and takes out two eight-by-ten glossies. She slides them across the desk. "I hope you're not just trying to get my phone number."

"I'll give them to some people. No guarantees."

I turn and start for Miss Blitman. She's doing one of those foot-tapping numbers on the floor.

"Mr. Quinlan," the receptionist says, "maybe I get too suspicious sometimes . . . Anyway, thanks."

I walk back to the receptionist. Miss Blitman says, "Mr. Quinlan!" but I ignore her.

"I hate to kill a good thing, but those who don't call me Mr. Quinlan and don't call me something a good deal worse usually call me Charlie."

"Let's get one thing straight," the receptionist says. "You don't wear a wedding ring. Can I take that at face value, or is it just a come-on?"

"Don't think I'm married, but I'll give it some thought."

"Don't strain yourself. I just hope you don't turn out to be some kind of freak."

"I hope so too. Call me Charlie?"

"Okay. Charlie. My name's Claude."

"Claude? Okay. Be seeing you, Claude."

I turn back to Miss Efficiency, who's giving us both a disapproving look. "Mr. Quinlan? Do you think you're ready to keep your appointment?"

"I'm all yours, Miss Blitman."

She does a crisp march down a wood-paneled hallway stuffed with offices. I rush to follow close behind her so I won't get lost.

"How'd Mr. Stockton get to his office?" I say. "He didn't come in through the reception room."

"Private elevator. It goes from the basement garage directly to his private office."

She stops in front of a door, and nobody in the world would ever guess who it belongs to if it weren't for the six-inch-high gold lettering saying MR. ETHAN STOCKTON as simple as simple can be.

Miss Blitman turns with her back to the door and says, "Since you haven't met Mr. Stockton before, I should warn you. He's a little under the weather this morning."

"Looped?"

"Pardon me?"

"Looped? Soused? Drunk?"

"Please don't be crude, Mr. Quinlan. It's unbecoming."

"Okay. I sure's hell don't want to be unbecoming."

She starts tapping her foot again.

"Mr. Quinlan, I'm not accustomed to being talked to in this manner. I can see you're a very crude man, but I expect you to conduct yourself with me on a higher level than you've been doing heretofore. Do you understand?"

"Yeah. I know. I don't like you, either."

"Liking has nothing to do with it. I will make every attempt to be civil with you. I expect the same courtesy in return. I hope you understand, because I won't take any more smart-aleck crap from you."

The lady has some spirit, after all. Could be I was wrong about her.

"Okay, Miss Blitman. Maybe you're right. Maybe I rubbed you the wrong way. Maybe you rubbed me the wrong way."

"I suppose it would be too much to expect an apology from you, Mr. Quinlan."

"I admitted you told me off. That's all you're going to get from me. Now I think I got an appointment with Mr. Stockton."

8

The old man sits at a desk large enough to hold a small swimming pool. He's barking rapid-fire into the phone, but pauses long enough to motion me toward a chair.

He's old. Still, he's younger than I expected. He punctuates his sentences with quick choppy hand movements and his head bobs continuously from side to side. He has the nervous energy of an eight-year-old. He ends his conversation by slamming the receiver onto its cradle.

He looks across the desk at me. Miss Blitman is standing a little over to the side.

"Quinlan?" he says. "I been on the phone twice since I sent for you. Guess it's a long trip from the reception room."

"Sorry I kept you waiting," I say.

"You met Miss Blitman?"

"I met her."

"The two of you get a chance to talk?"

He's testing me, but I'm not sure which way he wants me to go.

"We talked a little."

"Think the two of you could get along?"

"I don't think so."

He keeps his eyes on me for a long time without saying anything. He gives me enough time to figure I've just blown my new case. Then he looks past me. "Miss Blitman," he says, "Mr. Quinlan and me're about to discuss business. Move your ass out of here and close the door behind you."

I guessed right on that one.

He waits till she's gone, then says, "She doesn't like the idea maybe I got some things to talk about and I don't want her in on them. Miss Blitman likes to be in on everything. Sometimes that's useful. Not always. Want a cigarette?"

"I'll take one of those cigars, if you make the offer."

He slides a gilt-edged humidor across the desk. "Take all you want. Drink?"

"Too early in the day for me."

"Never too early, or too late." He stands up and ages at least fifteen years. From the waist down his body is stiff and creaky and he needs a cane to move the few steps to the bar. He fills a large pewter mug with Scotch. No water, no ice. The pewter mug looks like it could serve a lot of different purposes—if you cracked someone over the head with it, you wouldn't have to call a doctor. Just the coroner.

"It's a hell of a thing, growing old. You still want the same amount of liquor you drank when you were young, but you're not young. You spend your whole life working up your appetite for things, then you get too old and you can't satisfy yourself any more. Body can't take it."

"I saw a movie once. About Diamond Jim Brady. I think Edward Arnold played the part. Big and fat, and in the end he decided to kill himself. Ate himself to death."

"I saw that picture. You get too old for things. If they're going to pull that kind of trick on you, they might's well kill you off. Might be kinder."

"Think I'd rather be living."

"Yeah? You'll see, you get older. I never had reason to use a private detective before. Used to take care of these things myself. But those days're gone, for me. Got to accept it. That's what they say, don't they?"

"So I've heard."

15

"They're full of crap. Don't accept anything. No matter what they do to you, you got to stand there and shake your fist at them. You know what I mean?"

"You mean you're a tough old buzzard and you want me to know it, right off."

"Yeah. What about you?"

"I'm a tough young buzzard, Mr. Stockton. You want me to get up and shake my fist?"

"There'll be time enough for that later. Don't accept anything, Mr. Quinlan. Unless you're damn sure you *got* to accept it." He settles back into his chair. It looks like it pains him to do it and for a second I think I hear a bone crack. It must be my imagination. "I know there's some things I can't do any more. The thing is, finding someone who *can* do those things. And knowing that someone can be trusted. You can't trust too many people these days."

"I didn't know there ever were days you *could* trust too many people."

"You can trust yourself. That's about all. So what'm I doing talking to you?"

"You got some trouble you can't handle yourself, I guess."

"Larry Hibson told me you did some work for him. What'd he need you for?"

Now we play games. "I don't recall if he needed me at all."

"You can tell me. Larry and me're close friends, from way back."

"That case, you got questions, give your questions to him."

"I did. Didn't find out a fuckin' thing."

"You didn't really care, either. You still don't. You just want to see if I can keep my mouth shut."

"Some guys, over with the police, they said as private detectives go, you stack up okay."

"You talked to the wrong cops."

"Maybe. I heard you're in the business. Actor?"

"Used to be. Nothing big."

"I know actors. I don't know if I trust actors."

"I don't trust 'em myself. Besides, I got out of that."

"You're going to be in the business, you want to be a director, or a writer, or a producer. You don't want to be an actor."

"My father, he used to be a writer."

Forget it, Charlie, Don't go into it.

"A writer? In the business?"

"He wrote some films. In the forties. Nothing big."

"A screenwriter, huh? But he doesn't write films any more?"

"No. He's dead."

"I'm sorry."

"I'm sorry too, Mr. Stockton. He killed himself when I was fourteen."

Okay. You said it. Happy? Now shut up.

"Too bad," he says. "This's a hell of a city, huh?"

"It was a lot more'n just the city." Charlie! Shut up! "Mr. Stockton, what'm I doing here on a nice Monday morning?"

"This city's full of gossip. I don't see any reason to add to it. I figure, people in your business, you got to have some kind of ethics."

"I suppose we do but I wouldn't want to place any bets on it. Look, you want to hire me, you got a reason, so far you're trying to avoid it. If you're trying to avoid it, it must really worry you."

"I haven't hired you yet. You're acting like maybe you don't want the job."

If there's anything I want, I want this job. That's the problem. I want it too damn much.

"I don't know what the job is, Mr. Stockton. Whatever it is, I figure you don't want someone you can kick around the way you kick around Miss Blitman."

"Miss Blitman's a royal pain in the ass. That's the nicest thing I can say about her."

"The hell it is. If that's all there was to it, you wouldn't have her here at all."

"You're right. She's damn efficient. If I didn't treat her pretty rough, she'd start to think *she* runs this company. I think maybe she *could* run this company. Better not repeat that to anyone. What're your rates?"

For a man with your money?

"I go for three hundred a day plus expenses."

"That's sort of high."

"Plus, you pay me a minimum of three days."

He laughs. "You think you're worth that much?"

"You're rich enough to afford that much. I'm good enough to be worth that much."

"Okay. If you believe you're that good, maybe you are."

"Mr. Stockton, how can I help you?"

He takes another long drink from his pewter mug.

"Damn it," he says. "I don't like doing this. You better be worth it."

"How can I help you, Mr. Stockton?"

"My son's missing. I want you to find him. Damn it! I want you to find him!"

9

The door opens behind me and a man comes in pretty quick. He's dressed casually in the most up-to-date style. Like those who dress to look like movie stars and turn out to be insurance salesmen.

He sees me sitting there and he doesn't seem to care about it. He starts right off, speaking loudly. "Ethan!" he says. "I told you I was going to have trouble! And you didn't do anything about it, did you?"

Mr. Stockton looks at me. "Mr. Quinlan, please excuse the interruption." Then he looks at the newcomer. "All right, Howard. What's wrong?"

"It's that damn fuckin' idiot Fishman! He's supposed to be cutting my Delvin ad! He's taking too damn long! I want to give it to one of the other film editors!"

"Quiet down, Howard. Mr. Fishman's been cutting film for me for twenty years, and he cut a lot of film before he ever came to me, so I think we can agree he knows what he's doing. He's got the commercial? He'll cut it. You'll have to wait till he's finished."

18

"Ethan! He's too old! By the time he's finished I'll be ready to retire from this fuckin' business!"

"Mr. Fishman's five years younger'n me. You think I'm too old?"

Howard stands there and looks pretty uncomfortable. Mr. Stockton lets him stay that way for a moment.

"Howard, you leave Mr. Fishman alone. I'll talk to him. You better learn to have a little respect for someone you think's too old. Maybe the day'll come *you'll* be too old."

That sticks it to Howard pretty good.

"Well," he says, "you better do something fast. We're supposed to be on a schedule."

"I'll take care of things."

Howard turns and stares at me.

"Nice talking to you," I say.

He marches out of the office as abruptly as he came in.

"Working in this business's pretty hectic," Mr. Stockton says. "Sometimes it breeds rudeness."

"How long's your son been missing?" I say.

"He didn't show up for work last Monday. I did some checking. The last time anyone saw him was a week ago, Friday, in the afternoon. At least, far's I know, that's the last time."

"That makes ten days. Why's he missing?"

"How'd I know why he's missing? That's why I need you!"

"This going to be dangerous?"

"Why should it be dangerous?"

" 'Cause you just raised your voice. And with this guy Howard, just now, you didn't raise your voice once. So I'd like to know —is it going to be dangerous? Sometimes it helps if I know ahead of time."

"What'm I supposed to tell you?" He drinks some more of his Scotch. Whenever things get touchy, he goes for the Scotch. "My son's missing. I want you to find him. I don't have any reason to think it'll be dangerous."

"Good," I say. I take all this to mean there's a good chance it'll be dangerous. That's okay with me. In fact, that's fine with me. "Where's your son work?"

"He works here. He works for me."

"He any good at it?"

"It's none of your business."

"In other words, he isn't any good at it. You got any reason to think it's foul play?"

"No."

"But you asked the cops to look for him, I suppose. Before you gave me a call."

"No."

Yeah. It'll be dangerous.

"It's that bad, huh? No cops, and you got contacts with the cops, yet. Look, this's a job for the Missing Persons Bureau."

"I told you. I want to keep this quiet."

"Nothing's quiet when the cops know you been asking about the credentials of a private detective."

"I checked you out through intermediaries. Nobody'll trace it back to me."

"You're that good? Okay. What's your son's full name? Where's he live?"

"Jamie. Jamie Stockton. There's some information for you in this envelope. There's a picture. I'm afraid it isn't very recent. And you got his address, the license-plate number of his car, things like that."

I spread out the contents of the envelope on the desk. "What're these keys for?"

"I got 'em from his office desk. One of them's for his office. I guess the other's to his apartment."

"He been doing anything unusual lately?"

"He's been gambling a lot. And drinking. That's not exactly unusual. My family enjoys gambling and drinking, at least my children and I do. My wife never caught the bug. We usually gamble at the Summit. You ever been there?"

"I'm not a member. A friend deals blackjack there, he got me in on a guest pass once. Very fancy place, but a little too rich for me. I don't suppose they do much worrying about getting closed down."

"They got some pretty good connections. Henry Tyding, he's

the owner. He's a former business associate. He's a good guy to know if you ever need a favor."

"So? Why're you telling me this?"

"Henry told me Jamie's been gambling heavily lately, and losing. Henry doesn't care if Jamie owes him a lot of money. He always does, and Henry writes it off. Or I pay it. But the thing is, this time Jamie stopped playing there. Henry did some checking for me and found out Jamie's been gambling all over town. Cheap little places, some of them I never heard of before. You got a list of them there."

"Sounds like this guy Tyding knows more about your son'n *you* know about your son."

"I don't keep a watch over what Jamie's doing."

"Only when he's gone, huh? This stuff you just told me, you don't think it means anything, but you *do* think it means something. That's why you're telling me."

"You're a very suspicious guy, Mr. Quinlan."

"We're both suspicious."

"Yeah. Maybe we'll get along."

"What else's there? Your son got a steady girl friend?"

"No."

"No? Okay. You know any of the girls he goes out with?"

He doesn't say anything for a minute. "Far's I know, my son doesn't go out with girls."

We both know what my next question should be. He doesn't want me to ask it, so I don't. I already know I can ask somebody else about it.

"Okay," I say. "No girls you know about. Let's get on to something else. I mean, if you really want me to find your son, you can't keep things from me."

"What? What do you want? I told you what I know."

"Mr. Stockton, you hire me and don't tell me everything, you're throwing your money away. You got sources in the police department but you don't ask them to find your son. Okay. You're afraid if they look for your son they'll discover something you want kept quiet. If I look for your son I'll probably discover whatever it is. So if I know it right now, before things get too confused, and these things do have a habit of getting confused, it might help things along."

He thinks it over. Then he says, "If there's a crime, you got to report it?"

That's what I figured.

"Depends on the crime. I won't suppress evidence, but if you're my client I'll protect you and your family the best I can. That's if you play straight with me. I'll also protect my private investigator's license. If we're talking about murder or—"

"Oh, no! No! Nothing like that! Not at all!" He hits the Scotch again. "Let's say it's a matter of drugs."

"Selling or using?"

"Let's say using."

"Play it straight with me. I'll protect you if I can."

"Jamie disappeared once before. Several years ago. He was only twenty-three. He dropped out of college and started working here, but things didn't work out. Then he just disappeared. I didn't give it much concern. He was young. I thought being on his own might be good for him, might shape him up. It didn't. After six months he turned up in Las Vegas. He was on drugs and he got caught. I went up there and spent some money. Sometimes money helps. I put him in one of those asylums for four months or so and then he came home. I think it worked, I don't think he ever used drugs again. So don't get me wrong, I don't have any reason to think he's on drugs now. It's just . . . it happened last time. Maybe it could happen again. But I don't think it did. I think now he's clean."

"Why'd he disappear that time? Years ago?"

"He was working here, and it was no good. He was trying to find himself."

"Now he's working here again. Maybe he disappeared to find himself again."

"I don't know. Jamie had to take on some extra responsibilities early in the year. Something happened, so I made him take on a big advertising campaign. I thought it'd be good for him, but he couldn't handle it. So then I had to move him to something else, on accounts. I guess he felt he'd failed."

"Sounds like he did fail. So he disappeared and you're afraid he's on drugs again."

"I don't know. If he is, I don't want him hurt. I don't want him put in jail again."

"You want him back."

"Yeah."

"What if I find him and he doesn't want to come back?"

"Mr. Quinlan, I want to talk to Jamie. And I want to be sure he's not on drugs. If he comes back here or not, that's his decision. Find him. Then we'll see what happens. Please, Mr. Quinlan. Find him for me."

10

Jamie Stockton's office looks like a place nobody ever used for an office. I find nothing.

I walk down the hall to the reception area to tell Claude I can't take her to Indonesian food, after all.

Someone calls to me. It's the man who barged into Mr. Stockton's office. Howard. He's running toward me with his hand outstretched.

"I owe you an apology," he says as he shakes my arm off. "I guess I was rude before. I shouldn't've busted in that way. I was wrong. I really mean it. I really am sorry."

"Okay, you're sorry. I got the message. Leave me the arm. You think you ought to apologize to someone, go apologize to Mr. Stockton."

"Yeah. You're right. I ought to do that. I was just mad about something. I'm sorry."

"Okay. Okay. I forgot about it already."

"Yeah. Right. Sorry." He turns abruptly and disappears into an office.

That's what it's like at Stockton Film, Inc.

And that's what goes with the name—Ethan Stockton. I don't

know if I like him, but I hope when everything's done we'll be on the same side. I have a feeling it's safer that way.

I've seen three people who work for him. One of them has the nicest legs in town. The other two, I wouldn't bid on them at a garage sale.

11

I give all my photographic work to a place down the street from my office. I drop off the picture of Jamie Stockton and ask them to make duplicates. They say I can have them in a few hours.

My first phone call goes to George.

"Hello, George. It's Charlie Quinlan."

"Back in town? How'd the show go?"

"I was a smash."

"Standing ovations?"

"I got a sitting ovation."

"I didn't read any reviews in the papers."

"It's a small theater, couple hundred miles away. You awake enough to do some thinking?"

"Hell, I'm never that awake."

"Pretend you are. You're still dealing at the Summit?"

"The money they pay, you think I'm going to quit?"

"I'm going to talk to you about a guy. But you're not going to remember anything about our conversation after it's over."

"Oh, hell. You called me 'cause you're on a case."

"There's a family named Stockton. The old man's named Ethan Stockton."

"Jesus H. Christ! Ethan Stockton? You working for him? Hell, Charlie! Better charge an arm and a leg! He's worth more'n you and me and everyone we know and everyone *they* know, all put together."

"That I know. What about the family?"

"The old man's a relic. There's rumors he started the Spanish-American War. Tough old bastard. Real close to my boss. Either they love each other or they got so much dirt on each other they're afraid *not* to be friends. But forget the old man, he's just a lot of money. Stockton's wife's the one for me. You seen her? She's some dame."

"I heard the wife doesn't gamble."

"She don't. She just stands there and lets everyone look at her. She's like you, she used to be in movies, but *she* used to be a star. A real long time ago. She's still something to look at, for a lady in her sixties."

"Tell me about the rest of the family."

"The daughter's a born gambler. Like her daddy. But never big stakes. Nice conservative bets, and she loves to bluff. The mother's warm as toast but that girl's a cold fish. I get the shivers every time I see her coming over to my table. The odds favor the house but she still wins. We make it up with her husband, though. Schmuck. Every time he comes in he pulls out lots of money, and he don't leave with much of it. He doesn't give a damn. Maybe he likes going home with empty pockets. That's okay with me. And then there's the son. He's bananas."

"How so?"

"The son, I bet he's been playing cards regular most of his life. He still don't know the rules. I guess that's how it is. You got an old man rich's Ethan Stockton, maybe you never got to learn the rules."

"They tell me the son's been losing pretty bad lately."

"That's news? He always loses bad. Yeah, you're right. Lately he's been losing pretty heavy. For a while he's paying off in cash, then IOUs. We got a string of them, you could stretch them out end to end, they'll take you to Omaha."

"And now he isn't playing there, right?"

"Haven't seen him. Maybe a week, maybe two weeks. Guess he's on the clip joints now, the ones that take everyone for a ride. He doesn't have to come back to us far's I'm concerned. We do all right without him. That kid, he just don't know the rules."

"I hear he drinks."

"Big deal. The whole family drinks. They must keep a couple distilleries in business all by themselves."

"The kid—you think he's on drugs?"

"He don't need drugs. He's already looney."

"What kind of girl friends he got?"

"You got me. If he's got girl friends, I never seen them."

"Boy friends?"

"Never seen any of them, either."

"Uh huh. You think he's gay?"

"Doesn't make any difference to me what he likes. He ain't made any tries to pick *me* up."

"But you haven't seen him with anyone, male or female?"

"Don't think so. Don't think he's much interested in other people. Doesn't even seem too close to his family."

"He must have someone."

"Maybe he's got a dog. Play your cards right, maybe he'll take a liking to *you.*"

"I'll keep it in mind. After all, he's rich."

"You want to go after someone, go after the mother. The old man, he can't live forever. You ask me, one good knock on the head, the old guy'd be deader'n yesterday's news."

"You really like the old lady?"

"Wait'll you see her. You won't believe it. I'll tell you a story, the kind you like."

"Go ahead."

"They say he used to live down in South America, I don't know which country down there, and he got a look at one of her films, and he came all the way back here just to get her. You like the story?"

"Love it."

"Fuckin' romantic. Listen, one more thing. I got some advice. You're going to get involved with that family, keep an eye on the old man's bodyguard or whatever the hell he is. He's bad news."

"You mean a guy named Simson?"

"I don't know his name."

"Speaks kind of funny? Slow and measured."

"I don't know. I never heard this guy talk. You'll know him when you see him. Don't show him your back if you want to keep it."

26

"What about the kid? You think he's dangerous?"

"The kid? Wouldn't think so. But you never know, do you?"

"Sometimes when you know, it's too late."

12

I hang up the phone and dial another number. I'm going to do something I don't want to do. I'm going to use the Singer again.

"Tulley's Bar and Grill."

"Hello, Tulley. It's Charlie Quinlan."

"Charlie my boy! Charlie my boy! How you doing, Charlie my boy? Where you been?"

"Up north."

"Panning for gold?"

"I did a musical. Summer stock."

"Hey! You should've told me! I'd've gone with you! I'm the best tenor in town."

"Everyone wants to get into the act."

"Hey! I can do Durante, too! Want to hear?"

"Spare me. You got the Singer there?"

"Hey, the Singer may hit the booze a little heavy but even he don't start this early in the day."

"You expect him in, though."

"Why? Thought you and the Singer were on the outs after what happened that last time."

"I'm not planning to buy him a birthday present. I'm in the market for some songs, I want to see him."

I *don't* want to see him. But I'll see him.

"What kind of songs you want?" Tulley says. "Maybe I can hum a few bars for you."

"No. It'll involve some traveling music. If the Singer doesn't come in, can you get a message to him?"

"Like the pony express."

"I'm going out for a couple hours. Tell him to be at my office when I get back. I want him sober. Tell him to bring his shoes."

27

13

I lock up the office and walk the ten feet to the door with the orange and red lettering. The orange stuff says SUNLIGHT PRODUCTIONS and there's a drawing of the sun and three million spokes shooting off in two million directions. Under that, the red stuff says CARO-LYN VAN DUYN, PRODUCER.

I walk in without knocking. Carolyn's at her desk, snapping into a phone. She looks up, sees me and waves me forward.

Her two assistants, Larry and Sue, face each other from opposing sides of a big square desk which once played a major part in one of Carolyn's movies. They also snap into phones. Neither of them bothers to look up.

I settle into a chair near Carolyn and wait. My attention wanders to a new thing on her desk. It looks like an Academy Award made by a sculptor on a binge.

I listen to all the phone chatter from the three of them and tune out.

Carolyn's real name is Drexelhof. When she decided to become a movie producer she found Drexelhof left something to be desired when it came to wooing investors, so she changed her name to Van Duyn, which sounded more affluent. In the fifties she was a script girl at Warner Brothers. I worked on a few films there. We got to know each other. I got five days of work on *The FBI Story* and we spent the third, fourth and fifth nights together.

We never did set up house. I'm not sure why. But when I became a private investigator and she became an independent producer, we rented adjoining offices. We like to mix business with pleasure.

Carolyn spent about ten years at Warner Brothers. Being a woman didn't help her in terms of advancement. When she was working in the script department she came across a story the Warner brothers didn't like. When they dropped their option she picked it up. She raised some money, made the thing on a shoestring and got lucky. The film showed a small profit. She's been in the business for herself ever since.

Carolyn puts down the phone, stretches her arms out wide and yells, "Hold all calls! I got an important visitor!"

Nobody pays any attention to her.

"That's the way you run a business here?"

"Yeah. You on a new case today?"

"Does it show on my face?"

"I knew it! I knew you'd get a case today!"

Nobody keeps secrets from Carolyn.

"Okay. You knew it. What'd my horoscope say?"

"Hold it, I got it here. 'You will get a new case today.' "

"That's not what it says."

"Sure it does!"

"Bullshit. What's it really say?"

"Okay, here's what it says. 'You uncover obscure information. By acting promptly, you can advance your career and increase your earning power.' "

"How the hell does something like that tell you I got a case?"

"Simple. Uncover obscure information. That's got to be right on target for a detective. And if you're going to advance your career and increase your earning power, how you going to do it unless you got a case?"

"I don't see that as necessarily a logical progression of thought."

"Charlie, you got a new case?"

"Yeah."

"You got to believe what it says! The stars tell you everything! 'Increase your earning power' means you got a job working for someone with money. A *lot* of money. Right?"

Maybe she's got ESP? If there is ESP.

If there is ESP, she'd have it.

"Yeah. I got a client with a lot of money."

"Uh huh! Uh huh! Uh huh! Nonbeliever! It's in the stars, Charlie! It's all in the stars!"

"Bullshit."

"Who's the rich client?"

Carolyn doesn't waste any time.

"Can't tell you. It's confidential, and I think you'd know the name."

"Got a big one, huh?"

"It's money. It's the most money I ever met."

"Come on. Tell me. What's the money's name?"

"Sorry. Confidential."

"If your client's rich, get to know your client good. Maybe later your client'll want to invest in a film."

"I know what you mean. How's it going?"

"Look at this room! What an office! That's all I got to work with. No big studio for Carolyn Van Duyn, baby. Me, all I got's a cubbyhole decorated by the Salvation Army on one of their bad days. Listen, baby. A week from Wednesday. One week from Wednesday! Into production! I got 'em all signed. All the biggies. Hackman, Reynolds, Dunaway, Streisand and Phyllis Diller! All together! For the first time!"

"What a line-up. What's your budget?"

"Seven million!"

"Doing a Bible epic?"

"I don't know how the hell I'm going to pull it off, Charlie. All I got's three hundred fifty grand. I don't know where I'm going to get the rest of that fuckin' seven mill."

14

"What'll it really cost?" I say.

"I'm going at it just like Welles. I got the three fifty grand, so I'm telling the investors I can do it for that. Hell, we'll never bring it in for that. If I'm lucky, I might pull it together for half a mill. Where'll I get the rest of that money, Charlie?"

"You need at least five hundred grand?"

"I signed contracts already. There's no going back. What if I rent myself out by the hour? That ought to bring in something."

"Yeah, but not a hundred fifty grand."

"No, huh? I was afraid it wouldn't. We start shooting a week from Wednesday. We'll run through the money we got, and by then little old Carolyn better come up with the balance or jump out a window."

"Can't you hold off on production till you raise the rest?"

"I signed contracts. I had to sign 'em or lose the talent."

"What're the stars saying?"

" 'Go into production, Carolyn, before you lose the option on the story.' "

"Oh. I see. Good story?"

"Yeah. I got a script written by someone who knows English, this time. A woman who's out for revenge against half a dozen men. It won't win any awards, but revenge's a good theme. It'll sell."

"A woman out for revenge. I think Truffaut did that one. *The Bride Wore Black.*"

"That was ten years ago. Who remembers ten years?"

"Truffaut had Jeanne Moreau. You got Jeanne Moreau?"

"Not quite."

"Too bad. *I'd* like to have Jeanne Moreau."

"*You* got *me.*"

"You come close, but you don't speak French." I pick up the thing on her desk. It weighs a ton. "I must've missed something. When'd you win the Oscar?"

"Hey! Right! It's supposed to be an Oscar!"

"It looks drunk. Guess it's seen better days."

"Ain't we all? I picked it up in this little art shop out in Malibu. The guy that made it, he owns the shop. When I told him it looked like an Oscar, he said I was the first one to tell him that. Sold it to me for half price. Makes a nice paperweight."

"So does the real thing. Where you going to get the rest of the half mill?"

"Don't remind me. The way I got it figured, the actors, I pay them part now and part on deferral. And I got this young guy to direct. He's good but he's young. He's trying to make it out of TV and into movies, but nobody'll give him the chance, so I made him an offer. A little money now and he gets a percentage of the gross,

31

if there is one. He went for it. His fuckin' agent fought it, but he went for it. But I got to keep things down and close."

"Where you going to get the rest of the half mill?"

"Shut up! Okay. I'm trying to figure. Would it be easier to go to bed with one real rich guy for the whole one hundred fifty grand or ten semi-rich guys for fifteen grand each?"

"It's a tough decision."

"Seriously, Charlie, it's a good property. If I can just get all the front money, I already got a distribution deal almost completely set. I can make some money on this one."

"You told me that last year."

"Well, that didn't work out. This one'll sell."

"I hope so. Start shooting next week, huh?"

"Shut up! Like I said, a week from Wednesday."

Very casual now, Charlie. Slip it in casual.

"You all cast?" I say.

"Bastard."

"What?"

"Here I am, crying about all the money I got to raise—and all you want to know, you want to know if I'm all cast!"

"It's a simple question."

"Okay, Charlie! What happened? You met a girl?"

You're too quick for me, Carolyn.

15

I put the picture and résumé in front of her.

"She's pretty," Carolyn says. "She got good legs?"

"Sure."

"Like I had to ask. Her name's Claude? I don't suppose you know if she can act or not?"

"Nope. Just met her this morning."

"You're trying to make it with her?"

"If she photographs anywhere near the way she looks, she'll

be worth it to you. I'm not trying to use you. I saw a girl I liked and I thought I'd see if I could help her."

"Listen, baby. If you're horny, just give me a call. I'll take care of you. Don't go after actresses."

"Carolyn. You're getting jealous."

"Who the fuck are you?"

"Do I sense the verge of what they call a strained relationship?"

"Damn right. That's not all you'll get strained."

"Carolyn, this girl, she needs some help. I didn't make any guarantees. I'm just passing along the picture. If you can use her, fine. If not, that's the breaks. It's a tough business, right? That's all I got in mind."

"Yeah? Like hell. Okay. I don't believe you, but I'll see if I can do anything. But while we're trading favors, I want one too."

"Don't you always."

"I mean it about this film. I think if the director doesn't screw things up—I think this film'll make some money."

"I hope it does."

"What I'm saying, Charlie, if you'd listen, is this. If you got some money, it'd be a good investment."

"Carolyn, you bitch. You made up that horoscope. About increasing my earning power. Just so you could put the bite on me."

"Baby, you want to blow it? Go ahead and blow it. I'm telling you, I'm going to hit with this one."

"How much money?"

"If you can put in two thousand five, it'd be something."

"It sure would."

"Come on! That much, it wouldn't break you!"

"I'll give it some thought."

"What I'd like you to do is make it an even five grand. Just five grand. Forget your investigator's license and be my associate producer."

Once a woman starts going at you on something, she never gives up.

"I told you, Carolyn. I'm not interested in that."

"Hey. Charlie. Come on. You want to get back in the business! Come on! Fly with me!"

"I like the business I'm in."

"Bullshit! You're scared to come back in the business!"

"No."

"You ought to go see a shrink."

"You're the one in analysis, not me."

"You don't want to spend the money."

"I don't trust shrinks."

"You don't trust anyone. I think you're scared of shrinks."

"I am. Every time I meet a shrink, after I talk to him for five minutes I get the idea he ought to see a shrink."

"You ain't got the guts to try it, just like you ain't got the guts to come back into the business."

"Don't try that kind of psychology on me."

"Come on, Charlie! You aren't scared of the business? Okay. Show me you ain't scared. Come in with me—the water's fine!"

"I'm out, Carolyn. For good."

"You're still paid up with the Screen Actors Guild?"

"Yeah. I guess so."

"You still carry an Equity card?"

"Yeah."

"Just did some summer stock?"

Some day I'll win an argument with her. It won't be today.

"Forget it, Carolyn. I'm out of the business."

"Just 'cause you knew a couple people, they used to be in the business and they ended up killing themselves, you going to let that keep you out of what you really want to do?"

"Shut up."

"It wasn't the business killed them. It was other things."

No. I don't want to go into this. I've been fighting it all day.

"Shut up, Carolyn. I know what killed them."

"You do? So what're you scared of?"

"Carolyn, let it go! I'm not up to it. Not today."

She won't leave me alone. She just won't leave me alone. My own memory won't leave me alone.

Stop the world—I want to get off!

No. I don't. Not yet. I'm not through fighting yet.

I just wish I knew what the hell I'm fighting.

"I'm sorry," Carolyn says. "Okay, baby. I'm sorry. I didn't mean it."

Nobody means anything.

"Charlie. Come on. It's going to be my biggest film so far, if I ever get the rest of the money. I could use you. Associate producer. You'd be good."

"I'm good at what I'm doing."

"Charlie. You'll never learn."

"I learned. I got out. Can't you understand something? I like what I'm doing. I like being out of the business."

"How the hell can you like snooping into other people's lives?"

"Sometimes it works out."

"Let me tell you, baby. Guys get killed in your business, too."

"Guys get killed in every business. I can't talk to you. You make me think I'm a fuckin' banana. I got to go."

"I'm sorry, Charlie. For what I said. I'm sorry."

I know. But you still said it.

"Okay, Carolyn. Forget it. I'll still love you when you're old and gray."

"Going to invest in my film?"

"I'll take a look at my savings, see if I got two and a half grand stashed some place."

"We'll make some money. This one'll go all the way."

"Sweet. You'll win a real Oscar for it."

"I just want to make some money so I can keep on producing."

"Take the cash and let the credit go."

"Who's that from? Sam Goldwyn?"

"Guy named Omar the Tentmaker. Sometimes he used the alias Khayyám."

"Okay, Charlie. I'll see if I can do anything for your girl."

"Not my girl. Just a girl I met. Who needs some help."

"We all need help. Come on, Charlie. Come back to the movies. We can make happy endings in the movies. If we can raise enough money first. In the real stuff, private detectives sometimes get killed."

"But they get a chance to write their own scripts."

"Do they really?"

"Go raise money, Carolyn. I got work to do."

So I get out of there. But she's got me thinking about what that nice little horoscope said.

Uncover information . . .

Act promptly . . .

Increase earning power . . .

She probably made the whole thing up.

It doesn't tell me anything important. Like whether or not I'll make it through the day.

The stars don't know everything, I guess.

16

I go across the street to have some lunch. Then I drive out to North Hollywood.

Jamie Stockton lives in a two-level apartment complex which curves around a swimming pool. There's nobody sitting by the pool today and the surface of the water carries a fleet of dead bugs.

I look in the front window of the first-floor apartment and there's nobody home. I have the key, so I invite myself in.

The layer of dust in the living room tells me the place has been unused for at least several days. The furnishings are sparse and they hardly fit together in terms of color or style. The bookcase holds a set of spanking new hardbacks. They're there for display, not for reading.

The kitchen's bachelor-bare. When I open the refrigerator I'm met by the smell of milk turned sour many days earlier.

The bedroom's dominated by a king-size waterbed. The closet holds a wardrobe of denim running the gamut from faded jeans to fitted suits.

I sit at the desk in the living room and go through the drawers.

One holds back copies of sex magazines. So maybe Jamie likes girls, after all. I take a five-minute vacation from work and flip through the pages.

Another drawer contains a half-used model airplane kit.

Some old letters from friends give me a little reading to do. From what I read, Jamie's friends are duller than most.

I thumb through a small spiral notebook. It's a crudely made-up account book. A column for names, but there are no names, only initials. The next column lists dates. Then a column for amounts owed and another for amounts paid. Jamie's customers always pay the amounts in full. The date of the last transaction is twelve days ago.

I find a used checkbook and flip through the stubs. Electric company, telephone company, department stores, gasoline. Nothing unusual here.

The doorbell rings. I slip the spiral notebook into my pocket, put on my best smile and open the door. A young girl holding a baby on her hip smiles back at me. Her smile's a lot more nervous than mine.

"Oh!" she says. "I live across the way. I saw someone go in the apartment, I thought maybe it was Jamie."

"Nope," I say. "Just me."

"Are you one of Jamie's friends?"

"Yeah. Jamie and me, we go way back." How far back? Let's make it— "We're Army buddies."

"I didn't know Jamie'd been in the Army."

Figures. "He doesn't like to talk about it. He didn't like it. I didn't care for it much myself."

She wipes her baby's drooling mouth. "Are you supposed to meet Jamie here?"

"I just got to town, I figured I'd stop by to check a few things. You know when Jamie'll be back?"

"He left over a week ago. Said he'd be gone for two weeks, maybe longer. You didn't stop by to drop off a package, did you?"

"A package?"

She freezes. "Are you the police?"

So that's it. The spiral notebook. The initials.

I put my mind into gear. It settles onto Marlon Brando. Not the brooding, threatening Brando of *Streetcar* or *Wild One*. The other one—the silky, smiling Brando from *Guys and Dolls* and *Bedtime Story*. I don't want to go any heavier than that.

I laugh. "Not me, honey. I ain't the cops. Not on your life." I take out the key, insert it in the door lock and demonstrate how it works. "I told you, honey. Jamie and me're old buddies. I got a key to his apartment, he's got a key to mine, up in Vegas. Don't get worried. When the cops come, you'll know it. The cops come, they aren't exactly polite. But me, I'm a friend, you know? I got my own key. And you, you're a friend too. You been waitin' for a package."

"I thought maybe—"

"Hey, kid. Don't tighten up. Take it cool. You thought I was the delivery man, right? No. I never carry anythin', you know? Safer that way. I got others to make deliveries for me. What's the matter? Didn't Jamie ever tell you he's in business with a friend in Vegas?"

"No, he didn't tell me. I never asked any questions."

"Smart girl. That's the way to act. You know, I sent a guy down here last week. Maybe you saw him. Sent him down with a package for Jamie, but Jamie wasn't home. So then I started callin' but I didn't get an answer. So I figured I better come down myself and see if Jamie's okay. I mean, make sure he wasn't picked up or anythin'."

"No, I don't think he was. I hope not."

"Hey! Honey! Don't worry. It's nothin' like that. I got my contacts, you know? I already checked things out. Cops ain't got him. They ain't even lookin' for him. No problem there. But see, I don't know where he is. You ain't seen him?"

Give me something, lady. I need a clue. Please?

"The last time I saw him was a week ago last Friday. I don't know where he is. Excuse me, I think I better go."

Awwww. You won't give me anything?

"Look, lady, I mean . . ."

She's already walking away.

"Okay, honey. See you around. And don't worry. There's no trouble, you know? Everythin's cool."

I watch as she goes back to her apartment. She's pretty eager to get away from me. She doesn't look back once.

I guess I played Marlon too heavy.

I close the door behind me and walk along the side of the pool, whistling "Luck Be a Lady Tonight," and pause only to glance at her apartment door. Apartment 7. I check the mailboxes and apartment 7 belongs to Mr. and Mrs. Arthur Carson.

I check the spiral notebook. The initials A.C. reappear on several pages.

17

It's five o'clock by the time I pick up the duplicates of Jamie Stockton's picture.

My office is on the second floor of a postwar building on Western Avenue, halfway between Santa Monica and Sunset. It's a small office and I keep both doors locked. One door faces on the hall. The other opens on a smaller office I use for a waiting room.

This room is always open in case I get a client who feels like waiting around. I provide a brown vinyl sofa, red rug and drapes and a table with a *Reader's Digest* and a *Sports Illustrated* in case the client can read. I figure those are two magazines nobody will ever steal. Nobody ever does.

A scrawny little man in need of a shave sits cautiously on my brown vinyl sofa. His eyes are glassy as marbles and his first name is Rudy. Nobody knows his second name. The only purpose he serves for man or beast is to sell information. He always has plenty, and if he doesn't have the stuff you want, he'll go out and get it for you. This is the way he earns money and we call him the Singer. He scares the hell out of me.

"Hi, Mr. Quinlan," he says. "Nice to see you again. Tulley said you been up north with a show. Getting back into acting, huh?"

"Cut the crap, Rudy."

I open the door to my office and we go in. I sit down behind my desk. He stands. He tries to smile.

"You wanted to see me, right? Soon's Tulley told me, I come right over. Didn't think you wanted to see me any more, after—"

"Rudy, shut up and sit down."

He doesn't look good. I've made a mistake.

"Rudy, how long's it been since your last drink?"

"I'm trying to cut down, Mr. Quinlan. I'm trying my—"

"We used to have an agreement. If I buy information from you, I own it." Who am I kidding? "You don't run off to sell that information to someone else."

"Yeah, Mr. Quinlan. I know."

How the hell can I use this guy?

"So I figure I can rely on you," I say. "So I buy your information. And things go wrong. You resell the stuff."

"I needed more money, Mr. Quinlan. I needed it real bad. That was the only information I had. I didn't have anything else to sell."

It's like talking to a wall.

"You fucked me!" I say. "What the hell'd you need the money for? A bottle! Right?"

"I was in a bad way. I usually don't get that bad."

I'm not going to use him. I can't. It's too risky.

"All you got to do, Rudy, is get that bad once. And it's all over." Much too risky. "You resold the stuff, you bought another bottle and just about got me killed."

I'm really getting to him now. I'm getting carried away. I'm playing it like Hackman in *The French Connection*. Hackman ready to kick ass on New York streets. Busting junkies and pounding punks. This is fun.

"You're still pretty sore, huh, Mr. Quinlan?"

I'd like to put your head under water, Rudy. How would you like that?

"I don't have a right to be sore?"

"Yeah, Mr. Quinlan! You got a right. Sure you do!"

Rudy the Singer. I'm making a big mistake.

"I'm plenty sore. But I got no time for that kind of crap."

Well, I've made mistakes before. "I got a job for you. But don't fuck up! If you can do the job right, I'll use you. If you can't, I'll find myself another singer."

Another singer? What other singer? They're all as bad as Rudy.

"I'll do the job, Mr. Quinlan. I learned my lesson. Ask Snyder and Wentworth. I been doing okay for them. I'll do okay by you. I mean it!"

I'm going to use him. I'm a fool.

"It's probation, Rudy. Any mistakes, I'll run your arms through a meat grinder!"

"Thanks, Mr. Quinlan. I always liked working for you. You're a square guy."

"Rudy—you're nuts!" Hell. "We're both nuts." Yeah. And I'm a terminal case.

I give him one of the duplicate pictures and try to calm down. He doesn't recognize the face.

"His name's Jamie Stockton. I want to locate him. If you see him, you don't say *anything*. You call *me*. Right?"

"He done something, Mr. Quinlan?"

"Don't ask questions!" Brother. "Rudy, you got to know something, I'll make sure you know it. No, he didn't do anything. And even if he did do something, you don't want to know about it unless I want to tell you about it."

"Sorry, Mr. Quinlan. I just wondered if he's dangerous."

"Far's I know, he's not dangerous. That's far's I know. Doesn't mean it's so. Anyway, it doesn't concern you. If you see him, you don't even wink at him. That's how we work it."

"Gotcha, Mr. Quinlan."

"He likes to drink and gamble. He used to do it in expensive places, but no more. Maybe he's on the skids, maybe he's playing off the back of his wallet, maybe he just doesn't want to be recognized. I don't know. But he's hitting the cheapies."

I take out the list of gambling places Ethan Stockton gave me. There are a baker's dozen of them. Some of them I know, some I've heard about and some are complete surprises. I write out the first six names and give them to Rudy.

"Show the picture around as much's you got to," I say. "But try not to make too much noise about this. I don't want him to know I'm looking. If you don't run him down at any of these places, check out some of your own. You turn up anything, give me a call."

"Right, Mr. Quinlan. You'll hear from me."

Yeah. Sure.

May the Lord watch over us all when we get so stupid we rely on guys like Rudy the Singer.

Why doesn't someone come and lock me up for my own good?

18

At five forty-five I'm getting ready to leave when the phone rings. It's Mr. Simson.

"Please Mr. Quinlan . . . Mr. Ethan Stockton wish to know you have anything report . . ."

"No, Mr. Simson . . . I got nothing to report . . . Except to tell you I'm hungry and I plan to do something about it . . . in case you're interested . . . Goodbye, Mr. Simson."

Don't call me. I'll call you.

I go across the street and eat a high-protein dinner, topping it off with two cups of coffee in anticipation of a long night. Then I start to make my rounds.

I have the names of seven gambling spots scattered throughout the city. By ten o'clock I've been to the first five. There's always someone, a bartender or dealer, who recognizes the picture. Some of them know it's a guy named Jamie something, a guy who sometimes wins and usually loses. A guy who sometimes pays in cash and occasionally leaves an IOU if he can get away with it. A guy who never seems to be where I am. Not much of a pattern developing, except Jamie Stockton always comes into the spots alone and leaves alone.

I call my answering service. There's one message and it's from the Singer. He's having the same luck I am.

My next stop is a real dive in Venice. The doorman knows he hasn't seen me before and thinks I'm a cop. The second time today someone thinks I'm a cop. Maybe I parted my hair wrong this morning. The doorman bounces his hands around my body. I've no gun, no badge, and I'm not wired. He decides I can come in. I step into the main room and see Jamie Stockton standing at one of the blackjack tables.

I go to the bar and order vodka on the rocks. I say to the bartender, "Surprised to find you open. I heard they closed down a place around here the other night. Thought it might be this one."

"I didn't hear anything like that," he says.

"You don't get closed down?"

"We don't have no trouble. No trouble at all."

"My mistake. Must've been some other place."

"I don't think so. I think you just made it up."

"Maybe I did."

"You planning to be trouble?"

"I'm clean. I got the check at the door. Just want to be sure things're secure here, since I ain't been here before."

I keep an eye on Jamie Stockton. He appears to be alone. He also looks a little drunk. He keeps playing blackjack. He's getting plucked cleaner than a chicken. He looks like he doesn't even know it.

"All right," the bartender says. "Maybe you're just being cautious. You don't have to worry. Last time they closed us down, must've been over a year ago. Right after we opened. The boss learned his lesson. He patched things up. They ain't planning to close us down again."

"Good. I always like to know that, when I hit a new place. You know what's the worst thing in the world? Sitting down to play cards when you got to keep one eye on the front door to see if the cops're going to make an appearance."

"Got no worry here. Everything's been taken care of. We run an honest game, too. Oughta try your luck."

"Okay."

I walk over to the blackjack table. I stand over to the side for a few minutes and watch Jamie Stockton drop twenty dollars. Then the player beside him quits the game. I move in.

When I gamble, which isn't too often, I stick to blackjack and keep my bets conservative. George taught me how the dealer plays it, and I know enough to come out slightly ahead, if the game isn't rigged too bad. After five minutes Stockton's lost another twenty dollars and I've won nine. It's turning into a profitable case, but I decide it's time to get back to work. I act a little drunk and give Stockton a light elbow in the ribs.

"Been losing all night," I say. "All over town. Losing every place I been to. So look at this. Just won myself three straight. Could be you're bringing me some good luck, first time tonight."

"I'd rather bring *myself* some good luck," he says.

"Stick with me, friend. We'll do it together. I feel it coming."

We play another round. I win. He loses.

"See?" I say. "I'm on top of things now."

"So what? You're not spreading things my way."

He acts pretty sour. I decide we need to be simpatico, so I purposely lose on the next two deals. In this game that's pretty easy to do.

"What's the matter now?" I say. "I was winning, now I'm losing again. Ain't that the way it is? You get a little luck, first thing you know, it's flying out the window to somebody else."

"You win some, you lose some. The hell with it." He throws in his cards and walks away.

I'm pretty sure he's going to leave. I make a big show of quitting the game, brush past him brusquely and storm out the door, mumbling as I go. I make sure he knows I'm leaving before him.

I go to my car quickly and wait. He comes out soon enough, with a slight stagger, and climbs into a blue Buick LeSabre. I watch to see if anyone joins him.

The way it looks, he's alone.

19

I follow his car from a distance of two blocks. We end up at a sleazy hotel in Santa Monica. From the corner of the lobby I watch him get into an elevator. The dial above the door stops on number 2. I run up the stairs and reach the second floor in time to see him go through a door at the end of the hall. I walk down the hall and knock on the door. It opens a crack and Jamie Stockton peers out at me.

"How you like that?" I say. "You and me staying at the same hotel! Remember me? Playing blackjack. That joint in Venice, just before."

"What do you want?" he says.

"Here I am, getting my keys at the desk, and I turn around, who'd I see getting into the elevator? You! I shouted to you, guess you didn't hear me."

"Yeah, yeah. What do you want?"

"I got a bottle here. Want to kill it off with me?"

"Leave me alone. I want to go to bed." He begins to close the door.

I shove the door quite hard.

It flies open and he sails back into the room.

I step in and look around.

A table, some chairs, a bed, a nightstand, an open door to the bathroom; another closed door, probably to a closet; a half-open window.

Okay, Charlie. Things look peaceful enough. Play it nice. Don't go heavy on the macho.

I close the door behind me and wait for him to speak.

"Why'd you do that?" he says. "What the fuck you want?"

"Just some talk," I say.

He looks me over for a while. Then he sits down on the edge of the bed. That seems a good idea. The way he looks, he probably couldn't stay standing much longer.

"So where's the bottle?"

"Sorry. No bottle."

"No bottle? Why'd you say you got a bottle if there's no bottle?"

" 'Cause I lied."

"Oh. What do you want? Money? I don't have much. You can have it if you want it. Don't hurt me."

"I don't want to hurt you, Jamie."

"What? How'd you know my name?"

"I work for your father. He asked me to locate you."

"What're you talking about? You don't work for my father. *I* work for my father. I know everyone who works for my father."

"He hired me this morning. To find you."

"To find me? Shit. What the hell're you? Some kind of private eye?"

"You got it."

"Shit. What'd my father tell you to do to me?"

"Jamie, I'm not going to do anything to you. I only want to talk."

"Sure. You're going to play with me. That's what he told you to do. First you want to calm me down, so I'm quiet. Then you're going to hit me."

"I'm not going to hit you, Jamie. Why'd I want to hit you?"

"You know."

"No, I don't."

"You don't know? So what do you want with me?"

"Your father's worried about you. Where've you been for the last ten days?"

"I been around."

"You haven't been home."

"Says who?"

"I been to your apartment. The cobwebs're taking over."

"So? I been sleeping out. Who cares?"

"You don't go to your usual places. You don't go to work."

"A real snoop, huh? Look, they don't like me at work. I don't like them, either. And my father doesn't want me there. He doesn't trust me. So why should I go to work?"

"Your father told you he doesn't trust you?"

"My father doesn't tell me anything. I know how he feels

46

about me. You know what the hell it is, don't you? It's Howard. That's what the fuck it is. Him and his fuckin' accident. My father, he made me do that advertising campaign. After Howard had that fuckin' accident. They all knew I couldn't do it. My father knew I couldn't do it. He made me do it anyway!"

"What kind of accident?"

"Go to hell! Don't ask me any questions. You got to do something, go ahead and do it. Let's get it over with!"

"So you couldn't handle it. After the accident, you couldn't handle it."

"Of course I couldn't handle it! I never been able to handle crap like that. You know what my father did? He yelled at me. Right in front of the whole fuckin' crew. That's the kind of father I got. And *then* you know what happened? *Howard* suddenly decides he's all better, and he finished the thing himself. They tell me I don't have to do any more work on it, Howard'll take care of everything. Isn't that sweet? Real sweet. That's how they treat me at work. My own father, that's how he treats me. They all hate me."

"So you started drinking."

"What about it?"

"And gambling."

"Yeah! I *like* to gamble. So what?"

"And taking drugs."

"Who the fuck told you that?"

"I heard you're on drugs again."

"I'm not on drugs! Who told you I was on drugs? Oh yeah, now I got it. That's why you're here. You're supposed to prove I'm on drugs so they can put me in jail."

"No, Jamie. It's nothing like that. Your father's worried you might be on drugs again."

"The hell he is! He didn't care last time, did he? He didn't care when I ran away. He only cared when he had to get me out of jail and keep everything quiet. And he only did that because he was afraid my mother'd get mad at him if he didn't."

He's shouting on a regular basis now, so I keep quiet and give him some time to cool down. I don't care much for the things he's telling me. It's starting to sound a little complicated, but in the wrong ways. I wish I'd brought that bottle I told him about.

"Look, Jamie," I finally say, "I don't know what this's about. I'll tell you what I know. Your father wants to talk to you. He wants to be sure you're all right."

"He doesn't care. He'd like to see me kill myself on drugs, but he knows if I did it, my mother'd blame him for it. That's what worries him."

"Maybe you're wrong. Why don't you talk to your father about it? See what he's got to say."

"Yeah," he says. "Yeah. Okay, I want to talk to my father. Yeah! I want to talk to him right now!"

His sudden reversal takes me by surprise. "Okay, Jamie. Let's go see your father."

"No! On the phone. You want me to talk to him? I'll talk to him on the phone. Call him up!"

"No. I don't like phones. Let's go see him."

"No! I'll talk to him. You call him up."

"It's late, Jamie. Maybe he's asleep."

"He'll be awake. If he's home. You want me to talk to him? Call him up. Right now!"

Something's funny. Well, what the hell.

I dial the Stockton home and get an answer after two rings.

"This is the residence Mr. Ethan Stockton. This is Mr. Simson speaking. Please, who is calling, please?"

"This's Mr. Quinlan. I want to talk to Mr. Stockton. Tell him I located his son."

I hold the phone to my ear and wait.

"So you're really a private detective?" Jamie says.

"Yeah. As really as they come."

"What's it like? You carry a gun and everything?"

"Yeah, sometimes."

"What're you going to do? Bring me in with your gun?"

"I don't know. Am I going to need a gun with you?"

"No. I don't like guns. I'm a nice quiet guy. I want a cigarette. You want a cigarette?" His hand reaches inside his suit jacket. When it comes out it isn't holding a cigarette.

20

Ethan Stockton's voice comes over the line.

"Hello? Hello? Mr. Quinlan? You there?"

"Yeah, I'm here," I say. "Wish I wasn't."

"Mr. Simson said you found Jamie."

"Yeah. He's sitting across the table from me."

"Let me speak to him."

"I don't know if I can do that. He asked me to call you so he could talk to you, but I think he changed his mind."

"Changed his mind? I don't understand."

"I don't understand, either. Your son's pointing a .25-caliber pistol at me. He's got the muzzle about two inches away from my right eye. I'd say the barrel could use some cleaning."

"Are you serious?"

"Yeah, I'm serious. The question is, is *he* serious?"

"Mr. Quinlan, let me speak to him."

"Yeah, Mr. Stockton. I'd like to do that. What's your opinion? You think he'll use the gun? You told me he's not dangerous, but now things look a little dangerous."

"All right," Jamie says. "Hang up the phone."

"Come on, kid," I say. "You don't need the gun. The phone's all ready for you. Talk to your old man."

"Don't call me kid! Hang that fuckin' phone up or I'll blow your fuckin' head off!"

"Okay, I got the message." Then I say into the phone, "Good night, Mr. Stockton. Looks like this's the end of our conversation. Not my choice."

As I hang up the phone I hear the closet door open behind me. I really should've checked that closet when I came in. It's turning into a real screw-up, all right. My mind flashes to William Holden at the end of *Bridges of Toko-Ri*. Holden, trapped in the gully, with the Koreans closing in. Holden didn't get out of that one. I wipe it out of my mind.

"Don't turn around," Jamie says. "Keep your eyes on me."

"Okay. Don't get nervous with that gun. I sure hope you know how to handle one of those things. If you don't, you could get both of us into a lot of trouble. They don't make 'em right, you know? One time out of ten, you pull the trigger, the damn thing backfires on you. That's if it doesn't just blow apart in your hand. They never tell you that when you buy 'em."

Someone takes my arms from behind and holds me pinned against the chair. Whoever he is, he's big and strong and sweaty and I can't move. As soon as this fact is established, Jamie puts away the gun, takes a medical syringe from the nightstand and fills it from a small bottle.

"You really don't have to go through all this. You could just hit me on the head."

"Don't worry," Jamie says. "It'll hurt me more'n it hurts you."

"You got a license to practice?"

"You think you're funny?"

"Just scared. When I get scared I try to be funny. Sometimes it takes my mind off things."

"Listen, you shit. Next time give it some thought before you bust in a door."

"Yeah. Careful with that syringe. If you haven't done this before, be careful. You get an air bubble in that thing, you could kill me. It'd be a shame to kill me if you don't want to kill me."

"Don't worry. I'm an expert. Used to give myself shots all the time. Not with stuff like this, of course."

As he comes at me I react instinctively. I push off with my feet against the floor. I hit the big man with my shoulders against his chest.

The big man holds on, squeezing my arms tighter.

I shake my body from right to left, and then the big man swings me against the wall.

My head hits the wall and my head's full of sparks. I kick out my feet but they find nothing to kick against.

I snap my head back and it hits what might be a chin. The big man yells in pain.

That gives me an idea. I open my mouth and yell for all I'm worth.

50

The big man swings me against the wall again.

My eyes close, then open. I see Jamie Stockton coming at me. Then all I see is the point of the syringe.

I shake from right to left. The big man really has me.

I yell again.

Jamie slaps my face and jabs the syringe straight through my jacket sleeve.

I think I feel the needle entering my upper arm, but I'm not even sure I feel that.

21

It itches. My arm. It itches.

Something's sucking at my arm. Like a leech.

Bogart? What's Bogart doing here? Oh. He's sailing the *African Queen*. Down that river. Hepburn's giving him hell. The boat won't move. What's Bogart going to do? He's in the water. Moving the boat. The leeches attack. Leeches. They're sucking him. They're sucking me. Don't suck me! I'm not Bogart!

Itch. Itch. Like ants. Killer ants. Crawling across a jungle. They're after the plantation. They'll eat it up. No they won't. Charlton Heston won't let them. The ants—they want to destroy everything in sight. But they're no match for Heston. That's it! Kill the ants! Yeah! It doesn't itch any more!

But everything's too bright. The sun. That's what it is. The sun. It's Peter O'Toole. Out in the desert. It's the sun!

No! No? No. It's something else. Fuzzy mouth. Swollen tongue.

So this is what it's like. Losing my mind. Losing my mind is like a swollen tongue.

It's O'Toole again. He's back again. What's he still doing in the desert? Sand. And sun. O'Toole! Wise up! Get out of the desert!

Where's the water? I want water. I want water! *I Want Water!*

Water. Water. Thank you. I'm in water. Ahhhhh.

Gregory Peck. Gregory Peck? I'm Gregory Peck. With a wooden leg. I'm in the water now. But I'm strapped to that whale! The whale! He's diving? I'm going down—disappearing into water!

No, this isn't what I wanted! Someone didn't understand my instructions!

Where am I? Where am I?

My arm itches.

22

I think I'm . . .

I think I'm . . . No, I'm not! I'm not!

I'm lying belly up . . . on a bed. Yes I am . . . Yes I am. Belly up . . . on a bed.

My watch tells me seven o'clock . . . The birds tell me morning.

I stand up. Okay. I'm not falling over. Not yet.

My wallet's missing. No. It's on the table. They went through it. But they left it. Even the money. Very considerate.

The room's been . . . Uh oh . . . Here we go again. The room's been stripped of all clothes . . . and sundry articles belonging to Jamie . . . and his friend with the sweaty hands. Looks like the only personal effect they left behind . . . is me.

I wonder if they ever pulled this number on anyone else? . . . They sure did it sweet enough . . . with or without rehearsal.

Whew! Clear up, head! Clear up!

I take the elevator. Down. To the lobby. Spots keep coming before my eyes. They go away, too. But sometimes not quick enough.

I won't bother the desk clerk. With any deep questions. Like whether or not Jamie left. A forwarding address.

Brother.

I go home. Squeeze orange juice. I know how the orange feels.

Drop four eggs. Into the skillet. Scramble. Mix in chopped onion. And a teaspoon of mustard.

Hey! I'm doing this real good! Force of habit.

Two slices of toast. Spread with peanut butter. Perks me up. Some honey in the tea. Any energy I can find, baby.

Baby.

A shower. A shave. With the electric razor. No blade today. I'm not *that* dumb.

A little better. A little better.

I'll read the morning paper. Better check the obituaries. In case I'm there.

I'm not.

Not yet.

Eight thirty. Okay. I'm a little better. Almost human. I'll take a crack at the phone.

The Stockton house. Mr. Simson. He sounds like he doesn't know how to speak. What's wrong with him? Or is it me? Oh, yeah. Now I remember. That's the way Mr. Simson always speaks.

Mr. Stockton isn't up yet. I understand that much.

"Okay, Mr. Simson. This's how it is . . ."

Come on, Charlie! Will you please come on?

"I found Jamie, but he decided he didn't want to stay . . . Performed his midnight experiments on me. I didn't mind. After all, that's what I'm paid for . . . Am I making any sense? I got bored . . . and fell asleep. And Jamie flew the coop. Or something like that. Tell your boss he owes me some . . . information. Let him think about that for a while . . . I'll drop by his office later this after . . . this after . . . this afternoon. Nice speak . . . speak . . . speaking to you, Mr. Simson. We'll have to get together for drinks . . . for drinks . . . for drinks . . . sometime, Mr. Simson. Mr. Simson . . .? Mr. Simson?"

Where the hell . . . did he go? I was just . . . talking to . . . him.

Oh . . . I see . . . I hung up . . . the phone.

Hahahahahahahahahahahahahahahahahahahahahaha.

Oh no! Here it comes . . . again!

NO!

I think I'll go back. To the shower.

Where am I? Where am I?

I'm in the shower. The phone's ringing. Okay. The phone's ringing. Let it ring. It needs practice.

I'm out of the shower. Again. The phone's ringing. Again. If I don't answer it . . .

It might get mad.

"Hello? Is this the phone? Were you ringing?"

"What's going on?" It's Ethan Stockton's voice. "Mr. Simson gave me your message but I can't make hide nor hair of it!"

"That makes two of us . . . Mr. Stockton."

Cut it out!

"Mr. Quinlan? What the hell happened last night? What the hell's going on?"

"Answers," I say. "I want answers. From you. I'll be over to your office. Later. In the afternoon. Later."

"I don't want to wait till this afternoon," he says. "Tell me now! What happened?"

"I don't know," I say. "I don't know."

"You must know!"

"I'm not up to much," I say. "Not right now. I want to talk to you. I can't do it. Not right now. I'll talk to you. But later. And not on the phone. In person. You understand?"

I don't hear anything.

Is he still there? Is anyone still there?

"All right!" he says. "We'll have it your way. At least for now. But I expect action!"

"Good for you, Mr. Stockton. I expect answers. I expect . . ."

What happened? Where is he?

I lost my client!

Oh.

Afraid I hung up the phone again.

I'll try the shower.

Did I already try the shower?

I'll try the shower.

23

I feel a little better now. It's a few hours later and I'm sitting in my office. I'm trying to stay awake, against my better judgment. The phone rings.

"Mr. Charles Quinlan?"

"Yeah. This's Charlie Quinlan. You got him."

"How are you?"

"You ought to know."

"Hey, You know who this is?"

"I'm good at recognizing voices on the phone. I'm especially good at recognizing voices I got a reason to remember."

"I got your name and number from one of your business cards. Charles Quinlan. Investigations. Very nice printing."

"It's called 'Classic Peruvian.' Picked it out myself. Guess I ought to be happy you left the money and the wallet."

"Hey, I'm not a thief!"

"Glad to hear it. What the hell'd you put in that syringe?"

"Nothing lethal."

"Good. That must mean I'm not dead."

"I'm sorry about the whole thing."

"Yeah, I know. It hurt you more'n it hurt me."

"It wasn't my fault. You busted in on me."

"Yeah, I remember. You said you wanted to talk to your father. Why didn't you talk to him?"

"I changed my mind. I couldn't talk to him."

"Who's your friend with the big sweaty hands?"

"Just a friend. Why don't you leave me alone, Mr. Quinlan? You must have other cases which're more interesting."

"Nothing interests me more'n you, baby. Tell you what. Shape up and come over to my office. We'll have a talk. The two of us. Nobody else allowed. Play nice and I might spring for doughnuts."

"Maybe some other time."

I hear someone in my outer office. Steps come toward me. Carolyn Van Duyn née Drexelhof comes in and sits down.

"Still scared?" I say into the phone. "Your father says he only wants to know you're safe and sound. And clean. He says that's all."

"I told you I'm clean. I'm not on anything."

"That's what you told me. The way you acted makes me wonder. What're you doing with the syringe? Keeping in practice for old times sake?"

"I'm clean!"

"Call up your father and tell *him* that."

"I don't want to talk to him."

"So why're you calling me?"

"I thought I ought to apologize for last night. I want to make sure the shot didn't hurt you."

"Very generous of you."

"What's the story, Mr. Quinlan? You going to keep on looking for me?"

"You bet on it, baby. I'll find you, too."

"Yeah? What if I don't want to be found?"

"I'll still find you. And when I do, don't try cute tricks like last night. Any more syringes and I'll kick your butt from Burbank to Barstow."

I hang up the phone.

"Who're *you* supposed to be?" Carolyn says. "Clint Eastwood?"

"Arnold Stang."

"Syringe?"

"Don't ask."

"What's up, Charlie? I called you around midnight, you didn't answer."

"Wasn't there to answer. You could've called at five this morning and I wouldn't've been there."

"Slept out, huh?"

"Yeah."

"Anyone I know? That girl yesterday? Claude?"

"Last night Quinlan slept alone."

"Too bad. You didn't have to sleep alone."

"The way things worked out, I didn't have much choice.

Sorry. If I'd known you wanted me, I would've tried to be there. Just 'cause I got problems doesn't mean *you* got to sleep alone."

"Who says I slept alone?"

"Yeah? Anyone I know?"

"I don't tell tales out of school."

"You're a beaut, Carolyn."

"Actually, I wasn't calling about that. I already had someone lined up by midnight. Just called to tell you I got some more money last night. I got a guy to put in forty thousand."

"Before or after bedtime?"

"No, it was legitimate. He's not the one I ended up with last night."

"Well, you're getting closer to your half a mill."

"But not close enough. You ought to cough up a couple thousand, Charlie. We make this film right, it's got a chance to go through the roof."

"That's what they all say."

"Okay. You're missing a good one."

"That what you wanted?"

"No. I came by to make sure you're all right."

" 'Cause I didn't answer the phone at midnight?"

"I tried again at two. You didn't answer then, either."

"You called at two? What was that? A break in the action?"

"It was halftime."

"How's my horoscope today?"

"You really interested?"

"No. I don't go by that stuff."

"Stop by my office later. I'll check it for you."

I stop by her office and she tells me the horoscope says "Listen to the shifting opinions of others to have a better idea of where you stand and to make stronger progress."

"What the hell's that supposed to mean?" I say.

"Damned if I know," she says. "I just read 'em, I don't try to interpet 'em."

"I think it means don't sink any money into the movie business."

"Fuck you, Charlie."

24

What a fine-looking woman.

I sit in the restaurant across the street, mulling over the menu I face an average of three days a week every week in the year, when something makes me look up in time to see her coming in the door. She's the genuine article, and that's something to think about.

She is old and she is not. She's the type who don't get old. While other women face the constant struggle to keep in style, she is style.

They direct her toward my booth and I get up as she comes over.

"Mr. Quinlan?" she says. "I stopped by your office, but you'd left. Someone said I might find you in here."

"Someone was right, Mrs. Stockton."

She looks at me with surprise. "Have we met before?"

"Nope. You like a drink?"

"Yes. A margarita, please."

We sit looking at each other till the waiter brings two margaritas. Then we click glasses and drink.

I drink. She sips.

"I'll be frank," she says.

"Fine with me."

"I didn't think it'd be a good idea to hire you, Mr. Quinlan. It went on for a week. One day my husband said he was going to hire a detective, the next day he said he wasn't. Then he was, then he wasn't . . ."

"How'd it end up? Did he hire one or not?"

She looks at me.

"Sorry," I say.

"Mr. Quinlan, I assume private detectives are as honest as any man and I don't presume to question your integrity."

"And if you really mean that, you're the only person I ever met who felt that way. Okay, we'll agree I'm the salt of the earth. You're just worried I might discover the family secrets."

"You don't mince words, do you?"

"I can mince with the best of them, if that's what you want."

"We all have things we don't want made too public. We all need our privacy."

"Hollywood's the wrong town for privacy. Try Albuquerque."

"Are all private detectives this rude? Does it come naturally or do they have to train you for it?"

"Sorry. I apologize, Mrs. Stockton. I had a rough night and now you're beating around the bush and sometimes I forget to be patient. I'm sorry."

"This is a difficult thing. Let's not make it more difficult."

"You're right. But please come to your point."

She looks at me without a smile. She's got one of those faces that work without a smile.

"I'm being that transparent?"

"No, Mrs. Stockton, you're doing pretty good. You already got me to apologize and I don't do that so often, even though I probably should."

"Please tell my husband you have to leave this case for reasons of your own. I'll persuade Ethan to compensate you adequately for your time. More than adequately. Whatever you think's a fair amount."

"Uh huh."

"It's my experience, given time, some situations correct themselves. Without outside help. It'd be best to let that happen here, before anyone's hurt."

"Hurt? Is that a threat? If it's a threat, we better get it straight right now."

"No! I don't mean that!" She catches herself and goes back to normal. "I just think things would be better if they're left alone. That's all. Don't you understand?"

"Sure, Mrs. Stockton. That was fine. Couldn't've done it better myself."

"I'm sorry if I insulted you. I wanted—"

"You didn't insult me. But if you can get your husband to compensate me for my time, why don't you just get him to fire me? That'd be the neatest way to do it and a lot cheaper."

She doesn't say anything.

"That's what you ought to do. Go straight to your husband and get him to fire me. Unless, of course, you can't."

"My husband hired you. Once he makes a decision, he sticks to it. For some reason, you men think changing a decision makes you look weak."

"If I tell him I can't do the job, if I don't give any specific reasons, he'll accept it? He'll pay me off?"

"I'll see to it."

"It's always nice to know who controls the purse strings."

"Ethan controls the purse strings, Mr. Quinlan. Don't underestimate him."

I won't underestimate either of you.

"Okay. Guess it's my turn now. I'm probably supposed to tell you how I got a business and a reputation to protect. How I can't walk off a case unless it's over, that sort of thing. Nobody believes that kind of line any more. I don't myself. We'll skip over it and go on to something more interesting, like determining my price. Two thousand dollars? Could you swing it?"

"If you think two thousand dollars is a fair price, I'll talk to Ethan and see what I can do."

"A fair price? I been on the case about twenty-six hours. Some people might say two thousand's a little high for one day's work. Of course, for the record, I did find sonny boy last night and he did pull a gun on me. And for all I know, maybe he was ready to kill me, so I suppose my life's worth something. I don't think I'd get everybody in the world to agree on that, but if it's my decision, I'd have to say my life's worth something. Two thousand sound reasonable?"

"I'm sorry about whatever Jamie did last night. I'll see to it my husband pays you two thousand."

"Aww, it's no big deal. Happens all the time. I almost forgot about it. I didn't know two thousand'd be such an easy thing for you. Better let me think some more. Could you arrange four thousand? Your husband's loaded, he ought to be able to afford it."

She's too good for me. She sips her drink without a frown or a blush or a slap in my face.

"I was somewhat mistaken about you," she says. "Please tell me exactly how much you think you're worth."

"I don't know. Never been asked before. Two thousand'd be pretty good, but I was thinking ahead. When I leave the case your husband'll hire another detective, and when he does you're going to have to go through this whole thing again."

25

That shuts her up like a clam. I'll keep at it.

"Some other detective might be hungrier'n me. He might want four, six, even ten thousand. That's if you're lucky."

"You think my husband would just hire another detective."

"If I quit the case? After last night? Sure he would. The next detective, he might be worse'n me. The noble type, the type you can't buy off. There's really guys like that. I don't understand them. They stick to cases like it'd make some kind of difference. I say take the money and run. Right out of Woody Allen. Simpler that way. I understand you used to be a movie star."

"What? What're you talking about?"

Good. Caught her off guard. Come on, lady. Let's be friends for a while.

"They told me you used to be a star in the movies."

"I wasn't a star. It was a long time ago."

"Tell me about it. Maybe I saw some of your films."

"You wouldn't be interested."

"Sure I would. I been in some films myself."

"You were?"

"Lots of extra stuff. Day player. Next time they run *Spartacus* on TV, if you look real good at the right battle scene you can see me falling down a hill, but the way they cut it, about all you see's my left arm and leg."

"Are you serious?"

"Yeah. I take a nice fall. Tell me about *your* films."

"You're a little too young for my films. Maybe your parents saw them."

"I see a lot of films."

"I was only in two. I was in *Golden Girls,* they show that one on television occasionally. That was 1932, before you were born."

"Yeah, I wasn't around till 1940. What'd they call you back then?"

"Eve Carroll. That was my name before I was married."

"Eve Carroll? You made *Bigtime.* You starred in *Bigtime.*"

"Mary Moore starred, but I was in it."

"I remember. The one with the long blond hair. The gangster's girl."

"That was me."

"Yeah. I hear they're showing *Bigtime* around some more, now. One of those films the college kids picked up. A cult film."

"So I've been told."

"You only made those two films?"

"I left the business after *Bigtime.*"

"How come?"

"I married Ethan."

"He didn't want you in the movies?"

"I wasn't interested in staying in the business, once I got married."

"Your husband, I hear he was really something in those days."

"He was. He had dark hair and a big black mustache. There were lots of girls after him when he came back to California."

"The way I heard it, he came back 'cause he saw one of your films and he was after you."

"I think he heard business was good in California and he just wanted a change of scene."

"I think you're wrong. I think he came back here to marry Eve Carroll."

"Why're you so sure?"

" 'Cause I like it more that way. He made his money in the East, huh? New York?"

"I guess he did well in New York, but he inherited money too.

His parents owned some gold mines in Northern California. Around Oroville. After we were married we bought a ranch up there. It's very beautiful country."

"How come you came back to Los Angeles?"

"It wasn't any good for Ethan. He needs the activity, the hustle and bustle of a city. So we came back here and he started the company."

"Was that a good idea?"

"Those were the early 1940s. Difficult times. I don't think the company made much money at first, but Ethan needed something to do and he didn't have to worry about the money. He was still a young man, he wasn't even fifty. And he was interested in film. He had lots of friends who owned businesses, so he did some advertising for them. He's really very good at it. I think it surprised him to find out how good he was. Stockton Film got to be pretty big, and then he started into television commercials right away and that made him a lot of money. Ethan's always been very astute in business, very quick to go in the right direction. He was one of the first to produce television commercials for politicians."

"That's not much to be proud of. He ever use you in his stuff?"

"I never had any great talent as an actress. When I was young I had the looks for it. That was all."

"You still got the looks for it."

"Well, it's kind of you to say that. No, I never wanted to go back into the business. It was only something, an accident, really, which happened when I was young."

"The right place at the right time, huh?"

"Yes. A very fortunate accident. If it hadn't happened, I probably never would've met Ethan."

"Sometimes accidents turn out pretty lucky. Sometimes the business helps people out, and sometimes it doesn't."

"The time I spent working in movies, the little time I spent there, they were good times."

Throw it at her, Charlie.

"How long's your son been playing with guns?"

"Jamie doesn't play with— Oh, I thought you . . . So . . . I see. So you wanted to catch me off guard."

I don't say a thing.

"You were just waiting. Waiting to ask me about Jamie."

Lady, I never stopped asking about Jamie.

26

"I didn't come here to discuss Jamie," she says.

"Then you might's well get up and leave," I say.

She doesn't move.

"How'd he look last night? Did Jamie look well?"

"Hard to say. I never saw him before, I don't know how well he's supposed to look. A little haggard but acceptable. If you want to know if your son's on drugs, he says he isn't. Could be he's telling the truth, but we'll have to wait and see."

That's got her hooked.

"Are you a discreet man, Mr. Quinlan?"

"Holy cow! How the hell should *I* know?"

"That's not a very comforting answer."

"It's an honest answer. You want comfort, don't come to me. You want to help your son, I think you probably ought to tell me about him."

She sips tentatively at her drink, then puts the glass back down on the table. "Jamie's never been a good boy, but he's never been a bad boy, either. He's always been weak, very easily influenced."

"I think he's over that now. He was doing some fancy influencing last night—with a gun."

"I was surprised when I heard about that. I didn't know he still fooled with guns."

"I don't like the sound of this. You going to tell me he shoots people?"

"No! That's a ridiculous question!"

"Yeah, you're right. It was kind of ridiculous. You'll have to excuse me, I'm just the guy he pointed the gun at. I'm biased."

"He wouldn't't've used it. He's not that kind."

"*Nobody's* that kind, Mrs. Stockton. Till some day they *do* it. *Then,* all of a *sudden,* they're that kind."

She doesn't say anything. I try to calm down. Then I say, "I'm sorry. How long ago'd he start playing with guns?"

"Military school. They taught the students to shoot rifles."

"A worthwhile course. That'd be a long time ago."

"Jamie stuck with it. When he went to college he was on the rifle team."

"He do good in college?"

"He dropped out. No, he didn't drop out. His marks weren't good and the Army took him. He was a top marksman in the Army. That's about the only success he's ever had, his marksmanship. Ethan says Jamie must've inherited the talent from him."

"Your husband likes guns too? Your husband shoot people?"

No answer.

Looks like you can push this lady pretty far without her cracking. She starts her sipping act again. At the rate she's going, it'd probably take the better part of the day for her to finish the one margarita, and a guy like me would have little hope of getting another one into her.

I don't know what to make of Mrs. Ethan Stockton. But she doesn't know what to make of me, so I'm keeping the score even. Sometimes that's the best I can do.

"My husband had a great deal to do with guns when he was younger. Before we met. Your question was in poor taste, Mr. Quinlan."

"Don't take me so seriously. Your son was successful in the Army?"

"Only as a marksman. As for other things, he didn't seem properly suited. They asked him to leave."

"The Army doesn't ask its soldiers to leave."

"They asked my son to leave."

"Any of my business?"

"I don't think so."

"Of course it isn't. Why'd I bother to ask? I guess that's another question in poor taste, and there's probably some kind of

65

extenuating circumstance, as we say. And there's no connection with the business at hand."

"There's no connection."

"I didn't think there was." I'll let it go for now. "What'd Jamie do after he left the Army?"

"Ethan took Jamie into the business. Jamie was never right for the business."

"Maybe your husband figured he could keep Jamie out of trouble."

"I don't think that's quite the way to put it. Ethan just wanted to watch out for Jamie."

"He didn't do such a good job. Jamie disappeared, then he surfaced in Vegas, and when he came up for air he didn't look so hot."

"So you know about that. Very well. There were reasons for that."

"What're those reasons? Or maybe I'm not supposed to ask."

"They're irrelevant. They wouldn't have anything to do with why he disappeared now. I'm sure of that."

Good. That means you know why he disappeared before.

"Why'd he disappear now, Mrs. Stockton?"

"I don't know."

"You're a beaut, Mrs. Stockton. Tell you what I think. Maybe he *did* have the same reasons. Then and now. And that's what you're afraid I'll find out."

"No, Mr. Quinlan. It couldn't possibly be the same thing."

"Sure it's the same thing. That's why you want me off the case."

Chew on that for a while.

"This morning I heard you'd seen Jamie, and I heard about the gun. Jamie's a weak boy, Mr. Quinlan. If he's got a gun, he's scared."

"Scared of what?"

"You might hurt him. Without meaning to, of course. I don't want that to happen."

"If he pulls a gun on me again, I'll do everything I can not to hurt him."

"Will you stop looking for Jamie?"

"Why does your husband want me to find Jamie? Jamie says his father doesn't care about him. He says you're the only one who cares about him."

"Jamie told you that?"

"Yeah."

"That's nonsense. If it were my decision, Jamie could disappear forever and never come back."

27

Casually gulping down what's left of my margarita, I say, "Come on, Mrs. Stockton. Have a heart. I'm just a poor working stiff and I had a hard night. Let's try it one more time. You come here to see me, you say you want me off the case—okay, I'll buy that much. But tell me *why* you want me off the case and make it good enough so I don't have to ask you again, okay?"

"I love my husband more than anything in the world and I won't let him be hurt. He's not so strong any more. He's proud, he's always relied on himself, but things're different. Now he looks to other people to do the things he can't do himself."

"Like me."

"What? Oh, yes. Like you. But Ethan's not what he used to be. He tries to hide it, but he's an old man and he doesn't have the resilience he once had. If something were to happen, it might hit him harder than he thinks."

"What's going to hit him?"

"I don't want Ethan hurt."

"Something's hurting him right now."

"Ethan did the right thing when Jamie disappeared before. He didn't do anything. When Jamie turned up in jail, on drugs, Ethan went to Las Vegas and took care of it. He put Jamie in an asylum, and when they said he was well enough Ethan brought him back to the business. Ethan feels guilty about Jamie. As if Jamie's problems were his fault. That's why he hired you. He feels responsible for Jamie, and for what Jamie's done or may do. He wants to stop things because he's afraid they'll get worse, and because of that they probably will get worse."

"How'll that happen?"

"I don't know. I don't know where it'll lead, but I think wherever it leads Ethan's going to be disappointed."

"Your son's walking around Los Angeles with a gun in his hand, Mrs. Stockton. That's a problem and it won't go away. If you want to help your husband, you ought to help me. You don't help me, or you lie to me, it'll probably get worse."

"I don't know what to do."

"Your husband's got a man working for him, some guy named Howard. You know him?"

"Of course I know him. Howard Banner."

"Banner? That name means something to me. Howard Banner. Why do I know that name? Who is he?"

"He's my son-in-law. He doesn't have anything to do with this."

"Your son-in-law, huh? Tell me about his accident. The one he had recently."

"That's nothing to do with this."

"Jamie told me this guy Howard had an accident. I always like to know about accidents. What happened?"

"Nothing."

"Sure. Nothing. That's why Jamie told me about it, 'cause it's nothing. Come on, lady. If it's not important, you can tell me about it. If you can't tell me about it, I got to figure it's important. You really want me to figure it's important?"

"It's *not* important. Howard was driving to San Francisco last New Year's Eve and there was an accident on the road. A three-car collision. It was in the newspapers. That's probably where you know Howard's name from."

"No. I know the name Howard Banner, but it's something else. Don't try to put me off the track. Did he cause the accident?"

"The police investigated. They said it was one of the other drivers' fault."

"Your husband didn't pay off the cops to keep things quiet? Like he did in Vegas?"

"No! Ethan didn't do that. There were other people involved. Other people hurt. Ethan'd never pay to keep things quiet in a matter like that, with other people hurt!"

"How seriously was Howard hurt?"

"Sometimes Howard leads a charmed life. He wasn't scratched."

"Something must've happened. He didn't take on an advertising thing. Jamie had to take it over."

"It was something else. A girl was seriously disfigured in the accident. Howard felt responsible. He couldn't get his mind off it. That's why he couldn't work."

"You said the accident wasn't Howard's fault."

"It wasn't. This girl, she was riding in Howard's car."

"Uh huh. You mean, this girl, she wasn't your daughter?"

"It wasn't Amanda. It was a girl, some girl Howard picked up that evening."

"Howard does that sort of thing?"

"Mr. Quinlan, it's been my experience many married men do that sort of thing. Occasionally."

"How bad was the girl hurt?"

"I never saw her. They said her face was badly scarred. I understand she was very pretty before the accident. Howard arranged for a plastic surgeon to take care of her, but I guess the operation wasn't successful."

"Too bad. That's why Howard didn't do this advertising campaign?"

"He was depressed, he couldn't work."

"Must've bothered your daughter, too."

"Howard's a little like that. Amanda's learned to live with it. You either learn to live with it, or you leave. All wives have to learn to live with certain things if they want to go on living with their husbands."

"I guess husbands have to learn to live with some things themselves."

"Marriage is no bed of roses, Mr. Quinlan. With Howard,

69

sometimes he does things without really thinking too much about what he's doing. At heart he's a good boy. Ethan and I understand, and Amanda understands. You have to get used to Howard."

"I can believe that. I met him yesterday. Briefly. Very briefly. I can see how he'd take some getting used to. When your husband gave the advertising campaign to Jamie, did he really think Jamie could do it?"

"Ethan tried to help Jamie. I warned him it wouldn't work. He should've listened to me. Toward the end, when Howard took over, it was too late to salvage much. The spot was never used. I've seen it, it was quite bad. I guess Ethan finally realized he'd pushed Jamie too far."

"Jamie says his father yelled at him in front of some people."

"It was bad. Ethan apologized later, for what good it did."

"Apologies usually aren't worth too much. People make 'em 'cause they don't know what else to do. Your son-in-law, Howard, you like him, huh?"

"He's a good boy."

"He makes good commercials?"

"Excellent."

"When I saw him the other day he didn't look like much of a success."

"Howard's had some bad luck. He thinks he's a failure. Once you think you're a failure, pretty soon you are a failure."

"How come he's a failure?"

"He's not a failure. He's brilliant. If you'd seen some of those spots he made two years ago, you'd know what I mean. They were the best work Howard's ever done."

"How come I didn't see them?"

"They didn't run down here. Just in San Francisco. They were political commercials, for John Donhauser."

"He made commercials for Donhauser?"

"They were wonderful spots. Some people think Donhauser might've lost that election except for Howard's spots."

"I don't think much of politicians—in fact, I don't care for them at all. But John Donhauser's enough to give even politicians a bad name. He's sort of connected."

70

"What?"

"He's owned. By a San Francisco hood. A guy who likes to pretend he's the kind of guy Brando played in the movie."

"Oh. Yes, I know about that. It's rather a sore point in the family. Ethan didn't want to take the account, but Howard said he had some ideas he wanted to try out. That's why he wanted to do those spots. I only mean the spots he made, they were brilliant. The best work he's ever done."

"Sure. You shoot good film, it doesn't matter what the film's used for, right?"

"Maybe Howard didn't realize what he was doing at the time."

"That'd be a good trick. Donhauser's criminal ties weren't all that secret. People knew where his money was coming from."

"Howard didn't elect Donhauser. The people of San Francisco did that."

"Howard dressed up the package, he sold the soap. But he didn't force anyone to wash with it, huh?"

"He was paid to do a job. He did it extremely well."

"There's some jobs, maybe they shouldn't be done."

"You sound prejudiced."

"I am. I got reasons. Aww, the hell with it. Look, if those spots're so good, how come you said Howard's a failure?"

"He *is* a failure. But sometimes, if he lets himself go, he's brilliant. That's what Ethan sees in him."

"But he doesn't see it in your son."

"Jamie's different. Howard tried once, and maybe some day he'll try again. Jamie won't try."

"So you'd just's soon see Jamie disappear."

"Don't judge me, Mr. Quinlan. You don't understand what's going on."

"I probably don't. But I know you're afraid of me."

"I am?"

"Uh huh. You say you don't care if your son disappears forever, but you do care about your son-in-law, and I might feel the same way if I knew them both, but the way I see it, you're afraid

71

your son-in-law's the one who's going to get hurt by all of this. That's the problem."

"No, it's not Howard."

"Why'd the Army ask your son to leave?"

"I don't know."

"Oh, brother. The hell with this. Thanks for stopping by, Mrs. Stockton. I got a couple ways to see Army records. Don't worry, I'll get the whole story. Give my regards to your husband."

She doesn't move.

"Jamie was a bad soldier. That's all."

"The Army's full of bad soldiers. That's what makes it the Army. Jamie was a crack marksman. I think they'd keep him around."

"He couldn't follow orders."

"They'd make him follow orders."

"Then I don't know why they didn't want him."

"I know why."

"What?"

"I know why, Mrs. Stockton. They didn't want him 'cause he liked the other soldiers too much."

"What're you talking about?"

"Come on, he doesn't like girls. It's all over the office. Jamie's gay. He's queer. That's why they kicked him out of the Army."

"No he isn't! Jamie isn't that way!"

"It's not so serious, Mrs. Stockton. Some people're gay. It's nothing to be ashamed of. That must be why he got kicked out."

"No! They kicked him out because he stole things!"

28

Ahh. That's what I wanted. He stole things.

"What kind of things?" I say.

"Letters," she says. "Things like that. Nothing big, not money. Nothing important. Nothing of value."

"Oh. So all of a sudden you know all about it."

"Jamie always stole things. When he was a child he'd go through my desk, my bureau. And my husband's things. Just pins and costume jewelry, things like that. He couldn't help himself. The doctors couldn't cure him. When he was in the Army he stole rings, watches, I don't know what else. They found out it was him and they beat him. The other soldiers. It happened more than once."

"What'd the Army do? Court-martial him?"

"Dishonorable discharge."

"Your husband must've loved that."

"Ethan made sure it was kept quiet. That was all."

"He took Jamie into the business so he could keep an eye on him."

"Yes."

"What about your son-in-law, Howard? Was he working at the company then?"

"That was before Howard married Amanda. I'm not sure. Howard left the company for a while, but then he came back to work for Ethan again. I suppose he may've been back by then."

"How long did Jamie last before he disappeared?"

"A year. No, it must've been longer. Two years."

"Why'd he disappear?"

"You already asked me that."

"And you didn't tell me, so I'm asking again. That's how it works."

"It doesn't matter."

"So you do know the reason."

She drinks the rest of her margarita all in one swallow. "You mustn't tell Ethan we've met," she says. "We need time, that's all. If we could just have a little time, everything'll take care of itself."

"What if you're wrong?"

"What if *you're* wrong, Mr. Quinlan?"

She sits still for a moment and her face changes. Exactly what that change is, I couldn't say, but suddenly there's something different there, something you couldn't pin down.

"What a mess this is. I shouldn't've come here."

"So why'd you come?"

"My husband said you looked like a decent man."

"You're sounding pretty good now."

"What's that supposed to mean?"

"I don't know. I'm wondering out loud. What you're saying now—are you saying it 'cause you mean it or 'cause it sounds good?"

"You think I'm acting out a little scene for you?"

"Are you?" She sits quietly. "You said a lot of things. I don't know which things I believe, or if I believe any of them."

"I'm not used to being talked to this way."

"Yeah, maybe I ought to be sorry for saying something like that, and if I should be sorry, I *am* sorry. But right now I'm not sure. Maybe you're a little too clever for me."

"You're crazy."

"You won't get any argument from me on that. I'm even crazy in ways you don't know about. The question is, right now, am I being crazy in the right way?"

"You don't understand. You don't know anything about what's going on. You're an outsider, you're not part of it."

"And you're afraid if I stay around I *will* be part of it."

"Can't you just leave it alone?"

No. I can't. I really can't. I needed a case and now I've got it and I won't let go. I can't.

"You really want me to leave it alone?" I say.

"I hoped you were a man I could trust."

"Trust to do what?"

"Oh, you're impossible."

"You hoped I was someone you could come here and tell me what you wanted, I'd go out and do it, no questions asked. But you got the wrong guy."

"Please, at least keep your mouth shut about our conversation. I don't want Ethan to know I've seen you."

"That'd cause a problem, huh?"

"You're just impossible. Mr. Quinlan. If you can't leave things alone, don't let my husband be hurt. Please, you're working for him, you must protect him."

"Protect him or protect you?"

She doesn't like that. She stands, trying to make her face go back to the way it looked when she came in. She can't do it. She's good but not that good.

I've rattled her about something and maybe she figures if she stays any longer I'll figure out what it is. What can I throw at her to crack things up? She's a pretty strong lady and I don't know if that's good or—

"I'm not going to let anything happen to Ethan, Mr. Quinlan. You better understand that."

"Okay. Tell me how I can watch out for him."

She stands there, looking at me. "It's no good," she says. "I wanted to trust you. I don't think I can."

I reach for something else to say but I'm not quick enough. Everyone in the place looks up to watch her leave.

29

"Howard Banner?" Carolyn says. "Yeah, Charlie, I heard of him."

We're sitting in Carolyn's office, on either side of her statuette. The one that's supposed to be an Academy Award, but isn't.

"I heard of him too," I say. "But I don't know where."

"Made a couple films back in the sixties. Stinko. So I heard, I never saw them. No, I'm wrong. Did see one a couple years back. *Flower of Evil.* Pretty bad stuff."

"I must've missed it."

"Everybody did. He took a couple actors who'd been on TV awhile and weren't even good enough for that. That film finished them off. Must've finished off Banner, too. Never heard anything else about him, till just now."

"He's making commercials."

"Good. Hope he stays there. He's one of those guys, they don't direct, they steal stuff from other directors. And they don't even know enough to steal the good stuff."

"Was he with a studio?"

"Some of the studios, they're a little nuts, but they ain't *that* nuts. Banner, he must've made two, three pictures. I don't think any more'n that. Independent, all of them. Hell, he must've known someone with a lot of money. Wish I knew someone with a lot of money."

"Sign Howard Banner to direct for you. He'll tell you where he got his financing."

"I'd rather be poor."

"Carolyn? There's something you won't do for money?"

"Yeah. I won't hire a crap director like Howard Banner."

30

When I get to Stockton Film, Claude's on the phone, but she looks up and smiles when I walk in. That gives my spirits a lift.

The walls of the reception room are hung with stills from television commercials. One of the pictures shows a famous film actor who was in some of the greatest gangster movies of the 1930s. Now he smiles kindly at me and holds a can of coffee in his hands.

I sit down and listen to Claude's end of the phone conversation.

"Just a false alarm," she says. "Nobody gets the boot ... Yeah, we're all smiling at each other again ... Thanks for keeping your eyes open ... Yeah ... Okay. See you."

She hangs up the phone and we exchange smiles.

"You look happy today," I say. "That mean I got a better chance'n yesterday?"

"I wouldn't count on it."

"That's what I figured."

"You don't have to give up right away!"

"That sounds better. How's the career going?"

"Blech. Pretty much the same's yesterday. I heard about this company, they're looking for people for a film but they don't want to see any actresses unless you get submitted by an agent. So I figure I'll get my agent to submit me. So I call my agent. He's not even there. He's doing so well, he went down to Mexico for a week. Didn't even bother to tell me he's going. I got some agent."

"Least he's got enough money to get down to Mexico for a week."

"I don't suppose you gave my résumé to anyone."

"Gave one to a friend. Remember, no guarantees. If something happens, it happens. You never know."

"You really gave my résumé to someone? You didn't just throw it away?"

"I gave it to someone. Things're tough, lady. Both in the business and outside it. So maybe we help each other, we'll pull through."

"I usually hear it phrased other ways."

"What's going on with the phone call? Thinking of changing jobs?"

"Thought I was going to have to."

"Don't tell me Mr. Stockton doesn't like your short skirts?"

"He comes out here at least once a day, no matter how busy he gets, to see what I'm wearing. He says it's to stretch his legs. It's not *his* legs he's interested in. One of my first days here, I wore pants. He sent me a memo about that. A memo. No more pants. That's all it said."

"Gets to the crux of the matter, doesn't he?"

"Since then Mr. Stockton and me, we been on pretty good terms. Anything to keep the boss happy, you know."

"And the customers, too. So you're an actress, he's the boss, he likes you. How come he doesn't use you in his commercials?"

"That's the way it is. They could be looking for someone just like me for a spot, they wouldn't even think of using me. They just think of me as the receptionist. People in advertising, they're supposed to have imaginations, right? Well, those imaginations stop before they get to me."

"So you're thinking about leaving?"

"Thought I was going to have to."

"They don't pay you enough?"

"A receptionist never gets paid enough. No, that's not the problem. The new accountant came in last week to give his first

77

report on the books. There's money missing. Must be plenty. The story went through the building in less'n an hour. Everyone got scared the pink slips'd be coming around by the end of this week, so I told all my friends to look out for a new job for me."

"But now everything's okay? You had a false alarm?"

"It's funny. You work for a rich guy, after a while you stop thinking of him as a rich guy. Mr. Stockton's covering the whole thing and nobody gets the ax. He found out how worried we all were, so he sent out a memo this morning so we'd know there's no financial problems we have to worry about. He's a pretty good boss. Not like some I worked for."

"There's an old saying, I'm not sure if it's from Confucius or Jack Warner. It says when a new accountant finds money missing, maybe the old accountant's got a villa on the French Riviera."

"Confucius and Jack Warner are both off this time. If Harry took the money, nobody'll ever see it."

"Who's Harry?"

"Harry Spencer. Our old accountant."

"Why'd he leave?"

"He's dead. Died last month in a car accident."

"I'm hearing a lot about car accidents lately."

"Harry was a poor guy. I don't mean *poor* poor. I mean unlucky. And a rotten driver. About once a month he liked to get really plastered. And he wasn't a good driver when he was sober. I don't know how he ever got a driver's license. Must've paid someone off. He drove me home once, I thought we'd never make it. You'd meet him here at the office and you'd figure he's the quietest, meekest guy in the world. But you see him out on the road, he was a maniac."

"Glad I didn't know him. So you're staying on here."

"Yeah. I better get back to work before Miss Blitman comes out here and wants to know what I'm doing. What time's your appointment today?"

"No time. I don't exactly have an appointment."

"Yeah? So what're you doing here?"

"I wanted to see you."

"Uh huh?"

"I also want to see Mr. Stockton."

"Without an appointment? He won't see you."

"Sure he will. Ask him."

"You really think he'll see you? Are you that important?"

"Don't I look important?"

"I'm afraid to answer that."

"Call your boss."

"I never call my boss. I call Miss Blitman."

She picks up the phone and speaks to Miss Blitman. She frowns and whispers to me, "Miss Blitman isn't going to let you see him. Nobody gets by the dragon lady."

I take the phone and say, "Hello, Miss Blitman. Nice to speak to you again. I wouldn't want to get you in any trouble, but I'm in a bit of a rush. Tell Ethan I got to see him right away. Important stuff. You understand."

I hang up the phone before she can answer.

"You got to be kidding," Claude says. "You call him Ethan?"

"Only during business hours."

"You may get yourself thrown out of here."

"I been thrown out of places before. Some of 'em better'n this."

31

Miss Blitman appears in the doorway, keeping her eyes off me.

"Come this way, Mr. Quinlan."

I wink at Claude. Miss Blitman turns crisply and I follow her down the hall. She pokes her head into Mr. Stockton's office and I hear his voice grumble something. She pokes her head back out and paces quickly to her own office. Once she's at her door, she feels secure again. She turns and says, "Go in, Mr. Quinlan. Mr. Stockton would like to see you. And should you have the time, please be so kind as to screw yourself." And she shuts the door pretty loudly.

79

"You say something to Miss Blitman?" Mr. Stockton says. "She was in one hell of a snit just now."

"I just proposed marriage," I say. "She proposed something else."

There's a woman in the room. About my age. Slender and dark, in a tight black dress. You'd definitely look at least twice.

"Mr. Quinlan, this's my daughter, Mrs. Banner."

She holds out her hand. "Very nice to meet you, Mr. Quinlan. Do you think you can find my brother?"

I look over at Mr. Stockton. He gives me a small shrug that is supposed to mean something but I'm not sure what, so I decide it means I might as well go ahead and say whatever I feel like saying.

"Finding him's no big problem, Mrs. Banner. He's not trying too hard to hide himself. I already found him once. Doing more'n just finding him *could* be a problem."

"Is it true Jamie pulled a gun on you?"

There aren't many secrets kept in this family. I look back at Mr. Stockton. Still no clear message.

"Yeah, he pulled a gun," I say. "He was nervous."

"I'm sure he didn't mean to hurt you," she says. "You may've frightened him. Jamie's very high-strung. I hope, if you find him again, you'll be gentle with him."

"Don't worry, Mrs. Banner. I won't break him. Maybe if I'm lucky he won't break me, either."

"Jamie's not a bad boy. He won't hurt you."

"Maybe you could write me a little note to that effect. Next time I see Jamie I'll give him your note."

"You're not looking for a criminal, Mr. Quinlan. We're worried about Jamie. We want him back."

"Sorry, Mrs. Banner. I had a hard night. Maybe I'm making a bad impression on people today. I'm not interested in hurting your brother. If I can get him back, I'll get him back."

"Well, I guess you know your business. Jamie's a good boy. He's only confused, and sometimes he does things he doesn't really want to do."

"Don't we all."

She looks at me for another moment, then turns to her father. "I'll see you, Dad. I'm see you, Dad. I'm going to try to collect my husband. They say he's in the screening room, as usual. Goodbye, Mr. Quinlan."

As soon as she's closed the door, Mr. Stockton says, "What the hell's going on? What's all this crap about guns?"

He's a smart guy. He's going to take the offensive first. But only if I let him.

"Don't ask me," I say. "Ask your son, he's the one with the gun."

"I'd like to ask my son. I thought you were going to get him back for me."

"I thought so, too. Then he pulled a gun."

"So what the hell's going on?"

"I'll tell you what the hell's going on. You're not telling me crap, that's what's going on. You could've told me a couple things yesterday, maybe you'd have your son back now. But you *didn't* tell me some things, and he could've killed me last night. You want to get mad at someone? Get mad at yourself. I did what I was supposed to do. But I don't think *you* gave me what I needed to get the job done."

He sits quietly for a moment. Then he says, "You really think Jamie would've killed you?"

"If he wanted to kill me, he could've done it, so I figure that's not what he wanted to do. But next time I find him, he may have different plans. It's something I got to think about."

"I'm sorry about the gun, Mr. Quinlan. Really, I had no idea. Were you hurt?"

"You should've told me your son might have a gun."

"But how could I know?"

"Yesterday I asked if your son had a reason to disappear. You said you didn't know. You should've told me the truth."

"I told you the truth."

"You told me bullshit! Your son's been pocketing money from the firm."

He stiffens. "Who made that accusation?"

"Your son started to gamble with a lot of money. Then he

disappeared. Meanwhile your new accountant tells you the business's out a lot of money. Don't bother to deny it, it's an open secret around here. Everybody knew it but me. Including the guy who locks up at night. So you're missing a bundle. You going to tell me your son didn't take the money?"

"Don't be abrupt with me, young man. I'm the man you work for, remember? I pay the bills."

I've struck a raw nerve. It gives me the advantage, and Ethan Stockton knows it. He doesn't like it. He immediately regains his composure. He does it so automatically and effortlessly, it worries me. That gives him an advantage.

"Jamie may've taken the money," he says tonelessly. "Still, it could've been someone else. I probably should've told you about it yesterday."

"You didn't want the cops in on this. Not because of drugs. You were worried about this theft."

"Police can get noisy. I don't want the missing money to be public knowledge. I hoped you'd find Jamie without having to know about this. As for the gambling, I thought you might figure Jamie's got some other sources of income which'd explain it, and you wouldn't give it any thought."

"So you knew about that already."

"About what?"

"Jamie's other source of income. I found the account book in his apartment. Your son's dealing."

"Dealing? You mean he's selling drugs?"

"Probably marijuana. He's not making a hell of a lot of money at it, so my guess's marijuana."

"I didn't know about that. When you saw Jamie, did he look like he's on drugs?"

"I don't know. He didn't seem to be last night, but don't jump to conclusions. We'll have to wait till he's back."

"You think he'll come back?"

" I don't think he's got anywhere to go. Not if he's staying in town. But he's afraid to come back. He's afraid of you."

"Yeah. Jamie's always been afraid of me. Jamie's afraid of people. That's his nature."

"Maybe you push him to take on too much responsibility around here."

"Yeah. I suppose a lot of it's my fault."

"Maybe not, Mr. Stockton. Maybe Jamie stole the money and he's afraid of that. How much money you got missing?"

"A pretty good amount."

"Come on, Mr. Stockton. With what I know already, I want to do you some harm, I can do you some harm. Don't keep secrets. How much money?"

"Fifty thousand, seventy-five thousand. We're still not sure. It's very confusing. Padded expense accounts, things like that. For a while I thought the amount was even higher."

"Okay. If Jamie didn't take it, who did?"

"I don't know. It could be any of at least a dozen people."

"Like your old accountant? Harry Spencer?"

"Spencer? How could it be him? He's dead."

"So I heard. So what?"

"Yeah. I suppose so. Even him. Could've been anyone."

"You don't care about the money, do you?"

He gets up from his chair and hobbles over to the bar. I think he's stalling. Some Scotch goes into a pewter mug, and then down his throat. He finally works his way back to his chair and settles into it.

"Money's something the bankers count," he says. "I've had so much of it for so long, it's lost whatever meaning it's supposed to have. The thing that bothers me, it's not how much money's missing. It's that someone took it."

"You want to know who that someone is?"

"I guess I got to know. I'm the boss here. So I got to know. But I'm more concerned about the welfare of my son."

I have to go hard again. Despite all the trouble he's giving me, I'm getting to like him. And that right there is a big problem. You can't do the things you have to do if you get liking your clients too much. It gives you a blind spot. So I have to get a little tough with him again.

"You worried about your son 'cause you're *really* worried

about him, Mr. Stockton, or you just figure maybe you're supposed to *act* worried so I'll figure this's all legit?"

"You really like to play the role, don't you?"

"No. I don't like to play it. I just don't have any choice about it. Too many people give me too many lies, I need a little protective covering here and there, to keep off the slings and arrows of outrageous fortune."

"Mr. Quinlan, if you worked for me, I might fire you."

"I do work for you."

"Oh? You *do* work for me? Maybe I forgot. Maybe you forgot too."

"Sure. We both forgot. Except I don't forget anything, if I can help it. I just ignore some things. You're worried about your son, huh? Which is it? Love or guilt?"

He tries to laugh, but he isn't the type and it doesn't come out too well.

"That's it, Mr. Quinlan. Keep pushing. Till you get your answer. Maybe I should've been honest with you when I hired you. Don't seem to get anywhere being dishonest with you."

"Uh huh."

"I'm too used to dealing with weak sisters. That's what it is. Okay, it's some love and some guilt, and most of it's guilt. I guess the guilt part's got me worried about Jamie. That what you wanted to know?"

"You want me to stay on the case? If you want me off it, you better say so now. You may not get another chance."

"Find my son."

"You want me to bring him back to you if he doesn't want to come back?"

"Mr. Quinlan, some men, you give them a gun, it's okay, they know what to do with it. Or what *not* to do with it, which's even more important. I don't like the idea of Jamie with a gun. It could be he's sick, he needs help. I don't mean help from me. You know what I mean. Bring him back to me. Then I'll do whatever I can."

"Okay. I hope we understand each other. Anything else I should know? I get the feeling you're not so hot on keeping secrets.

What about your daughter? She know your son may've stolen money from you?"

"Why would Amanda know?"

"I don't know. She and her brother close? She sounded worried."

"They're brother and sister. She's concerned. The last time Jamie disappeared, she got pretty ill. Yeah, she's worried. She knows what happened last time."

"How about your son-in-law? You think he's worried?"

"Howard? I don't think Howard gives it much of a thought one way or the other. Howard's pretty much in his own world. Anyway, Howard and Jamie, they've never been friends."

"What about Howard? Could he've taken the money?"

"No, I don't think so. He could've done it, of course. But for what reason? I treat Howard like he's another son. He doesn't need money."

32

The fourth floor of Stockton Film is a collection of locked doors. Each door has a rectangular plastic title, black on white: Editing Room, Costume Room, Property Room, Film Library. Each door is locked and the hall is silent. Everyone's gone home.

On the third floor I find an open door. I walk up some stairs, which lead to a projection booth. One projector is humming away.

Beside it stands the projectionist, the kind of man I think of when I think about unions. He wears his gray hair in a short brush cut. A white T-shirt covers a belly protruding a yard over his belt buckle. His eyes hold a twinkle and his hands hold a can of beer and a fresh ham sandwich. It may be his first ham sandwich for the night but not his first beer.

"Howdy doody," he says. "What can I do you for?"

"Just looking over the building," I say.

"Don't believe it's for sale. Ain't seen you around. You workin' here?"

"Since yesterday."

"Welcome aboard. You inna production end?"

"Special project. Running some good film tonight?"

"I'm runnin' film."

"Not a good show?"

"Depends on what you mean. That's the screenin' room down there, below us. If you're talkin' about the show onna screen, I seen it a hundred times. It stinks. But if you're talkin' about the show inna seats, that a different story from Mother Goose. Can you keep your mouth shut?"

"I can try."

"Bop over to the window here and take a look. See the one inna orange pants and the flowered shirt? He's the old man's son-in-law, Howard Banner. The one inna black dress, she's his wife. Amanda Stockton Banner. That means she's both his wife and the old man's daughter. Got the picture? You put the two of 'em together down there, you got yourself a fruitcake. But you also got yourself quite a free show, once they get goin'. They're quiet now, but you wait around, it'll get interestin'. Howard plans to sit down there, get drunk and watch his old films. Me, I'm just sittin' up here and gettin' drunk. I had it with his fuckin' films. He likes 'em, though. He's a little off in the upstairs department, you know? Not quite playin' with a full deck. Those fuckin' films. Far's I'm concerned, they're borin' as hell, so if you wanna stay here and keep me company, you're welcome. Some nights, it gets so bad up here, I'm ready to take a flyin' fuck out the window."

He pauses to catch his breath, and I say, "What about his wife? She likes to watch his films?"

"Hey. This stuff I'm sayin', you ain't gonna tell anyone, like the old man, are you?"

"I'm just here to keep you company."

"Yeah. Okay. I wanna get that straight."

"What's the wife doin' down there?"

"She wants to get him outa here. Happens like this at least once a month. One time, I'm gonna get a camera up here, I'm gonna film the whole thing. I'll bet it'd be better'n some of them pornos they're showin' up on Hollywood."

86

"What's the film you're running here?"

"*Angel.* Directed by Mr. Howard Banner himself. One of the ten worst movies of 1961, in case you missed it and were wonderin' why. You don't wanna believe me, you don't have to. The critics were unanimous. They all said it's a piece of crap."

"How come you're showing it tonight?"

"Howard likes to look at it. It's like lookin' at an accident out onna freeway. I made somethin' this bad, I'd throw it away first chance I got."

"But Banner likes it?"

"I dunno. Guess so. Me and Bennie, the other projectionist, we take turns whenever he gets inna mood. I'll be here a couple hours, showin' this crap. Long's I'm here past six, I get time and a half, so I don't beef about it. You wanna beer? I got plenty inna refrigerator. Go ahead, take one. Make yourself a sandwich. I got alla fixins in there. I'm set for the fuckin' duration up here."

I take two cans of beer and give him one. Suddenly there's shouting from the screening room below. The projectionist nods his head at me. "Uh huh. I know my customers. Told you they wouldn't stay quiet long, didn't I?"

We look through the window. Below us the Banners are standing toe to toe, shouting at each other. Like two Muhammad Alis at the weigh-in. Then they stop and embrace passionately. Next Amanda steps back and slaps her husband square on the face. It's no love tap.

"She packs a pretty good punch," I say.

"Wait. This's just the prelims. I tell my missus what goes on, she thinks I make it up. Tells me I got a filthy mind. Shit. Wait around. It gets better."

"It's always like this?"

"Pretty close. Yeah, they're a number, all right. Oh hell. Take a look at the screen. This's the worst scene of all comin' up. A bunch of fags with angel wings, and girls dressed up like bats. The girls'll dance around and bite the fags onna neck. You ever seen black blood in a Technicolor film before? You'll see it here. Howard Banner, he calls it art. And he wonders why this crap didn't make any money. I can't watch it, not this part. Kills my appetite."

87

"His other films any better?"

"No, but they ain't got angels and bats with black blood. Whaddaya think could've been goin' through his mind when he made this stuff? He must've been sick, right? A normal guy, he'd never be able to turn out stuff like this."

"I can see why I never heard of this film."

"Fuckin' shame. The old man, Mr. Stockton, he's one of the few straight shooters inna business, but his two kids're losers. So the daughter gets married, look what she picks. She picks a banana. I sorta feel sorry for the old man. I got two kids myself, but they're good kids. They don't gimme any trouble. Well, a little trouble, like all kids do. You gotta expect that. But all in all, they're good kids."

"Look."

"Huh? What're they doin' now?"

"That scene. It's a steal from *North by Northwest.* Cary Grant hiding out from the plane, hiding in the cornfield."

"Yeah. The only good parts in his films're the stuff he steals."

"The way I heard it, Banner makes good commercials."

"Yeah. He's got the magic touch. Any commercial he makes, it's gonna sell the product. Even if it's manure for brushin' your teeth with. He's okay on commercials. But his films? El Crap-o-la. So I don't watch the screen. But sometimes I watch down there, what they're doin'. But I don't watch those films. The three of 'em, over and over and over. How much of that'm I supposed to take? They oughta gimme combat pay. Hey! Look at this! Willya look at what she's up to now!"

Below us, Howard is sitting again. Amanda is sitting across him, kissing him on the mouth. Her dress is hiked up well above her waist.

"Willya look at the body that dame's got! She gets tired of him, she can come up here and sit on *my* lap any time she wants. I won't keep my pants on, either. Hey, don't tell my wife I said that, huh?"

She's really giving her husband the workover, but she doesn't seem to be getting much back in return.

"What's the matter with him?" I say. "Doesn't seem too interested."

"If she was up there on film, then he'd be interested. He's always like this. Hot and cold. Changes from one minute to the next. Not just with her, with everyone. You start to think maybe he's an okay guy, then alla sudden he goes on you. Same thing with her. She's nuts. He's nuts. They're both nuts. Give 'em a little time, you'll see some real hot stuff."

I see, all right. As if on cue, Amanda's on her feet again, bumping and grinding to the music of the film, like a top-of-the-line stripper. The dress comes off slowly, followed by everything else. Howard pushes off the chair and they're both on the floor. No slaps on the face this time. It'd be hilarious if it wasn't so pathetic. Still, it's enough to mesmerize the projectionist and me. The next time he speaks, he's very quiet, as if he's afraid too much noise will stop them from doing what they're doing.

"You'd think they'd give a thought to me bein' up here," he says. "They don't care. They do whatever they wanna do. They don't care who sees 'em."

"What's this mean? You think she'll get him to go home now?"

"Hey. Don't talk so loud. No, he won't go home with her. If he did, it'd be the first time. Just look at that, willya? Can you believe it? Hell, you don't have to go see any pornos. Just come here and watch the action."

We watch silently, until the two lovers beneath us finally fall apart.

"Well, time for another beer. Sometimes I almost don't wanna watch 'em. Must be my religious upbringin'. I remember when Howard first came here, the end of the fifties. He wasn't so bad then. A real hotshot. The old man, he was gettin' on even then, and it was Howard put this company back on its feet. Then he went off to make his first stinko film. This one, the one that's runnin' now. With the black blood. But then he came back here, he was still okay. So the old man, he bankrolled him for another film. Stinko number two. Then the old man talked him inna marryin' his daughter. Amanda, she'd been after the poor guy for years. I think she's what did it to him. They went off for a while, off to Europe, for their honeymoon. Gone quite a long time, half a year,

I guess. By the time they got back he was in pretty bad shape. Guess she finished him off on that honeymoon. Must've been a honey of a honeymoon. He came back here, he started comin' in a couple nights a week to watch his old films. At least he didn't go out to make any *more* of that crap. But he'd be in here watchin' his old films. And me here havin' to run 'em for him. You know, there's somethin' sick there. Lookin' at his old films alla time. What's he lookin' for?"

"What're any of us lookin' for?"

"I dunno. I sure's hell don't look for whatever it is *he's* lookin' for."

The shouting from below begins again.

"What's up now?" I say.

"Nothin'. The final scene, that's what's up."

"There's more?"

"Not much. Par for the course, par for the course."

We look down into the screening room.

"Just 'cause they're gettin' together with each other there don't mean they'll stay together. Least, not in any way I'm used to stayin' together with my wife. Maybe it's 'cause I'm older, but I dunno. I don't understand what the hell they got goin' with each other. You just watch what goes on. Pretty soon one of 'em'll slap the other, then that'll be the last we see of Amanda Stockton Banner tonight."

He's right. She lets Howard have it with a strong right-handed slap. Then she's gone.

"See? You don't think I know my customers? I know my customers."

33

When I enter the screening room Howard is dressed and sitting again. He's watching his film and nursing a bottle of Scotch. I stand quietly for a while, over to the side. Finally he realizes I'm there.

"Hey!" he says. "This's private! What the hell you doing in here?"

"I was in the neighborhood," I say. "Never could stay away from the movies."

He looks at me carefully. "I know you. Your name's Quinlan. You're the detective, you're supposed to find Jamie. Yeah, I met you yesterday."

"You got it."

"What's the story? You going to find him?"

"I been giving it some thought. You care if I find him?"

"Me? I don't give a shit."

"I been watching your film from the projection booth."

"That so? You came down here to tell me how much you hate it, right?"

"Am I supposed to hate it?"

"Critics hated it. Everyone hated it. Hey, Quinlan, come on in, we'll take a look at something else." He picks up the phone at his side and snaps into it. "Hey, Sammy! You still awake up there? Shut this thing off and put on *Flame*."

I drop into the seat next to him and listen to him swallow Scotch. When the screen lights up with the opening credits of another film, he says, "This's something called *Flame of Youth*, Quinlan. This's my wildly acclaimed second film. Critics hated this one, too. Except *Time* magazine. *Time* called this film 'possibly a harbinger of a dynamic new Hollywood wave of surrealism, somewhat in the style of the work of Cocteau.' At least one critic understood something about what I was trying to do. I had some goals, some objectives, you know? I was trying to go for something. You try and go for something in this business, nobody cares. All they care is, you got some fights, some shooting, a little screwing around to keep the public interested. You go for something more'n that, they don't know what the hell you're doing."

"This the film Mr. Stockton produced?"

"Produced? *I* produced it. He just paid for it. To keep me on the reservation. Here at the company. And to get me to marry his daughter. That's why he paid for it. Too bad you didn't drop by earlier, Quinlan. You could've met my wife." He sits still a mo-

91

ment. "Yeah, you really missed something when you missed my wife."

"I didn't miss her. I saw her."

He snaps his head around at me. "You did?"

"Up in Mr. Stockton's office. She's an attractive woman."

"Attractive? Sure, attractive. She's made for show, you know? Hey, you like that? Made for show, you know. Not bad, huh?"

"You're a real wit."

"Amanda's made for show. Yeah, that's Amanda. She can't cook or keep a house clean, but she sure can make herself attractive. And she gets what she wants. She wanted me and she got me. Ain't life wonderful?"

"You really love your wife, huh?"

"Sure. All husbands love their wives. That's what it's all about." He takes in some more of the Scotch. "I don't love anyone. You think she's attractive? Would you say she's got class? Sure, she's got class. Private schools in the East, from the time she was sixteen. Vacations in Europe. That's class, right? Just like it's supposed to be, according to all the books? Class? Wrong, buddy. It's a joke. One big fat joke." He throws his head far back and stares at the dark ceiling.

"You're some comedian," I say. "You leave out the punch lines."

"There's no punch line. Amanda got into some kind of trouble once upon a time, so her mother sent her away to private schools in the East. That's all. Her mother wouldn't even let her come home for vacations. Send her to Europe! Keep her out of town! Class. Yeah, class. Amanda learned a lot in Europe. I can swear to that much. Why'm I going on about Amanda? You want a drink, Quinlan? I got pure-bred Scotch here." He pours some more of it down his throat. "One day my wife she came back from her private schools in the East, and her vacations in Europe, and I was here working for her father, and she wanted me, and that was that. Love. Marriage. I didn't love anyone, I didn't want to get married. I just wanted to make films. But she got me, all right. Signed, sealed and delivered. One Howard Banner to one Amanda Stockton. Please put your initials down here at the bottom, lady. Now you own one Howard Banner. But she sure's good in bed, I'll tell you that much. So I got something out of the deal." He picks up the phone by his side. Then puts it back down and says, "Quinlan, this's a good scene, huh? Good feel for color, nice movement."

"I liked it better when John Ford did it in *The Quiet Man*."

"Hey! This scene, it was my own idea!"

"Don't let it bug you. Lots of people steal from Ford."

"The hell with you!" He picks up the phone again. "Sammy, I don't want to see any more of this tonight. Take it off. Put on *Flower of Evil*."

The screen goes dark again, which is fine with me. I don't much care for the film he's shown me so far. It's pretty bad. I don't care for the things he's telling me, either. I don't have much choice about that. It doesn't matter if I like his stories or not. He's got something to say, and I want to hear it. I'm not sure what I want to hear, so I want to hear all I can.

34

"*Flower of Evil*?" I say. "Okay title, but I like *Touch of Evil* better."

"You like Welles?"

"Made some good films."

"Welles. Too big for this town. This town tried to destroy Welles."

"Welles still seems to be going."

"This town tries to destroy lots of people. Listen, I wanted to make another film, and Ethan wanted me to marry his daughter. I needed his money for the film, so I married Amanda. You got to pay if you want to play. I paid. I'm still paying."

"So you just married her 'cause you wanted money to make a film?"

"Yeah. What do you think of that?"

"I don't think I believe you."

"Believe what you want. I don't care." He goes quiet again.

I leave him that way. "Maybe, when we got married . . . I don't know . . . She *is* a good-looking woman. Lots of people say so. Maybe when we got married, maybe it wasn't just so I could make a film. What kind of guy would I be if I only married her for the money? I wouldn't be much of a guy, huh? So there must've been something else. I must've wanted to marry her for some other reason."

Silence. Then, "I don't know. Maybe not. Maybe I'm just a bastard. Maybe I don't care about anyone but myself. But they say —if you're going to care about anyone else, first you got to care about yourself. If you don't like yourself, they say you can't like anyone. Isn't that what they say?"

"Yeah, Mr. Banner. I heard that too."

"I don't know. We had a honeymoon in Europe. My only trip to Europe. They can keep it. Sweet little Amanda knew all about Europe and she took me to the high spots. She took me to this bordello in Amsterdam. Bordello. When you go to a real fancy cathouse where they charge you a lot of money, then they call it a bordello. Supposed to sound nicer. This place in Amsterdam, it was all sort of medieval, in an old castle. Make a great movie set. Hell, a guy could go in there with a camera, he could make a lot of money selling a film of that place.

"We didn't come out of that place for three days. You wouldn't believe some of the things they had in there. Makes Los Angeles look like part of the Bible Belt. You could pick anything you wanted and order it sent up to you. Place was packed. Everyone goes there. Men, women, men and women together, men and men, women and women. They'll serve up anything you want, long's you got the money to pay for it. I never seen anything like it. Anything you can think of, you can get it in that place."

"I'll look it up, my next trip to Amsterdam."

"I ought to go back there, make a film of that place. Then I'd be a big guy in this town. A film of that place, it'd make a lot of money. Then I'd be something in this town."

"So go back there with a camera."

"Amanda wants to go back there. Europe. Hell, they can have it. It's not for me."

The film begins. *Flower of Evil.*

"Here we are, Quinlan. My last film. Sort of an outgrowth of my honeymoon with my sweet little attractive classy wife. The *Time* critic really understood this one. Know what he wrote? '*Flower of Evil* lacks even a hint of the sparkling talent displayed in the director's earlier film, the much underrated *Flame of Youth*. This disappointing new film must be called what it is—a disturbing indulgence.' "

Quite a film. The opening shot shows a hanging.

"I get the idea," I say. "Think I'll be on my way, Mr. Banner. The gloom's a little thick in here. I don't get to meet too many in your league. You're a perfect solid-gold masochist. You hate your wife, your work, you hate yourself, you probably hate me, you hate—"

"No, I don't hate my work! I love my work! It's good work! My work's just's good as anyone's—its good as there is!" He starts yelling into the phone again. "Sammy, put on one of the Donhauser commercials . . . I don't care which one. Put on any one. Just get it up there!" Then he looks at me. "You think I don't like my work? Stay here, Quinlan. I'll show you the kind of work I can do. I'll show you what this business's all about."

The anger came to him suddenly and it leaves just as quickly. He collapses back into himself and pulls at the Scotch bottle. "You're wrong, Quinlan. I love my work. Maybe to some people it's not so great, 'cause it's only commercials, but commercials, you put a lot into them, they can be something. When my work's good —and sometimes it *is* good—I love it. I want to love it. And I want to love my wife, too. I want to love everyone. I don't know what the hell it is. Maybe I just don't know how. Maybe someone ought to give me lessons."

35

The room fills with stirring martial music and up on the screen I recognize the white teeth and silver hair of John Donhauser. Donhauser on horseback, buying ice cream for children, kissing babies and grandmothers, looking like the all-American boy, as clean and crisp as an unused tube of toothpaste. VOTE DONHAUSER! VOTE DONHAUSER! OF THE PEOPLE! FOR THE PEOPLE! MAYOR!

It's pretty impressive, in its way.

"Goddamn perfect," Howard Banner says. "He looks like a hero and he doesn't say a damn thing."

"And it worked. He got elected."

"Donhauser's people came to me, he didn't have a chance. The polls rated him at zero. Below zero. I figured I could make the greatest crap political commercials anyone'd ever seen, the company'd rake in a lot of money and I could work without everybody looking over my shoulder. Hell, Donhauser was supposed to be sunk. Everyone in San Francisco was supposed to know he was in with the Mafia, so it didn't make any difference *how* good my commercials were. So what went wrong? Did they really believe all that crap I showed them about that son of a bitch? How could they elect him?"

"You did a good selling job."

"I never thought he'd get elected. I never thought he'd win."

"But he *did* win."

"They voted for him, they got to live with him. It's not my fault. People should think for themselves. And you know what? I ended up with half the politicians and crooks in San Francisco as my friends. So who needs them?"

"Those're powerful connections."

"Yeah. Too powerful."

"They could finance another film for you."

"I don't need them. If I want to make another film, Ethan'll pay for it. All I need's the right idea. The right property."

"There's another election coming up next year. After what

Donhauser's done to San Francisco since he's been mayor, he's in a lot of trouble. You think you're good enough to get him elected this time?"

"Hey, I'm finished with that crap. One mistake was plenty. I'm not going back to that."

"No?"

"No. I'll never make another commercial for any politician. Never."

I lean toward him till our faces are an inch apart. I crowd in on him so suddenly and so completely, he doesn't know what I'm up to.

"How come you hate your brother-in-law so much?"

"I don't hate Jamie. Who told you I hate Jamie?"

"People're saying you want to get rid of him. They're saying you're behind his disappearance."

"What the fuck you talking about? That's crazy. Why should I care about Jamie?"

"People think you want to take over this company. But you're afraid Stockton'll give the company to Jamie."

"Quinlan, whoever told you that crap is crazy. Ethan likes me more'n he likes his own children. That's why he puts up with me. If Ethan ever retires, or dies, and I don't think he's ever going to do either, I'm going to get this business. And don't let anyone tell you different."

"Yeah, but you don't want to wait. You want the business *now.*"

"You're nuts! I don't know if I want it at all. The business can go to hell—I don't care."

I put my hand on his shoulder and push him against the back of his chair in my best tough-guy manner. "Don't give me any of this crap. You forced Jamie to run away, didn't you?"

"No! What the hell you think you're doing?"

"Like you forced him to run away before. You know what I mean. The time he ended up in Vegas."

"I didn't have anything to do with that. Take your hand off me!"

"Then why did Jamie run away years ago? If *you* didn't make him run off, what was his reason?"

"How the hell do I know? I wasn't even here then. I was in Europe. Who's been telling you these lies? It's all crap."

"So you think they're lies, huh?" I take my hand away from him and relax in my chair. Enough of that bit for a while. "Okay, Mr. Banner. I must've got you confused with someone else. Forget about it."

"What's this? You say I'm behind Jamie's disappearance. You say I want to take over the company. Those're lies! Goddamn lies! Who said those things about me?"

"I said them. Settle down, Mr. Banner. Have a drink. I took a little fishing trip, that's all. I asked you some questions to see what you'd say. I haven't been talking to anyone about you. Don't worry about it."

"What the fuck's this? You made all this up? All this crap, these accusations, you made it up?"

"I do that sometimes. Part of the business. Sometimes it works, sometimes it doesn't."

"You bastard! You son of a bitch bastard!" He stands up menacingly. "I ought to tear you apart."

"I agree with you. You ought to do that. But you won't. If you try it you'll get hurt, and neither one of us wants that." I look him straight in the eye and make it clear I mean business. I'm a lot better at staring people down than he is. "Sit down, Mr. Banner. I got you going for a minute, but it's not all that serious. Don't get too worked up over the wrong things. Save it for the times it counts."

"You fuckin' creep! Who the hell you supposed to be? Bogart?"

"Hmmm. Wouldn't mind being Bogart. If I got a choice, I'll take Bogart in *Casablanca*. He doesn't end up with the girl, but he ends up okay, there. I wouldn't want to be Bogart in *Caine Mutiny*, though. He really gets screwed at the end of *Caine Mutiny*."

"You ought to be Bogart in *Sierra Madre*. I'd like to see you end up the way he ends up in that one!"

"Yeah, I know. I ruffled your feathers. Sit down, Mr. Banner. Have some more Scotch. Ask Sammy to put on another movie."

He sits down and picks up the phone. "Sammy, I want to see *The Masked Casanova* . . . Damn it—I don't give a fuck what you think! Do as I say!" He slams the phone down and looks back at me. "Don't leave yet, Quinlan. This'll interest you. It's not one of *my* films. It's a little older vintage."

So I sit a little longer. *The Masked Casanova* turns out to be an old black-and-white porno film. The quality places it in the forties. The man wears a black mask, the lady has boots and spurs, and the bedroom is standard cheap hotel. It's a real hoot.

"I'll tell you the subject of my next film, Quinlan. The life story of an American hero. A man of money and a man of legend. A kid in the California gold fields. Orphaned but rich. He makes his way to New York City. Out of the stock market before the crash and into bootlegging, which turned out to be a lot more lucrative. The money rolls in but our hero gets restless. He tries Cuba, then he goes down to Argentina to do some gunrunning, which's also worth a buck here and there.

"Down in Argentina he joins forces with a young gunfighter —a real tough guy. A hell of a lot tougher'n you, in case you think you're tough, Quinlan. The two of them, they build an empire. But we got to have romance, right? After you have some killing, you got to have a little romance, too, or the folks won't come to see your film. That's what the rules say. So love calls our hero back to the States, where he marries a Hollywood starlet.

"Then world war erupts. But our hero, he's too old for it, so he becomes a film tycoon. This sound a little familiar, Quinlan? Stay with me, maybe we'll write in a part for you—later on. So our hero goes into films, in his own way, and he does well but he still wants a little more excitement. Our hero, at the end of the war, he starts to produce pornographic films. He gets in with some musicians, and they get *him* into the drug scene. And he wants power, too, so he helps politicians. Makes films for their campaigns. So what do you think? Where'll it all end? And what about his Hollywood starlet wife? Does she know about his pornographic films? Does she know that sometimes, not too often, mind you, but some-

99

times, he starred in those little flicks himself? Both him and his mistress? You think the wife'll ever find out about that?

"So tell me, Quinlan, what do you think of this film we're watching now? You recognize the masked Casanova? The hero in the black mask? I'll tell you one thing, it sure ain't the Lone Ranger. You think he's aged much in twenty years?"

It's my fault. I got Howard Banner pretty mad and now he wants to take it out on me. But he doesn't know how to do it, so he throws his anger at someone else.

I'm not interested. I'm already on my way out the door. I've had more than enough of Howard Banner for one night.

36

My answering service has a message from the Singer. He called in ten minutes ago and reported he spotted Jamie Stockton at Le Brigand.

Le Brigand is a good but not great restaurant in Hollywood. I don't mind if a client takes me there for dinner, but if I'm eating alone I refuse to pay those prices. Still, it's a popular eating place. Only regular gamblers and the cops know about Le Brigand's back room, and the cops make believe they don't know. The cops eat many free meals in the restaurant on a regular basis. To keep things even more secure, the manager of the place used to be a cop.

It takes me fifteen minutes to drive there. As I pull into the parking lot I notice the blue Buick LeSabre.

I don't know what Jamie might be up to tonight. I should take my gun with me, but I won't get into the place carrying a gun. And I have to go in. Okay. The gun stays in the car.

As I'm going up to the front door a voice calls to me.

"Hey! Mister!"

I look back into the shadows but can't see the face clearly.

"Hey! Those're nice boots you got there."

What the hell is this?

"How about it, mister? Wanna sell those boots? I sure like 'em."

"Not tonight, friend," I say as I enter the restaurant.

I don't see Jamie Stockton or the Singer.

I've never been in the back room but I know where it is. I walk toward the kitchen doors like I've done this lots of times before.

A large man who looks like a former wrestler sits at a small round table, drinking coffee. As I approach he points first at me and then at a chair beside him. He does it without the slightest flicker of emotion or concern, and from the way he looks he isn't the type who gets concerned over much. The finger he points with is quite large. If you cut it up for sausage, you could eat sausage for a month.

When I sit down he says, "You ain't been here before. Don't tell me you been here before, 'cause I got a good memory for faces and I say you ain't been here before. And when I say some guys ain't been here before, and they try to tell me they *have* been here before, I got to figure one of us's wrong. I don't like to be wrong. Most times it turns out the other guy's wrong. So the way I see it, you ain't been here before."

He pulls back his lips, smiles, and starts probing a toothpick into the spaces between his upper front teeth.

"My turn to speak?" I say.

The words "Don't get cute" come from somewhere behind the toothpick.

"I been here to the restaurant once or twice, but I never been to the back room."

He looks me over. "That could be. Guys come just to eat in the restaurant, I don't care about that part. All I care, I care when they come back here." He pokes the toothpick into the recesses of his jaw. "Okay. What do you want?"

I wait for him to finish his surgery, then say, "I want to play cards and I don't have the air fare for Vegas."

"Take a bus."

"Takes too much time that way."

"Oh yeah? I never thought of that. You in a hurry?"

"I came to gamble. Not to talk."

"Tough, huh? Maybe I don't like tough. Maybe I want to talk. Maybe you don't want to talk. Maybe you got some objections."

"If I got any, I'll keep them to myself. Till you lose about two hundred pounds. Then maybe I'll give you a go."

"So you're not so tough, after all."

"Probably to you, nobody's tough."

The toothpick disappears into his mouth. He starts to chew on it. "Now maybe you're getting a little smarter. I'm sitting here having a little coffee, I don't want to have to get up to do anything else. If I sit here and drink my coffee nice and peaceful, maybe we'll both be happier. Now—you tell me you're clean and I'll see if I believe you."

"I'm clean."

"Yeah. That's the way I want to hear it. Just a couple words, short and to the point. You're clean, you ain't here for trouble."

"No trouble. Just an honest wager."

He believes me. He believes me after he runs his heavy hand along my body and is sure I'm not carrying a gun.

"People lie to me," he says, "I got to do something about it. Later. That's what they pay me for."

"I'm sure you're worth every penny."

"I am. Okay. It'll cost you ten."

I fold a ten-dollar bill in half lengthwise and place it next to his coffee cup. He waits to see if it'll jump up and bite him. When it doesn't, he flicks a switch on the wall behind him and says, "Remember, no trouble. We don't like trouble." He points at a door behind me.

The back room is smaller than I expected. Someone's buying chips. They sell for much more than I expected. I lean against the side wall and the Singer comes over.

"Evening, Mr. Quinlan. You sure got here fast."

"Would've been here sooner but I had to sit outside for a while with the animal. Victor McLaglen's stand-in."

"That's Max. He's okay, long's you don't cross him."

"Wasn't any problem. I showed him he was boss and we got along fine. What's going on, Rudy? I don't see our boy."

102

"He's here. And he's winning. Went into the men's room just before you came in."

"You see anyone else with him? Someone big?"

"I ain't seen nobody."

"Okay. I hope you're right."

"I did okay, huh, Mr. Quinlan? You told me to find the guy and I found him. And I ain't been talking to nobody about it."

"So far, so good, Rudy. But don't get big-headed and screw up."

"No, Mr. Quinlan. I'm okay now. You want me to do a job, I'll do it. I'll do it right. You can count on me."

Rudy's telling me he wants some encouragement, a few words to tell him he's doing things the way he's supposed to do them. But if I fall for it and start the congratulation bit, he'll get carried away with how good he is and then suddenly he won't be doing so well. That's the problem and I've seen it before. When Rudy starts fishing for compliments, it's time to keep your eyes open.

"Rudy, you're a good man. *Maybe*. Let's wait and see how things turn out. You're still on probation."

"Yeah, but so far I'm okay, huh?"

" You're peaches and cream. Let's not leave our boy alone too long. Go in and make sure he's all right. I'll catch him on the way out."

I watch him go into the men's room.

I've got one thing on my mind. It sits there and it won't go away. One question—I wonder who will screw up first—Rudy or me?

37

Jamie Stockton comes out, stumbling drunkenly. I go over and get close to him before he sees me. I hold his arm above the elbow and pat the sides of his chest.

"Hey, what's going on?" he says.

"What's the matter, Jamie?" I say. "You're not packing a gun tonight?"

"What's going on?"

"You remember me, Jamie. We're old friends."

"Oh, yeah. Quinlan. Charles Quinlan. Didn't think I'd be seeing you again."

The hell you didn't.

"Anyway," he says, "not this soon. You're still following me around, huh?"

"Can't stand to see you lonely. You had a little too much to drink tonight. Better come with me."

I begin to steer him toward the door.

"Come on, Quinlan. Have a heart. I'm winning tonight. You know how long it's been since I been on a winning streak? Come on, let me keep playing. The least you can do, you can wait till I start losing."

"Sorry, Jamie. You're not allowed to stay out this late."

"Hey, Quinlan—I got my pockets full of chips! You got to stop and let me cash in my chips!"

Come on, Charlie. Keep him moving.

"Jamie," I say, "maybe if you play nice, we'll come back tomorrow night. You can cash 'em in then."

I get him past the door and guide him slowly through the restaurant. His legs are growing more wobbly and his sense of balance isn't the best, but nobody stops us. We make it through the place with a minimum of fuss.

All I have to do is get him to the door. Then out across the parking lot. Then home free.

But halfway out the front door we hit our first real obstacle. A large man—pressed up against me. At first I think he's a pickpocket and I feel for my wallet, but it's still there. I reach back to steady Jamie, who's listing to the side, and I feel the gun in my ribs.

Schmuck. I didn't keep my eyes open.

I look up at the large man's face. I've seen him around. In a city of cheap thugs he's still the cheapest. His name's Pastrano.

Jamie suddenly becomes very agile for a drunk. He pulls away from me.

It's a setup. I've been taken again.

"This guy's bugging me," Jamie says. "He's a real drag. Wouldn't even give me a chance to cash in my chips. And I was doing pretty well tonight. Can you take care of him for me?"

"I can take care of this guy," Pastrano says. "He don't look like much." He pushes the gun a little deeper into me. Then he points with his free hand toward a back alley behind the restaurant.

Charlie, if you get out of this, do me a favor, huh? Give five grand to Carolyn. Be an associate producer, huh? Go back to the movies.

Pastrano shoves his hand against my back, sailing me forward about two yards.

"Surprised to see you out tonight," I say. "Thought you spent all your evenings hiding in closets."

"Skip the conversation and keep walkin'."

I turn and he gives me a quick look at his gun. It's nice and big and I won't argue with it. I follow orders and lead the way.

"Cops don't like trouble at this place," I say. "Better watch it, Pastrano."

"Hey! Who told you my name?"

That's it. I have to shake him up.

"What's the matter, Pastrano? Didn't think I knew you? You're famous, Pastrano. Everybody in town knows *you*. Don't you know what everybody says about you?"

"What's everybody say?"

"That's you're all muscle, no brains. A real dummy."

The hand shoves into my back again. "That's what they say, huh? Keep movin'."

"Yeah, Pastrano. They say you're a guy who never uses his head. What do you think? Think it's true?"

"You're askin' for it, ain't you?"

"Yeah, and you're going to give it to me. Right here, you're going to blow me open with that cannon. And the cops'll be after you so fast, you won't even have time to put away the gun. This ain't a place to kill a guy. You got to do it somewhere out in the middle of nowhere. Not behind a restaurant. You got a lot to learn, Pastrano."

"Seems to me *you* ain't lookin' so smart right about now."

You said it. "I know. I'm a real dummy too. I got to be a dummy if I let someone like you get me this way."

"That's right. Now keep moving."

Charlie—try something else. This ain't working.

"What're you doing, hooked up with a kid like Jamie Stockton? He doesn't have any money. His father has it all. Why aren't you working for some guy with a lot of cash to throw your way? If you're going to do muscle work, you really ought to get paid for it."

"I get paid okay. Don't worry about me. I get paid."

Thanks for the information, Pastrano. That's exactly what I wanted to know.

What am I doing? Trying for clues? The hell with that! He's got a gun on you, schmuck!

We're in the back alley now, with all the garbage from the kitchen. I turn and face Pastrano. We're several feet apart.

"Okay, Pastrano. Let's see you shoot me, you think you're so smart. Then we'll see how fast the cops come."

Charlie! That's the best you can do?

He gives me a long look. Ha! It worked! Whatever he has in mind, I've pretty much screwed things up for him. He puts his gun into his jacket pocket. And takes out a set of brass knuckles.

I've seen what brass knuckles can do to a man's face. Come on, Charlie, it's now or never.

As he fits the knuckles across his right hand I step forward and kick into his groin, hard enough to lift him off the ground. He doubles over and I catch his chin with an uppercut. He staggers against the building and slides down to the concrete.

His face shows confusion. He's disoriented. He tries to get up, but it's giving him trouble. For support he reaches his hand along the inside of an open doorway. That's the wrong move.

Do it, Charlie. Don't stop to think. Just *do* it!

I take the door and slam it hard. His mouth opens wide but the scream never comes out. When I open the door his hand's become a bloody pulp. The brass knuckles are still there, but now you can't see them any more.

I like it. I'm not supposed to like it, but I do. I can't help it.

I lean toward him and swing a strong backhand against the side of his jaw. That's the end of it.

Okay, Charlie. You had to do it. Settle down. That's enough John Wayne. Settle down.

I take out my pocket handkerchief and cover my right hand. I draw the gun from his pocket without getting my fingerprints on it. When I lean down I get a better look at his bloody hand.

Brother. What a lousy business I'm in.

The hell with it. Every business is lousy.

As I walk out of the alley I drop the gun in a garbage can.

38

Jamie Stockton is sitting behind the wheel of the big blue Buick. His eyes light up when he sees me coming toward him.

That's right, friend. It takes more than one goon to polish off Charlie Quinlan.

He turns on the motor and guns his car out of the parking lot. He won't get far.

I unlock my car door. A voice calls to me. I've heard the voice before.

"Hey, mister! Hey, hey, whaddaya say? Don't take off! I want you to stay!"

He comes toward me, out of the shadows.

"Hey hey hey! I like those boots!"

He's not alone. He's got six friends with him.

"Now if you want, mister, you can just give us those boots. Then there won't be no trouble."

He's shorter than the others. They stick close together.

"We don't really care, though. It don't make much difference."

Now they start to fan out into a half-circle.

"If we gotta take 'em from you, mister, we're ready to take 'em from you."

I've got a gun inside the car. But to get to it I'd have to open the door, and I'd have my back to them for at least three seconds. I'd never get to the gun in time. They've got me.

"So whaddaya say, mister? Whaddaya say? What's it gonna be?"

They curve their half-circle around me, closing me in against my car. Now I can see them. They're a spooky bunch. Maybe they're on drugs, but they probably aren't. They're doing this 'cause they like to do it. Not one of them looks to be over fourteen years old.

They're closing in on me. Here they come.

It happens quickly. Now I'm lying on my back. I can hear a police siren. It doesn't mean a thing. It won't get to me in time.

I feel myself passing out. I feel the boots being pulled off my feet. I feel another fist in my stomach. Things are going black.

Yessir. It takes more than one goon to polish off Charlie Quinlan.

Not much more.

39

Half a dozen cops sit around trying to keep awake. I fill out a complaint sheet like I think it'll make a difference. Trying not to look like an ass while I'm standing in my stockinged feet isn't easy. My head feels like a flat tire with multiple ruptures. I don't have a spare.

Things take a turn for the worst. The turn is called Gilley. He's a homicide sergeant. He walks over, throws some papers across the desk and looks at me.

"Quinlan."

"What?"

"What the fuck you doin' here?"

"Nothing."

"Terrific. Keep up the good work."

Gilley thinks he's funny but his bank account of wit is perpetually overdrawn.

"You're the guy got mugged for the shoes, huh? Better go back to the movies." He rubs his thumb along the side of my cheek. "Dried blood. I'll clean if off for you."

I can feel the cut reopen. Tonight's the night for everyone to exercise their boredom on Charlie Quinlan.

Gilley slaps lightly at the cut. I don't move. He bounces on his toes, throws light punches into the air. "Come on, Quinlan. Let's mix it up a little."

There are almost a dozen cops in the room now. They've been watching, but not carefully. None of them says a thing. Cops.

Gilley comes close, fakes left, slaps right. I block it but don't slap back.

He shuffles his feet back and forth. "I get my moves from Ali! Watch!" In the middle of it he throws a slap. All he gets is air.

"See *Body and Soul*, Gilley. John Garfield'll show you how to move like a pro."

"I was just thinkin', Quinlan. About that Manning thing."

"That's dead and buried, isn't it?"

"Only thing got dead and buried was Manning." He comes close, slapping. "Remember?"

"I remember you tried to pin it on the girl. I remember it didn't work."

I shouldn't've said it. Gilley doesn't smile. Doesn't dance. Doesn't slap.

"I made a mistake. Everybody makes mistakes." He drops his hands to his sides, walks slowly toward me.

The other cops are quieter than a coffin with the dirt piled thick on top. I look at one I know. He looks away.

"Look, Gilley—"

He swings toward my face. I move to block it and he slams his shoe onto my foot. "Son of a bitch! Got you with that one, huh, Quinlan?"

Then he sticks his chin out. He wants me to hit him. He'd give anything for an excuse to tear me apart.

"One of you guys better pull him off."

Nothing. Cops are cops. You can't figure on a cop stepping in to stop something some other cop's behind. Once they put on the uniform they start thinking it's them against us.

"Come on, Quinlan. You want to do it, right?"

Right.

"I'll give you a shot. One good shot."

It's stupid to hit a cop, no matter what the reason. This cop wants me to hit him. It's insane.

He's smiling like he can read my mind. The bastard.

He slaps me again. Knocks me against the desk.

Damn it. I'm going to do it. His stomach. Hard and fast. I'm going to be the biggest idiot in Los Angeles. I don't care.

I lower my eyes to three inches above his belt buckle. I'm going to do it, damn it.

But the belt buckle's moving away.

Gilley can't put it together. Confusion's on his face. His shirt collar's cutting into his throat. Someone's taken him by the back of his shirt collar and yanked him off his feet.

Gilley goes over on his back like a sack of potatoes dumped into the corner. He hits the linoleum, grunts, starts to come up with his fists round as baseballs. Then we both see what's going on and he stays on the floor.

"You're a real fucker tonight, aren't you, Gilley?" When Lieutenant Jake Barnes talks that quietly, most people know to keep quieter. Jake turns to me. "Quinlan? You going to forget about this?"

"I already forgot."

"That's nice." Jake turns to Gilley. "Go do some work, schmuck."

"I wasn't—"

"What? You say somethin, schmuck?"

Gilley gets up and walks out.

The other cops get up and walk out.

Jake turns to me. "I better see you in my office before someone taps you on the head with a goddamn baseball bat, schmuck."

110

40

Jake sits behind his desk and points to a chair for me. "Busted up?"

"Yeah. A little."

"Go be an actor. You ain't tough enough for this business."

"Who's tough enough? You?"

"I ain't tough enough. You ain't tough enough. Hell, nobody's tough enough. Coffee?"

"It'd only keep me awake."

"Grass?"

"Will you arrest me?"

"I might."

"In that case, forget it."

"Can't win against Gilley. Nobody wins against a badge."

"Maybe tonight I'm just in a mood to hit someone."

"Schmuck. Want me to call the police psychiatrist for you?"

"Or maybe I felt ready to let someone hand my teeth to me."

"Looks like that already happened. They're laughin' upstairs. Some dumb p.i. asshole got his shoes stolen in a parkin' lot out in Hollywood. By a couple kids."

"I heard about it. Seven kids. Seven vicious kids. I thought cops're paid to keep the streets safe for law-abiding citizens."

"Find me a law-abidin' citizen, I'll see what I can do for him."

"Two patrolmen scare off the kids too late to do me any good. They see I carry a p.i. license. They tell me to come down and swear out a complaint or else they'll put down I was uncooperative and see what they can do about my license."

Jake smiles. He thinks that's funny.

"Those kids ever find out I filed against them, they're going to kill me."

Another smile.

"I'm paid to look for blackmailers. Missing husbands. Things like that. I'm not paid to take my life in my hands. Christ, hunting down kids's cop business."

"I always wondered what cop business was. Now I know. It's

huntin' down kids." Jake pulls open a drawer. "You don't want coffee, you don't want grass. Drink?"

"What've you got?"

"Scotch. Sorry, no vodka tonight."

"Just's well. No thanks."

Jake pours Scotch but leaves the glass sitting on his desk.

"What the matter, Jake? Troubles?"

"I never got troubles." He lets the glass sit there. I see what's going on. He's in a lot worse shape than I am.

"Janie?"

"Janie. The time I get home she'll be asleep. The time I get up tomorrow she'll be gone."

"She working?"

"Teachin' again. We figured we'd go down across the border last weekend. Just the two of us. Friday mornin' I get this case, po-lit-i-cal connections. They're breathin' down my neck, clear the damn thing up. That took care of Mexico."

"Janie give you hell?"

"She don't blame me for it. That's the fuckin' thing. Christ, she got mad, she yelled at me, least then I could get mad and yell back. We'd have a fight. That'd be it. Get it over with. But we never had that fight. She tells me she understands. Hell, how can she understand? *I* don't understand. Someone shoots someone, someone's got a little pull, you got to forget about Mexico. And Janie says she understands. You can figure how that made me feel."

I want to say something. I don't know what to say. He leaves the glass sitting on his desk.

"She ought to get smart, Charlie. Ought to take a walk."

"You're in great shape tonight."

"Ain't so bad. I took some of it out on Gilley, thanks to you. I was supposed to be out of here an hour ago. Waitin' for a report from a guy. Lucky for you. Wasn't for me, you'd be decoratin' the walls out there."

"A dozen cops watching us out there."

"You fuckin' civilian. You think a cop like Gilley gets a little out of line, someone's goin' to step in? Schmuck."

"Uh huh."

112

"We protect our own. Even when our own's got his head up his ass. Shit, we don't protect our own, who's goin' to do it? You? Fuckin' civilian. Somethin' goes wrong with someone, you think we're goin' to jump on him. What the hell do you know about it? You hear some cop's on the take, you think it's the end of the world. What the fuck do you know? We know how goddamn easy it is to fuck up. Maybe we try to watch out for the guy a little. You guys yell cover-up. Corruption. Shit. Sure, it's corruption. But maybe that cop's done somethin' good once upon a time. So maybe now he's bad. Maybe he's not *that* bad. So maybe we stand by him 'cause we're the only guys he's *got* to stand by him."

"I'm glad you called me in here."

"Why?"

"Wasn't for me, you'd be telling it to the walls."

"The hell with you."

"A nice speech like that, they'll put you in public relations. You won't have to be a cop any more."

"Fuck you! I want to tell you somethin', I'll fuckin' tell you somethin'! Understand?"

"Sure."

"Hell. I'm goin' off the wall." He opens one of his desk drawers. Slams it shut. Looks away.

"Jake? You feeling unappreciated? Want someone to come in here and tell you how you're doing a good job?"

"Yeah. Maybe."

"I'd like that, myself. Someone comes in some day, says Charlie, good job. You had a hard job to do. You did it."

"Uh huh."

"Fortunately, I don't sit around and wait for that. I go out and do the job. I figure there's no thanks. There's never going to *be* any thanks."

"You sound worse'n me. And you ain't even drunk. Tom Benson. Remember him?"

"I used to see him around."

"Good cop. Hadn't've been a good cop, he'd still be here."

"I remember. He had guts."

"Had a hell of a lot more'n just guts."

"I never knew him."

"Nice funeral. Mayor made a nice speech. Said Tom was a good cop. The best. But Tom was still alive, the mayor ever call him up to say thanks? Nope. The mayor had some nice words to say over his grave, though. That was a good time to say 'em. Plenty of TV around to make sure everyone saw the nice words the mayor was sayin'. So much for Tom Benson."

"I got an idea."

"Let's go out and get screwed."

"Let's hire some guy. He'll go around telling people they've done a good job."

"Yeah?"

"Sure. He'll hand out medals."

"Shiny medals? I hate medals that don't shine."

"You solve a tough case, we'll have a ceremony. Take some pictures. This guy'll shake your hand, give you a medal."

"On TV. Somethin' like that happens, it's got to happen on TV or they'll say it didn't happen."

"TV'll cost extra."

"So what? Some guy in Detroit puttin' in steerin' wheels on the assembly line, nobody gives a fuck about him, right? Our medal guy goes up to him. Hey, steerin'-wheel guy. You're doin' a good job. I got a medal for you. Maybe you figured nobody cares. You're wrong. I care. Keep up the good work!"

"I don't know. You can't do a hell of a lot with a medal."

"He'll give out bottles of whiskey. Some housewife, Charlie, she never hears nothin' from nobody. He'll go to see her. Thank you, housewife. I'm here to tell you you been ignored too long. I'm here to tell you you're doin' a good job. Thank you!"

"This's on TV?"

"Everything's on TV. Everyone!"

"Okay, but it'll cost. What's she get? A medal or whiskey?"

"Whiskey!"

"It'll never work."

"What? Why not?"

"Who's going to congratulate the guy going all around giving out the medals and whiskey? We got to get a second guy to congratulate him. And a third guy to congratulate the second guy."

"Shit."

We sit, thinking about things. And looking at the glass of whiskey on Jake's desk.

"Idea didn't sound half bad for a while there, Charlie."

"Next time you do something right, give me a call. I'll bring you a bottle of whiskey."

"What if *you* do something right? I got to bring you vodka?"

"That's the deal."

"Fine. I'll get the better of that deal."

"Better yet, give me Gilley's head. On a platter."

"You and Gilley. Two schmucks. He wasn't even mad at you tonight. He fucked somethin' up today and he got caught on it. That's why he was givin' it to you."

"What?"

"Guess he figured pushin' you around might make him feel a little better. We been workin' on this nice, sweet homicide. We know who did it. A little more evidence, we're goin' to send the guy away for a long time. But Gilley, he sees the way things're goin' to go, sometimes he don't know enough to wait till we got evidence. He fucked it up. We'll never make it now. There's nothin' left to prosecute. Now we got a killer he's free's a fuckin' bird 'cause Gilley got anxious. Gilley knows he fucked up. And *I* know he fucked up. And I know he'll fuck up again."

"Get rid of him."

"He's in. Once he's in, nobody gets rid of him. Schmuck."

"You had to stop him out there, didn't you?"

"I'm a schmuck too. There's nothin' I can do about Gilley. I figure, you fuck around with people the way he does, there comes a day you got to pay."

"You really think that?"

"I wish I did."

"Some night."

"I sure's hell didn't need you here. I was goin' nuts before you got here."

"You don't want me here?"

115

"I don't want you nowhere."

"See you around?"

"Try to keep yourself in less'n three pieces."

"Try my best."

I start for the door. Jake lets me get almost out, then he speaks. He times these things perfectly. "By the way, Charlie. What's your case?"

I turn and look at him. No expression on his face at all.

Sometimes we get to talking and I almost forget he's a cop. He doesn't forget.

41

"Who says I got a case?" I say.

I already know it won't do me any good.

"Someone's askin' about your credentials last week. I put in a good word for you, naturally."

"Naturally?"

"Almost naturally. I couldn't find out who's makin' the inquiries. Been curious about it."

"Curiosity's good for you. Keeps you young and good-looking. Except with you it'd be starting a little late."

"Probably. What's the case?"

"Maybe I got a case. Maybe I don't. I had one, I wouldn't be talking about it to people."

"Who the fuck's doin' the fancy inquirin'?"

The hell with it. I'll throw him something. Maybe it'll be enough. Anyway, I've got to talk to someone.

"Say I had a case right now. It'd probably be driving me nuts."

"That's better."

"Nothing adding up the way it's supposed to. People leading me in circles."

"Ahh. Like you're leading me."

"Pretty much."

"This case you don't have, nobody's breakin' any laws?"

"Maybe, I'm lucky, it'll turn out that way."

"Not with your luck, Charlie. I hope, you had a case and it turned out to involve cops—I hope you'd be smart enough to let the cops in on it."

"I might be. We'll have to wait and see."

Jake goes back to looking at his glass of whiskey. He takes out the bottle, puts it on his desk. Very carefully he pours the contents of the glass back into the bottle. He doesn't spill a drop.

"Some guys like to keep whiskey around for drinking. You keep it around for pouring. Back and forth."

"Just remembered, I don't like to drink on duty. Anyway, Janie's been at me. To cut down. I'll get along without it. Charlie, I won't press you right now, but I get the feelin' you know a little too much for anyone's good."

"And not enough for my own good?"

"Uh huh."

"I got some people, Jake. They got some trouble. I'm going to try to stop it. It's nothing for you."

"You might be smart. You get into somethin', you might give a cop a call. Unless you don't like cops."

"I'm horny for cops."

"You look it. Watch where you're goin'. Try not to step in it."

"Give my regards to Janie."

"Sure. I happen to get lucky, I bump into her sometime, I'll do that."

42

Something's wrong.

I know it as soon as I step into my apartment. Either someone's been here, or someone's still here. I don't turn on the lights. I stand still and look and think.

There's a light on down the hall. In the bedroom. I've had

117

enough problems for tonight. Maybe I'm going to have some more. They don't even give you time to sleep, do they?

I move quietly along the wall to Old Granddad. Old Granddad is a six-foot-tall grandfather clock which I got from my mother when she married her oilman and moved to San Francisco.

I slide my hand along Old Granddad's back till I reach the small wooden ledge I put there five years ago. My hand closes around a Smith & Wesson .32-caliber short-barrel revolver.

Okay, Charlie. Let's go see who's in the bedroom.

I move quietly down the hall. I don't hear a thing. I should've gone to a motel tonight. Live and learn.

I'm next to the door. I've got the gun at my waist. Here we go.

I come halfway around the corner of the door and keep the gun level.

"About time you got home, baby." Carolyn's lying on the bed reading a film script. "You going to shoot me?"

"What the fuck you doing here?"

"That's what I'm doing here, all right. You must be paranoid, Charlie. I came over thinking about *Last Tango in Paris*. You come in ready for *High Noon*."

"Okay. Give me a minute. I'll change movies and join you. You usually call first."

"I called. You weren't here. I came over anyway. What happened to your face?"

"Don't ask."

"How come you're not wearing shoes?"

"Don't ask."

"Why don't you get into a new business?"

"Don't ask."

"You're screwy."

"Yeah, I know. I'm all talked out. Let's just turn off the lights."

"Just like a man. You don't even stop to ask my last name."

43

I'm finally falling asleep and Carolyn lets me have it in the ribs.

"You still awake?" she says.

"Huh?"

"Charlie, I sat down with my budget. My real budget. It comes to an even half million."

"So?"

"Will you go over it in the morning? See if you can see something maybe I can't see? See if you can cut it back from half a mill?"

"Okay. Can we go to sleep now?"

"I signed contracts. But I don't have the money. I got to cut the budget!"

"Sure. In the morning."

I try to fall asleep again. But now I can't. Because I know she can't. I roll back to face her in the dark.

"What's the matter, Carolyn?"

"I lost forty thousand today."

"You lost your sugar daddy?"

"His wife found out. She told him if he's going to give out forty thousand to put in a movie, he's got to take her to Europe."

"So? If he can give you the forty thousand, why can't he take his wife to Europe?"

"He likes the idea of being in the movies. He doesn't like the idea of being *anywhere* with his wife. Especially Europe."

"Why can't he tell his wife to screw off?"

"It's her money. Actually, it's her father's money. The guy married into an insurance company, you know? He can't give me the forty thousand."

"Lady, you can pick 'em."

"I got three hundred fifty grand, but I don't know if I can pull the film together without the whole half a mill. I don't know if I got time to raise the rest."

"You'll raise it."

"How? I can't even get five grand from you. I've signed contracts, you know? I got to go with it."

"We'll look over the budget. Maybe we'll see some fat to cut. Things'll look brighter in the morning."

"You're full of bullshit."

"I think I already been told that a couple times tonight."

"I want to kill myself."

"I won't let you."

"You won't?"

"They're out to get us, Carolyn. You and me. We got to hang together. I let you kill yourself, they'll get me next."

We don't say anything for a while. Then, "Screw this!" Carolyn says.

"I'm going to bust this fuckin' town, Charlie! I'm going to raise the rest of that money, I'm going to make that film, it's going to go through the roof, Charlie! I'm going to go all the way!"

"You're a tiger, Carolyn. You just forgot it for a second. But you don't have to yell about it."

"They're not going to beat me, Charlie. I'm going to show this business who I am. Carolyn Van Duyn's going to show 'em all."

I roll on top of her and kiss her.

I have to do something. She'll wake up the neighbors, and I don't want to see any more cops tonight.

"Charlie?"

"Yeah?"

"I'm scared, Charlie. I'm really scared. I shouldn't've signed those contracts."

44

I crack eggs into the skillet and make the omelets. Carolyn sits there reading the paper. She doesn't even look up.

"What's the matter?" I say. "You dissatisfied with the service this morning, or last night?"

"It's nothing," she says.

"Carolyn, we'll cut the budget. It'll work out."

"No. It's not that."

She sits there, looking at the paper.

What's wrong? What's she got on her mind? What's in the paper?

Uh huh. Now I think I got it.

"Okay, Carolyn. Read me the horoscope."

"Listen, the stars, they don't know anything."

"What's it say?"

" 'Things come to a crisis. Make your views clear. Fulfill an old promise. For every contact you lose, you gain three.' "

"Your horoscope or mine?"

"Yours."

"Things are going to come to a crisis?"

"Please, Charlie, be careful today. Promise. I get scared about things like this."

"Crisis. Good. It'll be an interesting day."

45

I sit at my desk with Carolyn's budget spread out as far as the eye can see. I hate dealing with this much paper. She sits next to me, pretending to watch. She's still worried about that horoscope.

Screw the horoscope, Carolyn. Let the stars say whatever they want to say. For good or bad, whatever happens, we do it ourselves.

She put together a pretty good budget. There's not much fat. She knows what she's doing. I push at the buttons of my pocket calculator like I know what *I'm* doing.

"What can you make it come down to?"

"You really go thin, you can slice off something close to thirty, maybe forty grand. With a real sharp knife you *might* even cut fifty."

"You really think so?"

"No. I think you're stuck at half a mill, no matter what."

"You're a lot of help."

"Sorry. Best I can do. You already had it pretty far down to the bone. If you want to make the film and you want to make it this way, it's going to cost you five hundred grand."

She sticks her tongue out at me.

"Carolyn, you better show some spirit and get out there for the hustle."

She gives me another gesture to show her gratitude.

"Come on, baby! You can do it! I know you can!"

She pulls all the paper off my desk in a big swirling motion and suddenly I'm sitting in the eye of the hurricane.

"You bet I can, baby! You bet I can! Okay, Charlie. Thanks. If we can't cut the fuckin' thing, then that's the way it goes. I'm going to raise a hundred fifty grand by Wednesday if I got to hock the family jewels, which I don't even have any more. I don't have time to sit here feeling depressed. I got to get going."

She storms to my door, then turns back toward me. "Charlie, listen to the stars. You got a crisis coming today. Don't let it gobble you up."

"Why shouldn't I?"

" 'Cause I'll need you for your five grand!"

46

Women never leave you alone. Once one gets finished with you, there's always another waiting in the wings.

I'm sitting in my office at twelve noon and I have a visitor. Amanda Banner. She's dressed to kill and showing just enough leg to keep me interested.

She wants something from me and it's not five grand.

"Mr. Quinlan," she says, "what happened to your face?"

"Someone tried to improve it last night."

"You mean my brother?"

"If Jamie could've done it, I guess he might've, but he didn't get the chance. I got other friends besides Jamie."

"How's your investigation coming?"

"Going great guns."

"But Jamie's still missing. You haven't found him."

"I found him. Last night. Second night in a row. I told you, finding Jamie's no big problem. He hasn't disappeared very seriously."

"But I don't understand. You didn't bring him home?"

"Nope. Not yet."

She looks me over some more. I look her over. She looked pretty good last night in the screening room with her husband. And she looks pretty good now. And what's she up to?

"I don't understand why Jamie's doing this."

"Me neither. I wasn't hired to find out. All I got to do's bring him home to Papa."

"Mr. Quinlan, I don't understand you."

Good. That's how I like it.

"I don't understand how your mind works," she says.

"Sometimes it doesn't work at all."

"You're very suspicious, aren't you?"

"That's right. You thinking about giving me something new to be suspicious about?"

That shuts her up for a minute.

Why is it every time I get talking to someone about this case, I get the feeling we're spending all our time jockeying for position? And I don't even have any way to tell if I'm ending up in the right position.

"Mr. Quinlan, my husband told me you'd accused him of causing Jamie's disappearance."

"I said that? Could be your husband got confused."

"You upset him! He made some long-distance calls, and then he drove to San Francisco to look over locations up there for some advertising campaign. When he gets upset he likes to go driving."

"Yeah, I heard your husband likes to drive up the coast late at night. I hope he had a nice drive."

She doesn't flicker at that.

"You've seen Howard. You see how he is. Sometimes he's emotionally unstable. He's gone through several analysts, but they didn't do him any good. You've got to be careful with Howard. Things upset him."

"You really think so, huh?"

"Mr. Quinlan, the way I heard it, you were very rough on Howard last night. You can't continue that way. You could hurt him. Without meaning to, of course."

"Lady, what *is* this? Yesterday you asked me to treat your brother gently—I said I'd try to do that. Today you want me to do the same with your husband. You don't know me, lady. I wouldn't hurt a fly."

"You must understand something. My father's very fond of Howard. He wouldn't be very happy if you . . ."

She doesn't finish the sentence. She thinks it's more effective that way.

"Okay. So your husband's got nothing to do with this."

"With Jamie? Of course not!"

"Come off it, Mrs. Banner! When wives come to tell me their husbands're innocent, I start thinking just the opposite."

"Howard's not involved!"

"Not involved in what?"

"Mr. Quinlan, I know about the missing money."

You do, huh?

"But I don't think Jamie took it. And I know Howard didn't take it."

Careful, Charlie. Walk carefully.

"Okay," I say. "How'd you know about the money?"

"My father told me."

"Didn't know you were part of the business," I say. "Your father tell you everything going on down there?"

"No. We discussed the question, the possibility, of some relationship between the missing money and Jamie's disappearance. That's all."

"What conclusion did you reach?"

"I'm *sure* Jamie wouldn't take the money!"

"Your brother doesn't do that sort of thing? Steal things?"

She goes silent for a moment. She's pretty good.

"He has no need for money," she says.

"Okay. So why couldn't it be your husband?"

"Jamie didn't take the money. Howard didn't take it. Neither

124

one of them needs money. If they did, my father has plenty to give them. It must be someone else."

"Let's say you're right. It wasn't either of them. *Jamie* didn't take it, *Howard* didn't take it. So who took the money?"

"I don't know. Who?"

"Your father."

"That's absurd."

"He's got tax problems."

"No he doesn't!"

"Or maybe he wants everyone to think *somebody else's* been into the kitty. A setup, you know?"

"No! You're wrong!"

"Yeah? How do you know I'm wrong? Unless you know who took the money."

Silence. Then, "This is ridiculous."

"Mrs. Banner, the money's not my job. I don't care about it and it looks like your father doesn't care about it either. But there *is* something I'm interested in. I *would* like to know why your brother disappeared."

"So would I."

"I don't mean this time. I mean last time. Why'd Jamie disappear years ago?"

"I don't know."

"You're not much help at all, Mrs. Banner. Can't you give me any clues or something? You're his sister. It's been a lot of years. In all that time you must've figured out something about it." She says nothing. "Come on, if you don't know anything, at least make up something for me to think about."

She doesn't seem to like my approach.

"I've asked Jamie about it," she says. "He's never told me. The only thing I know, he was confused and upset over something. And he ran away."

"That doesn't help much. You care about your brother?"

"Yes. Very much."

"You didn't like it when he disappeared last time. Your father told me you were pretty sick over it."

"Jamie'd never done anything like that before."

125

"Well, this time you don't have to worry. You been through it all before, you know what to expect."

I wonder how far I'll have to go before she'll hit me like she hit her husband last night.

"Mr. Quinlan," she says, "I find you a very insulting man."

"I'm not the kind of guy you had in mind?"

"Definitely not."

"Uh huh. I was told your father had some trouble deciding whether or not to hire a detective. But he ended up deciding to hire me. I think you helped him on that one."

"Of course I did! I don't want my brother ending up on drugs again. But I don't think you'll be much help."

"Having second thoughts? 'Cause I'm sniffing in your husband's direction?"

"Understand this, Mr. Quinlan. You weren't hired to attack Howard."

"Worried, huh? Worried 'cause you know your husband's innocent, or 'cause you're beginning to think he's guilty?"

"Guilty of what? My husband doesn't have anything to do with Jamie's disappearance."

"But you don't know why Jamie's gone?"

"No."

"Then how do you know it's not because of your husband?"

"It's not because of Howard!"

"You could be wrong."

"I'm not wrong! You're being paid to find Jamie. Find him. Please, do it my way, Mr. Quinlan. I'm sure it's the best way."

"You haven't persuaded me."

"So how do I persuade you? With money? If that'll stop you from attacking Howard with ridiculous accusations, I'll get some money for you."

"That's what you think when you're rich, I guess. When you want something, all you got to do's pay for it. Tell you what. I got a friend, she needs a quarter of a million. You got a quarter of a million for me?"

"I can't give you that much!"

126

"Too bad. Almost had yourself a deal. Okay, you'll have to offer me something else."

"What? What're you talking about?"

"Information. That's what I want." No, it's not what I want. Maybe it's what I'll settle for. "Tell me why Jamie disappeared last time."

"I told you! I don't *know* why he disappeared before!"

"That's too bad. You can't give me money. You can't give me information."

Charlie, are you going to be a bastard? Yeah. Probably.

"You ain't got anything I want," I say. "How're you going to persuade me to leave your husband alone?"

We sit quietly. We've been going at each other pretty carefully. When you play that kind of game, the two of you get pulled together close. Like boxers in a ring, looking for an opening.

Some people say you never get to know a person until you get into some kind of fight with them. Maybe Mrs. Banner and I aren't exactly in a fight. But we each want something from the other. She isn't getting it from me, and I'm not getting it from her. So maybe we'll settle for something else instead.

We sit there and think about it in silence. And we start to know each other. Maybe too well.

She comes around the side of the desk, sits on my lap and kisses me on the lips.

She does it suddenly, almost without a thought. But she's still thinking. And I'm thinking.

And then I'm not thinking.

We kiss again, hold it, and pull back, looking at each other.

And I want her.

And I know better.

47

For a moment I'm gone. But then I'm back.

"No thanks, Mrs. Banner," I say. "I don't want that, either."

It catches her completely off guard. All her defenses are down. Then she recovers and moves off my lap.

"You son of a bitch!" she says.

I watch her hand swing back, then forward. "Come on," I say. "You can do better'n that. If you're really mad at me, you *got* to do better'n that. I know you can. I saw you in the screening room with your husband last night. When you really want to slap, you can slap pretty good. I guess you can do a lot of things pretty good."

That does it. She slaps me again. A good deal harder. There are some people who like this sort of thing. I hope I'm not one of them.

"That's more like it," I say. "Now I know you mean business."

"You bastard! I only came here because I love my husband! I'm warning you, Mr. Quinlan! Stay away from Howard!"

"That's much better, Mrs. Banner. Quite effective."

She doesn't like that, either. She throws a small compact at me and slams the door on her way out. Before she can get too far away, I yell after her, "Mrs. Banner! Please! Come back here!"

I listen to myself yell. All I hear is Brandon de Wilde yelling after Shane. I feel like a creep.

"Mrs. Banner? Please?"

There's no sound. No high heels going away from the door. I wait. Maybe I overplayed my hand. Or maybe I threw down the wrong cards.

She throws open the door and looks at me.

Okay, Charlie. One more try. Keep it civil.

"Mrs. Banner, maybe you don't like me much. That's the way it goes. As for me, I don't like this case. Every time I ask questions, you people don't give me the right answers. Or if I'm wrong, and you *are* giving me the right answers, they aren't the answers I like.

I haven't quite figured that part out yet. Someone's playing tricks on me, and I'm trying to figure out who it is."

"What do you mean?"

"If you know what's going on, I don't have to explain it. If you *don't* know, then it'd be stupid of me to tell you. Maybe I ought to forget this whole thing and just dump this case. You want to find your brother? Hunt for him yourself. You think you'd be good, doing that sort of thing by yourself?"

She stands in the doorway, not moving. Finally she says, "No."

"Then don't put stumbling blocks in my way. All I hear from you is 'Don't hurt Jamie,' 'Don't hurt Howard.' Lady, I don't want to hurt nobody. I'll try to straighten all this stuff out, but to do it I got to do it my own way. If you want me off the job, tell me."

"No. I don't want you off the job."

"Okay. So that's that. Anything more to say?"

"I don't think you can be trusted, Mr. Quinlan."

"You're right. But I'm all you got. So wish me luck."

She doesn't wish me luck. She just leaves.

That should take care of her for a while.

She's got some of the looks of her mother. She's got lots of parts of her mother, but I don't know if they're the good parts or the bad parts.

What a family it is. Some of them try to buy you off, some try to kiss you off, some show you their movies, some put you to sleep with a syringe—and none of them tell you anything if they can help it. So what do you make of it? Can *you* trust any of *them*?

And what about you, Charlie Quinlan? What kind of heel are you? What are you doing for the Stocktons? Are you helping them or just making things worse?

You don't know, do you? You're starting to get ideas, but you don't know.

Push on, Charlie. Do what you can.

I hope you're doing the right things.

I hope you're not just a creep.

48

Ethan Stockton's on the phone making small talk about whether or not I'm making any progress. I think I better push it.

"Mr. Stockton," I say, "you're a busy man and I can't give you any information right now. What is it you really want?"

"I don't know," he says. "Thought I'd just check with you."

"You calling to fire me?"

He doesn't answer. He doesn't sound so sure of himself. What's up?

"Mr. Quinlan," he says, "has anyone been talking to you? Maybe about stopping you from handling this thing?"

Yeah. I talked to your wife, your daughter, your son-in-law, and in passing, I talked a little to your son. None of them seems too happy with me.

"I don't know what you're talking about," I say. "Who'd want me off the case?"

"I thought maybe someone's been giving you trouble. About the way you're handling things."

"You want me to stop doing whatever it is I'm doing?"

"Mr. Quinlan, you stay on this case. You get to the bottom of it. No matter what happens, you get to the bottom of it."

Hmmm. Guess he's not going to fire me. Guess this isn't Carolyn's crisis.

"Mr. Stockton, I'm working for you. Nobody else. I'm going to try to bring back your son, if I can."

"Yeah," he says. "No matter what, we got to find out what's going on. Keep me posted, Mr. Quinlan."

He sounded funny. Something's bothering him, all right.

I'll try lunch. Maybe I can get through that without any trouble.

49

After lunch I return to my office and find I have a client. His name's Johnson and he wants me to track down a salesman who sold him a worthless insurance policy, apply some muscle and retrieve his money. He's willing to pay.

I explain I don't do that sort of work and send him on his way.

I spend the rest of the afternoon sitting at my desk, trying to fit the pieces together. After several hours I'm nowhere.

At five-thirty I call Tulley's Bar and speak to the Singer. He tells me he saw Jamie Stockton take off from the parking lot last night. That means he also saw my altercation with the boy scouts, but he's smart enough not to say anything about that. I tell him to finish his drink and start making rounds again.

I open my desk drawer and take out my harmonica. After five minutes there's a knock on the door. It's Bernstein.

Amos Bernstein is a sharp little lawyer who works out of the office next door to mine. On occasion he throws me a client, and his clients usually can pay. As a rule, I don't trust lawyers. I trust Bernstein.

He pokes his head around the corner of the door and says, "I heard you playing that thing again, Charlie. Thought I'd say hello. You and me must be the only ones in the building this late. Incidentally, if you're not on a case and you're not planning to stand around in a TV show tomorrow, I could use some help."

"I'm on a case, but thanks for the thought."

"I was here around lunchtime, Charlie. Saw a real sharp-looking broad come in to see you. She your case?"

"Forget it, Amos. She's married."

"So what?"

"Believe me, you don't want to fool around with her. It's a screwed-up case and she's one of the screw-ups."

"How complicated does that make it?"

"I haven't got it figured yet. Amos, how do I help people when they lie to me?"

"Got me. I'm a lawyer, all I hear is lies. Sometimes, even from judges. If it isn't a secret, what were you playing on that thing?"

"Christmas carols. I can't seem to figure out notes to anything but Christmas carols." I play a few bars of "Jingle Bells" for him. Bernstein signals me to stop. "Invest in some music lessons, Charlie. That's terrible."

"That mean no record contract?" I say.

"You going to play some more?"

"Maybe. It helps me think."

I try to run a scale on my harmonica. Amos winces.

"I got to leave," he says. "Nothing personal. Remember, you're free tomorrow, let me know."

Something must be wrong with Bernstein. "Jingle Bells" doesn't sound so bad to me. Anyway, it helps to clear the brain. But not enough to get me anywhere. The hell with it. Time to lock up.

The phone rings.

"Mr. Quinlan please . . ."

Ahhh. I know who this is.

"This is Mr. Simson speaking. I am speaking for Mr. Ethan Stockton . . ."

I never would've guessed.

"Mr. Ethan Stockton say he just receive telephone call from Mr. Joseph Button at Button Club in Santa Monica. Mr. Button say Mr. Jamie Stockton at Button Club, but no money."

"No money?" I say.

"Mr. Joseph Button say Mr. Jamie Stockton want to play on credit."

"Oh. What'd your boss say?"

"Mr. Ethan Stockton say Mr. Joseph Button extend credit. Mr. Ethan Stockton cover Mr. Jamie Stockton losses . . ."

If the building were burning and Mr. Simson was given the responsibility to call the fire department, he'd get them there in time to count the cinders.

"Mr. Simson," I say, "is Button going to keep Jamie there for me?"

"Mr. Ethan Stockton believe if Mr. Joseph Button extend credit, this keep Mr. Jamie Stockton at Button Club until—"

"Good. Okay. I got the picture. All sounds pretty convenient, wouldn't you say?"

"Beg pardon?"

"Nothing. Forget it. You got anything else to tell me?"

"Mr. Ethan Stockton request you go to Button Club, request you—"

"I'm on my way."

50

No, I'm not.

As I hang up the phone a man enters my office. He's fat as Sidney Greenstreet, at least two feet shorter, and moves slowly, like a turtle. He somehow wedges himself into a chair without breaking it.

"Mr. Quinlan?"

I don't need this one. Not now.

"I'm Quinlan's assistant," I say, "He stepped out for the day. Give me your name and number. I'll have him call you tomorrow."

"What's the matter? You going some place?" the Turtle says.

"Yeah. I want to go eat some dinner. Don't worry, I'll see Mr. Quinlan gets your message."

"Mr. Quinlan already has my message."

I'm stuck.

"Okay, friend," I say. "What've you got on your mind?"

"Good news, Mr. Quinlan. My boss wants to see you about a job."

"Do I know your boss?"

"I got a car."

"I'd like to help, but I got a date. She's a real honey and she hates to wait. Tell your boss to drop by tomorrow. I keep regular office hours."

"It won't wait till tomorrow."

"Friend," I say, "it'll wait."

I get up, put on my jacket and walk around the side of the desk.

The Turtle reaches out and closes his hand around my wrist. He leans partway out of his chair and swings me back around the desk.

"You don't understand," the Turtle says. "The boss doesn't like to wait. Mr. Quinlan, you'll come with me, please. Okay?"

I stand behind the desk where he can't reach me. I want to get the hell out of here. But not with him.

"Get lost," I say.

"That won't do, Mr. Quinlan. Please, no trouble. It'll be worth money to you."

We look at each other for a while. He doesn't smile. He doesn't even blink. Must be hereditary.

"Friend, there's a lawyer working in the next office," I say.

"He went home five minutes ago. I was waiting on him. I checked out the building, Mr. Quinlan. Everybody but you's gone home to dinner."

He knows his business.

"Not the janitors," I say. "Not the night watchman."

"Mr. Quinlan, please don't make a big thing out of this. I'm just here to take you to my boss. It'll be a nice proposition. I guarantee it. Don't get nervous. And besides, I checked things out. There's no janitor or night watchman around. I been told to bring you. I got to bring you."

I sit down at my desk and smile at him. "I can sit here all night," I say.

"Please, Mr. Quinlan. Don't you want to make some money?"

"I already got things to do."

"Just come with me. I don't mean you any trouble."

Okay, Turtle. You get one more chance.

"I want to leave here," I say. "And I don't want to leave here with you!"

"Mr. Quinlan. Please. Come with me. It'll be okay. Don't get so nervous."

Subtlety isn't going to work.

134

On the underside of my desk top there's a small wire cage attached with four screws. I keep a Smith & Wesson there. I take it out and point it at him. "I'm really sorry to do this," I say. "I got to go. Come back and try me tomorrow."

"Come on, Mr. Quinlan. Please. Put away the gun. You won't use it."

"Friend, we live in a dangerous age. Every city's plagued with burglars and killers. You came into my office, and fortunately, I had a gun. I shot you. Maybe dead. No jury in the country'll convict me. That's what the statistics show."

"Mr. Quinlan. Please. Don't play games."

I keep the gun on him and take a pair of handcuffs from my desk drawer. Then I come around the side of the desk again.

"Just the left hand," I say. "Stick it out, and don't move anything else."

He shrugs his shoulders and sticks out his left hand. I keep the gun pointed at his head. I reach down to snap the handcuffs onto his wrist.

He takes my wrist, and without moving from his chair, flips me across the front of his body, sending me flying against the side wall.

51

I don't know where the gun went. It must be some place. I'm lying on the floor with my back to the wall.

The Turtle has somehow managed to get out of the chair and he's looking down at me. "You going to come with me?" he says. "Please?"

"Get lost."

"Okay," he says. "I guess we'll have to mix it up a little, Mr. Quinlan. But please remember, it's your choice, not mine."

He lets me get to my feet. Then we start to circle. I figure if I can get close to the door, I can make a run for it.

He figures the same way. He keeps cutting me off. Things have looked better.

I try a few feints to his body and head. He's quicker than he looks. He blocks me pretty easily. But he always blocks low. I get in one quick right to his face. It doesn't have much effect. While I'm thinking that over he puts his left into my stomach and I'm against the wall again.

We try some more circling. I can't make it to the door.

I slap his left ear.

"Hey!" he says. "Don't do that!"

I slap his left ear. I slap his right ear. He doesn't like it. He's too slow, he can't block the slaps. I keep at it.

It must sting him. He pulls up both hands and covers his ears. I move in quickly, throw a right to his stomach, a left to his stomach, a right to his stomach.

He hits me against the shoulder with the flat of his hand and I'm against the wall again.

Going for the stomach won't do a thing. I get up and slap his ears a few times. It's fun and it does something, but it's not going to get me out of here.

I've got to get to the Button Club. I feint toward his stomach, he moves down to block and I get in two quick slaps to his ears.

"Damn it! Don't do that!"

That's all I have to hear. I try some more slaps. But I move in too close and he grabs me in a bear hug. For a second I can see through the door, out to the other office. I think I see someone out there. Then I don't see anything.

"Come on, Mr. Quinlan. Let's knock this off."

I hear something. It sounds like a slap.

Then I hear it again. I guess the Turtle hears it too. He turns around, swinging a slow backhand at someone or something.

This time I see what it is. It's Carolyn. She's slapping him on the back. He hits her across the face and I see her go tumbling onto the floor of my outer office.

The Turtle has his back to me. I kick him in the ass.

He turns around quickly. "Don't do that!" he says.

The Turtle and I circle.

"Carolyn!" I say. "You okay?"

"Charlie!" she says. "What can I do?"

"Get the hell out of here!"

I slap at the Turtle. He blocks my slap.

I hear footsteps going out of the office. The Turtle turns to see what's happening and I kick him again.

"Come on," he says as he turns back to face me. "Let's cut this out! I'm getting mad!"

I get in a good punch to his stomach. He wasn't expecting anything that quick. I move away from him even quicker.

I slap his ear. This time he blocks it and hits me. For a second I don't feel a thing. Then I feel it, all right.

I'm on the floor, against the wall. He's looking down at me. He's pulling back his fist. I think I'm going to throw up.

There's an awful crack.

The Turtle starts to turn around, slowly.

There's another crack. Twice as loud as the first.

The Turtle pitches forward on his face and hits the floor, almost going through to the office below.

"Should I hit him again?" Carolyn says. She's standing there looking down at him. She's got something big in her hands.

"No," I say. "I think you finished the job."

The thing in her hands falls apart when she drops it.

52

I hold the remains of the thing Carolyn used to smash in the back of the Turtle's head. "You'll never get this glued together." I say. "Not so it'd look anything like an Oscar again."

"I don't care about the fuckin' Oscar," Carolyn says. "If I want an Oscar, I'll win a real one. You okay?"

"Peachy."

"Get me a drink."

I put Carolyn in a chair and some brandy into Carolyn.

The Turtle's really out. Inside his jacket there's a gun—.38-

caliber. I open my safe and lock it in there. Then I find the hand-cuffs and cuff his hands.

"Is he dead?" Carolyn says.

"No. Better luck next time."

"Thank God. I was scared I might've killed him."

"You didn't even come close."

"Where'd he come from? A Sam Peckinpah film? I thought he was going to kill you."

"He just came by to make me a business proposition."

"Wouldn't it've been smarter to accept his proposition?"

"Probably. It didn't seem so at the time. He picked a bad moment to ask me to do business, there's complications."

"How's my face look?"

"Left side's pretty red. Hurt much?"

"Give me some more brandy and I won't care."

"He didn't cut you. That's what you got to watch for. Cuts. You're lucky you don't bruise easy. Put a little makeup on it, nobody'll know."

"I'll know."

"Only if you laugh. So don't laugh."

"I told you, Charlie! I warned you!"

"Told me what?"

"The stars said you'd have a crisis today. That's why I stopped by. To see if you'd had the crisis yet."

"Okay. Finish the brandy. We better get out of here. We don't want to be here when he wakes up."

"You've got him handcuffed."

"That may not make much difference. Anyway, I got a place to go to."

"Yours or mine?"

"No. I got business."

"Some thanks I get for saving your life."

"Carolyn, I love you. I love you I love you I love you. Now let's get the hell out of here."

"You're so romantic."

"Let's go!"

"Something really scares me."

"Yeah?"

"This was fun."

Brother.

"I mean, it wasn't fun when I thought I might've killed him. Or when I was worried he was going to kill you. Still, it was fun."

"Carolyn, I got to go."

"I really cracked him good, didn't I?"

"Terrific. But don't start thinking about it too hard. Look, I got to go some place. We'll discuss it another time."

"Going to your case?"

"Right."

"Take me with you."

"Carolyn, I got to go do some things."

"I'll go with you. We'll do 'em together."

"I thought you had to raise a hundred fifty grand."

"This'll give me a break. Come on! If it wasn't for me—"

"Carolyn, you want to be a private detective, go out and get yourself a license. I got things to do."

"What're you scared of?"

"I'm scared of you. And I'm scared of that guy lying on the floor. Scared he's going to wake up before we get out of here. And I got things to do!"

"Charlie, you're no fun at all."

"Damn it! You had a little action, now you can't come down."

"Is that it? Is it always like this?"

"I don't know. Sometimes. Maybe usually. I don't know."

"It's weird."

"Please, Carolyn. Let's get out of here."

She sits there sucking at the brandy bottle.

"I don't know, Charlie. I don't know if I like it feeling so good. It's scary. You know?"

"I know. I know. Carolyn, get out of here! I'm going—I got work to do."

"Yeah. Okay, Charlie. Go ahead. I'll see you around. I'll go pretty soon. I just want to sit here a little. I sure cracked him a good one, didn't I?"

Women and Turtles. They'll drive you nuts.

53

By the time I get to the Button Club, Jamie Stockton is long gone.

Joe Button tells me Jamie looked pretty drunk and left immediately when he found out Joe had called his father to check his credit.

I don't like any of this.

I decide to head home for dinner and some quiet.

I feel like I'm not doing anyone any good at all.

54

The phone's ringing when I get home, but it stops as I'm unlocking the door.

I'm in the kitchen working on dinner when the phone rings again. It's the Singer. He's back at Le Brigand and he's located Jamie Stockton, drunk as a lord.

I make good time and pull into the Le Brigand parking lot fifteen minutes later. A crowd is gathering in an open area and I walk over to see what's going on.

Jamie Stockton is sprawled across the concrete with blood spattered all around him. Any fool can see he's dead.

I think I've found my crisis.

When Charlie Quinlan takes a case, he knows just how to go about it.

Drop your problems on his shoulders and relax. He'll take care of everything. He'll know how to help you.

He might even know how to get you killed.

55

Someone's pulling at the sleeve of my coat and he won't shake off. It's the Singer. We move away from the crowd and then the cops drive up. The Singer and I stay in the shadows.

"I couldn't do anything about it, Mr. Quinlan. A couple minutes after I called you, he starts to leave. He was real drunk, staggering all over the dining room. I couldn't do anything. I followed, he comes out here, to the parking lot, and POW! This car's pulling out, it hits him straight on. Splat! He walked right into it. Never knew what hit him. The car didn't have no chance to swerve, even. I was the only one who saw it."

"Okay, Rudy. It wasn't your fault. What about the driver?"

"The driver stopped a sec, took a look back, took off. Don't think he saw me. Must've figured he better hop it before anyone came out. Hell, it wasn't the driver's fault, but who'd believe it?"

Maybe I won't believe it. Right now maybe I won't believe anything. Maybe . . . I don't know.

"Hit and run," I say. "This's just dandy. What've you got for me, Rudy?"

"Brown Chevy hardtop. I wrote the license-plate number here, on this matchbox."

"Damn it! I was starting to think I was on to something. We got one hell of a mess here."

"I did something else, Mr. Quinlan. Maybe I did wrong. Before anyone else came out, I went through his pockets. All I could find was this wallet."

Rudy, I love you. But I won't tell you that or you won't be any good to me at all.

The wallet contains thirty-two dollars in cash. There's also a driver's license, social security card and a half-dozen credit cards all made out to James Edward Stockton.

"You did right, Rudy. There's thirty-two dollars here. It's yours. Let's say I owe you another twenty. Get lost and keep quiet."

"You really mean it, Mr. Quinlan? I did okay for you?"

Don't go too far, Charlie.

"You did fine. I just wish I could say the same about myself. Go on. Beat it."

I see one of the patrolmen approaching, so I slip into the restaurant and use one of the pay phones. This is going to be a very hard call.

"Good evening. The residence Mr. Ethan Stockton."

"Mr. Simson, this's Quinlan. I got to speak to your boss."

A long two minutes pass. Long enough for a lot of things to go through my mind. None of them make me feel any better about the part I've played in this thing.

"Good evening, Mr. Quinlan. I been waiting for your call. What news've you got?"

Don't get dramatic. Just give it to him straight. It's the best way.

"Mr. Stockton, I'm afraid I got some bad news. Your son's dead."

I'm sorry. I'm sorry. That doesn't do any good, does it?

He doesn't say anything.

I'm in a hurry, but I take time and wait for him to say something.

"Mr. Quinlan? Are you sure?"

"Yeah. By the time I got to the Button Club he was gone. But I got a tip he was at Le Brigand, out in Hollywood. So I came out here but I was too late. He was dead by the time I got here."

"How'd it happen?"

"Hit-and-run. I got the license-plate number."

"I thought you got there after it happened."

"Yeah, I did. But I still got the number."

"Hit-and-run. An accident, you mean?"

"Looks like it."

"You're absolutely sure Jamie's dead?"

"I'm afraid so."

He's quiet for a long time. Then, "All right, Mr. Quinlan. I understand. Then there's nothing to be done."

"There's something, Mr. Stockton. The cops may have some trouble making the identification. I got your son's wallet and I don't think he was carrying any other identification. I also don't think the people here know your son by name."

"What'll the police do?"

"They'll just take him to the morgue," I say. "They'll check his fingerprints. When they make an identification they'll contact next of kin to make a personal identification. This'll take some hours. Right now they're still waiting for the van to take him downtown."

"What're you telling me, Mr. Quinlan?"

"If I talk to the cops now, if I tell them who they got, it'll save them a lot of time."

"Yeah?"

"It won't help them catch the hit-and-run driver, but it'll start the newspapers asking questions. The cops know I was here last night. I got into some trouble here, they'll try to make a connection."

"I think I understand. Are you required to tell the police your information right now?"

"I'm supposed to do that. That doesn't mean I will."

I'm stupid if I keep quiet. I'm risking a lot if I play it that way. I'm risking my license. But it's up to you, Mr. Stockton. I owe you at least that much, I guess. Unless you let me off the hook.

"All right," he says. "Thank you for your consideration, Mr. Quinlan. Don't say anything to the police. Go immediately to the morgue and wait there."

56

Los Angeles is turning into a slow drizzle. I drive quickly and reach my destination well ahead of the morgue wagon. As I open my car door a man in a raincoat approaches.

"Quinlan?"

"Who?"

"Yeah, you're Quinlan."

"I'm George Washington. Do I know you?"

143

"Come on. In here."

I don't like the looks of this but I follow him into the building. He's wearing a nice raincoat. Plenty of leather, buckles and rings. I estimate it costs more than my entire wardrobe. I wonder what you do to own a nice raincoat like that. Probably steal it.

Raincoat stuffs dimes into the coffee machine, waits for the lights to go through their on-and-off sequence, then hands me one of the paper cups. He leads me back outside. I follow like he's the Pied Piper of some place. He likes that.

We lean against the front wall of the building and count raindrops.

"What do you make of all this, Quinlan?"

"Not much. I usually drop by the morgue on nights I'm feeling depressed."

"Don't be so paranoid. I'm on your side. What's going on?"

"Give me your name, rank and serial number first."

"Private detectives. Got to play like it all means something."

"Okay. You got me. I'll tell you everything I know. How about the combined batting average of the Los Angeles Rams?"

"Last I heard, the Rams're still playing football."

"My mistake."

"All right. I'm not that interested."

The hell you aren't.

That's the way it is. Someone asks you a question and you play sappy and careful because if you give them an answer, later on you find you blew the whole thing. Some people think I'm playing tough. Others figure I'm paranoid. I have to follow my instincts. I stop doing that, I'm left trusting nobody.

And there's something about this guy I don't like. I can smell it.

When the van arrives, Raincoat directs me into the shadows and goes out to meet it. He flashes some identification and says some words. Whatever it is it's enough to send the attendants into the building without a question. Now I'm sure I don't like him.

When the attendants get inside, Raincoat waves toward the left. A gray limousine. I should've noticed it before. Like a fool, I was too busy not liking Raincoat.

The door on the driver's side swings open. Someone gets out. He moves quickly. A spring in his step. It sure isn't Ethan Stockton. A big man. Strong, firm strides. I think I know who this one is.

Raincoat already has the back doors of the morgue wagon open. They look in. I see some light which I take to be coming from a flashlight. Soon the new man sprints back to the limousine and disappears inside it.

Raincoat calls the attendants and watches as they carry the remains of Jamie Stockton into the morgue. Then Raincoat comes over to me and laughs. "Too bad for you, Quinlan. You screwed this one up. You're wanted in the car."

He gives me another small laugh, then walks off.

57

I walk to the limousine and get in the front. The man behind the wheel is muscular, with a craggy face and a jaw built like the prow of a tugboat but somewhat stronger. I wouldn't want to follow him into any dark alleys. I place his age in the sixties.

"Mr. Simson?"

"You are Mr. Quinlan, yes? I am Mr. Simson. So nice meet you."

He sits like a block of granite. No expression on his face, no movement in his body. He sits. And looks.

Mr. Stockton is in the back, drinking from a large pewter mug. He looks tired and drawn. He's not the same man I saw at his office. This man can be beaten. Not without a fight, but he can be beaten.

"Mr. Stockton? You okay?"

"I got a call tonight telling me my son's dead! You think I should be okay?"

"I'm sorry."

"No. I'm sorry. I shouldn't be jumping at you."

He never would've said anything like that to me before.

"Least you had sense enough to call me. There's some, they

would've gone out and got drunk first. Till they got up some nerve. Mr. Simson, do the honors. You might want to join us yourself."

Mr. Simson takes two mugs from a compartment in front of him and pours. Each mug holds about five gallons. Scotch, which I'm not too partial toward. Tonight I'm ready for it. I take a good swallow and turn toward Mr. Stockton again. It's taking its toll on him, all right.

"Who's your man in the raincoat?" I say to be saying something.

"You don't want to know his name. He's got some influence. He owes me some favors."

"He likes to ask questions."

"So do you, Mr. Quinlan."

He sits and looks at me.

"What is it, Mr. Stockton?"

"Lots of things. Maybe too much."

He goes quiet again. I feel rotten.

"I was wrong. Bringing you into this. Wrong to tell you anything about my affairs."

What the hell's going on? What's he doing? He wants to tell me something, maybe something he's been afraid to tell me before. Maybe about his phone call telling me to stay on the case?

"I'm sorry about the way things turned out, Mr. Stockton."

"Sorry doesn't get us very far. Why the hell didn't you get to Jamie at the Button Club? I told you he was there."

"I couldn't get there in time."

"Who the hell bought you off!"

"Nobody bought me off! Who the hell do you think wanted to buy me off?" No, Charlie. Settle down. "Nobody bought me off. That's the truth."

"You can't count on people. You think you know someone, you find you don't." He stops for a moment, looks at Mr. Simson. "Sometimes, you're lucky, you find someone you can count on. Sometimes. It's very rare."

"We been playing with a stacked deck, haven't we?"

"What? What do you mean? I don't know what you mean."

I look back and forth between him and Mr. Simson.

146

"Someone knows what I mean."

"I don't!"

58

"I'll tell you who I trust," Mr. Stockton says. "That guy you don't like. In the raincoat. He knows enough to move when I want him to move. He's got any thoughts on this matter, he'll keep them to himself. I know what makes him tick."

"That's the way you like it. A guy who's loyal without thinking about it."

Mr. Stockton laughs. For the first time tonight I see the man I met at the office—the man who knew he was in charge of things. "No, Mr. Quinlan. I can count on him 'cause he's a politician."

"I should've figured that's what he is."

"You don't like politicians?"

"Of the many things I don't like, I don't like politicians."

Especially on nights like this when I'm thinking about death. Especially then, I don't like politicians.

"You read all the things in the papers these days, you figure all politicians're rotten, huh?"

"No. It goes back some years." Let it go, Charlie. Don't go into it, keep your mind on the matter at hand. "I don't like politicians, but it goes a lot closer to home."

"Don't waste your hate on politicians, Mr. Quinlan. They don't do that much harm."

"I remember once, they did a lot of harm."

"That one, I've helped him some. I can help him again if I want to. Politicians ain't exactly the bravest people in the world. They don't do things on their own if they can help it."

I know. They like to travel in packs when they hunt.

"They do things on their own, they make enemies. They're too smart for that. A man like that one, you know exactly what he is, what he wants, you can count on him. Anything he does, first he'll put his finger in the wind and make damn sure it's safe for him to do it that way."

"Sometimes they're so busy following the wind, they don't bother about facts. Or who they hurt."

"Yeah. But I understand what drives that kind of guy. Ambition. Ambition's a hard thing. You got to have it or you won't get anywhere in this world. But once you got it, it makes you want things. Wanting things makes you do things. Some of them you know you shouldn't do. You do 'em anyway. And then, later, maybe you end up where you thought you wanted to end up. Then some night a guy calls you and says your son's dead. And for no reason at all, you start thinking about all those things you did to get wherever the hell it is you are. You wonder if you should've done some of those things. You wonder if it's all been worth it. What about you, Mr. Quinlan? What the hell *you* do it for? For nights like this?"

Not for nights like this. Death. Politicians. No, not for nights like this.

"I didn't like it, I wouldn't do it. Mr. Stockton, we all screw up somewhere along the line. I don't think tonight's the night for us to go back and look at those things. You're worried. You want to tell me something. You want to trust me. I want to trust you. But we can't quite get there."

"We seem to be having our troubles."

"Listen to me. Your politician saw your son in that van. He saw me. He might try to find out if that means something. Politicians like to look for advantages."

"Maybe you *are* looking out for me."

"I'm trying, damn it."

"Don't worry about that man. He can't pressure me. He talks big but he hasn't got the guts. Tell me what you think about tonight."

"I think I screwed up but I don't know where."

"You figure you got my son killed?"

"No. It's not the hit-and-run I'm talking about."

"You're sure it was an accident."

No. I'm not.

"It probably was. Anyway, I couldn't've done a thing about that. It's something else. Something's going on here. I haven't nailed it down yet."

"A stacked deck. Who do you think stacked it?"

Maybe you. No, I don't think so.

"I had some ideas. Now I don't know."

He passes his pewter mug to Mr. Simson, who refills it and passes it back. He drinks some more, still trying to make up his mind about me. I can't do anything till he does.

"Don't like to follow orders, do you, Mr. Quinlan?"

"I'll follow 'em if I think they're right. I pick my own roads to travel. I find it's the only way."

"I didn't get anywhere in the world by doing what I was told to do. I made my own rules. Sometimes those rules were lousy. I been thinking about that a lot, tonight. You make mistakes, but no man can live by someone else's rules. Maybe I don't understand you but I understand that part of you. I understood it the first day you came to my office. And before that, Larry Hibson, he told me that's the way you are. That's why I hired you. Then, later on, I started to get stupid. I figured maybe I made a mistake. Now I can't be sure either way. You still on my payroll?"

I can't let myself get suckered again.

"You got something to tell me?"

"I liked the way you called me tonight. You could've talked to the cops, but you talked to me." He's trying to convince himself. "I like guys who don't play it safe all the time. You don't let me push you. Lots of guys just let me push 'em." He wants to tell me. He's going to tell me. "If you're willing, I'd like you to stick with this."

"What've you got?"

"Mr. Simson says the dead man isn't my son."

It hits me square in the face and sticks there.

149

59

I knew I'd been taken for a ride. I thought I was on to something. Now it looks like something else.

Okay, Charlie. Shift into gear and get going. Put all the other crap out of your mind. No time for that, not any more.

"Let's get some ground under our feet," I say as soon as I'm ready to say something. "Mr. Simson? You're absolutely sure it's not Jamie?"

"I look very carefully," Mr. Simson says. "I shine flashlight on face. The man someone else. I swear."

"But he *looks* like Jamie?"

"He look very much Mr. Jamie Stockton. Very much. Thinner face. Someone else. I look carefully."

"That dead man's the guy I been following the last three days."

"What do you make of it?" Mr. Stockton says.

"It answers some things. We know why he didn't want to talk to you on the phone the other night. Someone's gone to a lot of trouble here, Mr. Stockton. I got to have straight answers right now, and I don't care if it hurts."

"What?"

"What about before? When you thought it *was* Jamie. Did you care if he was dead?"

"He's my son!"

"So what?"

Mr. Simson moves.

"No!" Mr. Stockton says. "No, Mr. Simson. Let it go."

Mr. Simson turns off like a switch.

"Jamie's my son. How was I supposed to feel?"

"Do you *love* him?"

He's quiet for a moment. "That's a hard question to answer."

"You just answered it. I figured, whatever it was, it wasn't what it's supposed to be. I had to be sure."

"Maybe it's my fault. That there's so little between us."

"Let it go for now. We're going to have enough problems

150

figuring this thing out. I knew this was a phony business almost from the start, but I didn't think along these lines."

"Phony business? What do you mean?"

"The first night I busted in on him, he was ready for me. He had a gun in his pocket, a slob hiding in the closet and a medical syringe in the nightstand. He couldn't've spotted me at that gambling house. I'm not that bad. Unless someone'd already told him to look for me. I think he knew I was coming to find him, he led me away from the gambling house and back to his hotel room, which's where he wanted me. Then he played his act and put me to sleep."

"Why?"

"I had to think he was Jamie Stockton so I'd keep following him. But if I'd brought him back to you, the game'd be over. Trouble was, I thought it was Jamie who was playing the game."

"Why didn't you tell me about this?"

"You hired me to find your son. Not to tell you what I thought was going on. And I didn't *know* what was going on. I still don't. I got to know who's pulling strings. Let's say I *had* told you what I thought. Who'd you tell? Maybe someone who already knew too much. Someone who knew you were trying to find your son. Knew you'd hired me. Someone who'd passed that information on. I didn't want that someone to know anything else. Who knew I was looking for Jamie? You, your daughter, your son-in-law. Mr. Simson. Who else?"

"My wife knows. And my lawyer. And my new accountant. I think they're the only ones."

"Servants?"

"I don't keep servants. Just my wife's maid. I didn't tell her. Hell, you never know what maids know."

"They usually know everything. People at your office? Miss Blitman?"

"I didn't tell her anything. Hell, that doesn't mean anything. She knows the damndest things."

"You already got so many people in on this, even if you didn't tell anyone else, who knows who they told? Mr. Simson? You tell anyone?"

"I quiet. Always."

I can believe that.

"You thought Jamie was playing a game with you," Mr. Stockton says.

"I figured someone'd tipped him off and he was leading me in circles for a little joke."

"What do you think now?"

"I don't know what the hell I think. Someone didn't want me to find Jamie. They gave me a double to follow. I followed."

"But why'd anyone do that?"

"Maybe for time to do something. Before anyone discovers it."

"Do what?"

"I don't know. Maybe spend the money stolen from your business. Maybe to get more money to pay you back. Maybe it's got nothing to do with the money. Maybe time's needed for your son to disappear so he'll never be found." Then I say what I have to say. "There's at least one other possibility."

"What's that?"

"There's no particular reason to think it's true. But it's possible your son's already dead and someone wanted us to think he's still alive."

I watch his face. No change.

"I understand, Mr. Quinlan. You want me to be prepared in case that turns out to be the way it is."

"The dead man was leaving me a pretty clear trail. I wasn't supposed to look in any other directions. Now everything's up for grabs. The thing is, whoever's behind this may not know this guy's dead. They'll find out soon enough. They'll have to come up with a new plan."

"Then we got to do something. We got to do something right now! But what can we do?"

Now's the time to hit him with it.

"Who do you think's been trying to buy me off the case?"

He doesn't say anything.

"Give me a chance. Tell me who you think wants me off the case."

152

He slumps against the back of the car seat.

"Follow up the leads you got. See what you can find."

"And you hope there's something I *won't* find."

"I hope there's something I'm wrong about. I got to wait and see what you come up with."

It's no use. He suspects something and he's afraid if he tells me what it is, it'll come true. I won't get it out of him. Not now.

"Go home and get some sleep, Mr. Stockton. I got some things in mind. I'll work on them."

"What'll you do now?"

"The first thing, I'll try to find out who the hell got himself run over tonight."

60

This is one place I can roam the halls without getting asked a lot of questions. Around the morgue they don't worry about people coming in to steal things.

It takes about ten minutes to find her. Then I turn a corner and she's walking down the hall away from me, which means I recognize her immediately. I don't want to raise my voice, so I say nothing till I catch up with her.

"Hello, Allie," I say.

"What the hell're *you* doin' here?"

"Nice to see you, too, Allie."

"You said you'd give me a call. You don't make calls any more?"

"Sorry. I was out of town for a while."

"I didn't think you'd call."

"Okay. I screwed up."

"What're you doin' here? You come to pick someone up? Or's this business?"

"I need some information."

"Asshole. You're always on a case, huh? That's your life? A bunch of cases?"

"John Doe. Hit-and-run. Came in about half 'n hour ago. From Hollywood."

"Now you're a fuckin' ambulance chaser. Didn't even know you passed the bar exam."

"Can you help me?"

"We got rules, Charlie. Giving out that kind of information's worth my job."

"No good will for old times' sake?"

"If I were you I'd keep my mouth shut. It'll cost you."

"Twenty?"

"Got it now?"

I give her two ten-dollar bills.

"Okay, Charlie. You caught me in the middle of my shift. Hang around, make yourself at home."

"At home in a morgue?"

"Yeah. You ought to feel nice and cozy here."

It seems like the middle of next month by the time I see Allie again. I've read a week-old newspaper from front to back and sideways, and I'm struggling carelessly with the crossword puzzle. Where I can't figure out the words to write in, I'm blacking out the spaces.

She walks by and taps me on the shoulder. She leads me down the hall and around corners till we end up in a windowless room filled with shelves of microscopes and test tubes.

She's got a large paper in her hand but she doesn't give it to me.

"What's the matter, Charlie? You can't even make a goddamn phone call any more? Carolyn got you on a leash?"

"It wasn't her fault. It's mine. I should've called. I meant to."

"I could fill a diary with men who meant to. Just don't start treating me like a one-night stand, Charlie. Either break it off or show me you care. That's all I want."

"Okay, Allie. I got the message. I screwed up. I feel like crap, okay?"

"Good. That's how I want you to feel. If you want to feel better, maybe you'll come see me sometime. What's the matter with men today? You guys never think about anybody but your-selves."

"Allie. Cut it. It's a two-way street. You got my number. You know where I live. There's no lock on my door. You're so interested? Pay me a visit sometime."

"No. I don't want to walk in on you and Carolyn."

"If she's there when you come, I'll ask her to leave."

"That'll be the day."

"Okay. I'll come to your place."

"Yeah. Tonight you're thinking about me. Tomorrow you'll be thinking about something else. You'll probably be on a goddamn case or something."

"Yeah."

"Shut up, Charlie. I don't want to get in a fuckin' argument with you. Here's your information. Give me a kiss."

I give it to her. She gives it back to me.

"Well, drop by sometime if you get lonely, but I won't stay up waitin' for you."

She's right. I'd like to stop by and see her, but I probably won't do it. She's right.

Time to get to work. Come on, Charlie. Get back to work.

Okay. Here we are. The information on my dead friend is enough to give me a start. His name's Austin Bedloe.

Born 1951 in Schenectady, New York.

Corporal, United States Army, Medical Corps. That explains his talent with the syringe.

Stationed two years in Vietnam. Him and thousands of other guys. None of them politicians. Okay. Skip it.

Hair: original color light brown, currently dyed dark brown.

Skin on face, neck, hands and arms: recently chemically treated to appear a darker color.

Someone went to a lot of trouble here. But who? And why?

Okay. A name. Austin Bedloe. No big surprises here, but at least I got a name.

I use a pay phone to call the cops. I report having seen a hit-and-run accident in the parking lot of Le Brigand earlier in the evening at approximately ten minutes past nine o'clock. I report

155

the license-plate number of the car. I hope the Singer wrote down the right number.

The desk sergeant wants to know why I waited so long to call. He wants to know my name. I don't think I want to tell him. I hang up the telephone and go home for some sleep.

61

I try my best but I still wake up at seven o'clock. When I can't fall back asleep I give up and climb into the shower. That almost does the job.

Grapefruit and my usual toast with peanut butter give me enough energy to look up Austin Bedloe in the phone book and begin dialing.

"Hello. Who's calling?" The voice on the other end of the line is soft and gentle, but predominantly male.

"Good morning," I say. "Is this Austin Bedloe?"

"Austin isn't here. Is there a message?"

So far, so good.

"This's Mr. Gilmartin," I say. It's a name I can do things with. "Austin had an appointment with me yesterday afternoon at four-thirty. But he didn't show. I may've confused the days. I thought I told him yesterday."

"Yesterday?" the soft voice says. "Are you calling from here in Los Angeles?"

"Yeah."

"Austin couldn't see you yesterday in Los Angeles. He's been in Las Vegas for two weeks."

I see. This is going to be tricky.

"Nope," I say. "I saw Austin three days ago, here in Los Angeles."

He doesn't like the sound of that.

"How can that be?" he says. "Austin told me he'd be gone several weeks. If he's back in town, he'd certainly contact me. I mean, he lives here. If he's in Los Angeles, where would he be staying?"

Good question.

"I don't know," I say.

"Are you sure it's Austin you saw?"

"What'd you say your name was?"

"Alfred."

"Look, Alfred, I was having drinks out in Hollywood. Three nights ago. Over comes this boy, a really nice boy. Says his name's Austin Bedloe. We kind of hit it off. I told him to drop by my office yesterday at four-thirty. I don't know why he didn't keep the appointment. We had a lot of fun out in Hollywood the other night."

"Yes. I see."

I bet you do.

"So anyway," I say, "he's supposed to meet me yesterday, but he didn't show. But the other night he said I could reach him at this phone number."

"Mr. Gilmartin . . . are you in the business?"

That's it. I should've guessed. No wonder he played Jamie Stockton so well.

"Yeah," I say. "I'm in the business. Independent. A production company."

"I don't mean to be pushy, Mr. Gilmartin, but if you're looking for someone of Austin's type and age range, I'm sure I'd be right. We're very similar. Actually, I've had more experience."

"Yeah?"

"More experience?"

"I've done several commercials. And a couple of TV things."

"I see. That's very nice. Alfred, right?"

"Alfred Harlan. H-a-r-l-a-n. If you like, I can send you a picture and résumé."

"We'll have to get together. I'll give you a call. Afraid I'll be tied up for the next couple days, though. Look, Alfred, I'd really like to get in touch with Austin. You got any ideas how I could reach him? Maybe he *is* in town, and he's tried to reach you, but

157

for some reason he couldn't do it. That kind of thing happens sometimes."

"The other night in Hollywood . . . when you saw him . . ."

"Yeah?"

"Well, I mean . . . was he alone?"

"Oh, yeah. He was alone. When I saw him, he was alone."

"Oh . . . Have you tried his answering service?"

"That's a good idea, Alfred. Problem is, I don't think I got the number."

"Hollywood 5-6500. You can reach me through the same service."

"Thanks, Alfred. You been a lot of help. I'll be in touch."

I hang up and dial again.

"Good morning. Hollywood 5-6500. Actor service. May we help you?"

"This's Mr. Gilmartin," I say. "I want to contact Austin Bedloe. You know how I can get in touch?"

"Yes, Mr. Gilmartin. This is a professional service. Is this business? We are not allowed to take personal messages."

"This's business."

"Yes, Mr. Gilmartin. What kind of business, please?"

I'd like to sell him a coffin. I can get him a good price.

"I'm an independent producer," I say. "I tried reaching Mr. Bedloe at home, but I didn't have any luck. The only other number I got on him's this one."

"Yes, Mr. Gilmartin. I can leave your message for when Mr. Bedloe calls in."

Lady, he won't call.

"Look," I say, "Bedloe got an agent? I wouldn't want to put you to any trouble, but maybe he's got an agent?"

"Yes, Mr. Gilmartin. Mr. Bedloe's agent is Ellen Bessie. Should we contact her for you?"

"I'll get in touch with her myself. Thanks."

62

Nobody answers the phone at Carolyn's apartment, so I try her office.

"How come you're at work so early?" I say.

"Baby, I got a film ready to fly in less'n a week," she says. "We're on all four burners here. How you doing?"

"I'm okay."

"When I got in this morning I sent Larry into your office to check things out. You'll be happy to know that fat guy's not there any more."

"Too bad. If he'd stayed the night I could charge him rent."

"You got many other friends like that?"

"He just came in to make small talk. How're the bruises on your face?"

"They give me the 'I mean business' look. Very scary. People figure they better not fool with me. Ahh, it'll go away by tomorrow. Doesn't hurt."

"You come down yet?"

"Listen, that little fight in your office, it got me charged up. I was pissed you wouldn't take me with you last night. But it worked out."

"What do you mean?"

"I was so worked up, I was ready to take on anything. So I started hitting the bars. Hollywood was dead last night."

"Some of it was deader than you think."

"So," she says, "I went down to some places in Santa Monica. I hitched up with this young guy, turns out he's a hairdresser. You got any idea how much those hairdressers make?"

"How much did you get him to invest in your film?"

"I was so hot after that thing in your office, I was coming on like gang busters. Baby, you should've seen me in action. About an hour later I got him writing me a check for twenty-five grand. Just like that. Doesn't have to check with his partners, his wife, nothing."

"You cashed the check yet?"

"I already sent Sue to the bank with it. No grass grows between Carolyn's toes. You know, Charlie, all in all, I had a hot time last night."

"You're a tiger."

"You do okay? I mean, after that crisis?"

"The fat man in my office wasn't the crisis."

"Shit. It got worse?"

"Don't ask."

"Sorry. You okay, baby?"

"I'm fine. You ever hear about an actor Austin Bedloe?"

"Never heard of him."

"Alfred Harlan?"

"Nope."

"How about an agent Ellen Bessie?"

"Yeah, I talked to her a couple times. She's been around awhile. She sends me some people sometimes, but her client list ain't too hot. I figure she must be hanging on by the skin of the old teeth."

"Think she might recognize me?"

"From all your starring roles? I don't know. She might pick you as an actor she's seen somewhere. Why? You don't want her to know you act?"

"I don't want her to know who I am. Right now I'm doing some checking, I don't want anyone to know who I am."

"Dress up like King Kong. They'll never know."

"Go pick up the rest of your half mill, lady. I'll see you sometime."

"Not so fast. Got something for you. 'Ask for favors. Work changes include filling in for others and scheduled interruptions.' "

"My horoscope or yours?"

"Yours, Charlie. There's a little more. Want to hear it?"

"Probably not."

"It also says 'Stop screwing around with the private detective business and give Carolyn the beautiful broad five grand for her film.' "

She never gives up.

63

Once you see the way your face looks in the mirror enough times, you get used to it. But it never gets any better. One good thing. I heal pretty quickly. The marks from the mugging at Le Brigand are pretty much gone. I'm back to looking like the same old Charlie. So I need a few changes. If it worked for Austin Bedloe, it'll work for me.

I dab some spirit gum onto my chin and upper lip and build myself a nice little understated mustache and beard. By the time it's set I look like my bank account just went up fifty thousand dollars.

I poke through my wardrobe for something resembling the touch of tweed. Something closer to Gilmartin and further away from Quinlan. I settle on a nice beige suit, bland and nondescript. And a striped tie which might connect me to some old school some place. To top it off, I put on an off-white country-style cap.

When I figure I look good enough for the front cover of a stylish magazine, I go for a drive.

Ellen Bessie doesn't work for any of the major talent agencies that are slowly but surely taking control of the Hollywood film studios. Ellen Bessie is an independent, which means she works out of a cramped third-floor office in a building too far up on Hollywood Boulevard. She employs one girl who probably spends her working hours with a phone glued to her left ear and the remains of a pencil stub stuck in her right hand. Ellen Bessie's office is a way station for actors on their way up, on their way down, or more probably on their way nowhere.

Ellen Bessie is glad to see me. She'd be glad to see anyone. I say I'm an independent film producer and she ushers me into her office. Her office makes my office look good.

I settle into a straight-back chair and give her my most expensive-looking smile. It's my imitation of David Niven.

"I must confess," she says, "I'm not familiar with your name, Mr. Gilmartin. Do you have a card?"

"Don't believe in cards," I say. "Too pretentious, don't you think?"

"It's strange I'm not familiar with your name."

"Quite new out here. Been doing a spot of work in London, actually."

My Niven needs a lot of work.

"Ahhhh. But you're not British, are you?"

Lady, I'm trying like hell to be British. I can't help it if it's not my style.

"You have the British look," she says, "but you seem so American."

I never could do an English dialect. Okay. Make changes.

"Quite so," I say. "New York, originally."

"I see. I'm sure I've seen some of your films. If you'd just mention some of the names. I try to see everything . . . Mr. Gilmartin?"

She doesn't believe me. Agents in this town get burned by so many phony producers. She doesn't believe me.

"British television," I say, "actually. None of it exported here, yet. Got some deals in the works, of course."

"Uh huh." She's ready to pick me apart. "You like it over there, in London?"

"Marvelous place to work. None of this Hollywood hustle bustle. My associates asked me to come over. Look things up and down, don't you know. Since I'm American and they're all British. My associates and I, we have some money available. We're contemplating a series of films."

"I'm surprised I haven't read about your projects in the trade papers."

Come on, lady. You got out-of-work actors, right? Don't push me. I'm here with jobs. Jobs! Come on! Jump at me!

"Hush hush, right now," I say. "Allows me to move freely, so we mustn't let the cat out of the bag too soon."

"Mr. Gilmartin, you *are* quite sure you'll be doing films here? I mean, sometimes—"

"Sometimes people say they're going to make some films. But

162

they don't make them. They say they have the money, but they don't have the money. And everything goes up in smoke. *Poof.*"

"Yeah. That happens sometimes."

"Exactly so, Mrs. Bessie. So we keep our plans secret. We don't want to end up with *poof.*"

"So you *are* in a position to hire actors."

"Mrs. Bessie, a sharp agent is the lifeblood of this business."

I hit the soft spot. I got you hooked, lady.

"That is, a *sharp* agent," I say. "I like an aggressive, independent agent, Mrs. Bessie."

"It's Miss Bessie."

"Ahh. How much nicer. I was an agent myself. Several years. New York. People don't realize. They do not realize. A grueling job. I know. Cats and dogs and all that, Miss Bessie."

"Call me Ellen."

"I'd be pleased to call you Ellen. My first name's Ernest, but please don't make it Ernie. So American, don't you know. Call me Gil."

"It's a tough profession, Gil. And tougher for a woman. But you work through me, you can count on me. You're looking for good actors? I'll get 'em for you. Young or old, fat or thin, I got it."

"I've been told some interesting things about this young one, Austin Bedloe."

She sits still. She's puzzled, but she doesn't want me to know it.

I'm worried. She looks like she already knows Bedloe's dead.

64

"Austin Bedloe?" she says.

"Yes. I'm told he's a good actor."

She sits still some more. "Yeah, sure he is. Who told you about him?"

"I hear things. Around town. Why? Isn't he available?"

"You want him? I'll make sure he's available. It's just—Austin Bedloe, he hasn't done much yet. I don't mean he's not good. He's good, you don't have to worry about that. I'm just surprised you knew to ask about him."

Now I know something. Bedloe must've been lousy.

"Well," I say, "someone said some things about him, made him sound perfect for one of the leads in our first film. Of course, if you don't think he's good enough to handle something big . . ."

"No, he's good. Austin's good. You're interested in Austin, you're interested in quality."

He must've been the kiss of death.

"Austin'd be perfect for almost any type of part," she says. "He's out of town right now, up in Vegas, but I can get in touch with him." No you can't. "I'll get him down here soon's you like."

"I don't have to meet him right away. Perhaps you have a picture I could see."

"Pictures never tell you much, Gil."

"Don't you have his picture?"

She pulls a glossy from her files and gives it to me. Austin Bedloe seems a pleasant-looking young man in his early twenties. There are small pictures inset along the side that show him in makeup, ranging from a seventeenth-century fop to a twentieth-century Nazi.

"Very nice," I say. "Big on makeup."

"Good character man. But he can play straight leads. Dynamite. You ask me, he's going to be very big . . . one of these days."

Every actor in Hollywood is going to be very big . . . one of these days.

Bedloe's credits are listed on the back of the picture. Now I know why Ellen Bessie was so surprised when I asked for him. His credits are all in nonprofessional theater, the kinds where the producers never lose very much money because the actors are never paid anything. The way it looks, as an actor, Austin Bedloe was a complete bust.

It could be the only good acting he ever did was for an audience of one. Me.

Ellen Bessie knows the credits are killers. She's all warmed up to tell me things are better than they look when her assistant slips past me and whispers into Ellen's ear. I can't make out any words, but we have some more whispers, followed by a hopeless groan.

"Ellen?" I say. "Something the matter?"

"I don't believe it!" she says.

She must've just been told Bedloe's dead.

"I just don't believe it!" she says.

The assistant doesn't waste any time getting back to the safety of her cubbyhole in the other office. But I don't have any place to hide.

"Actors!" she says. "How the hell can you count on 'em?"

"What's the matter, Ellen?" My goose is about to be cooked.

"I been working over a month to get a commercial for one of my girls. And I *got* it for her. They're all set to shoot the spot tomorrow, and now the girl's overdosed on drugs. Can you believe it? That stupid bitch! She couldn't wait till the weekend? The things you got to live with in this business! The first job I been able to get her in six months—*she's* got to go out and pop pills to celebrate!"

I've been reprieved.

"Is it serious?" I say.

"Serious? I'll say it's serious! Oh, she's not going to die, if that's what you mean. She'll be okay. But she won't be okay tomorrow, and tomorrow's the day they shoot the spot. You know who gets the blame for this, don't you? Me! 'Cause I can't deliver her tomorrow. I'll never get a call from them again. That stupid bitch!"

She's almost in tears, but she's too tough for that.

"Can't they use one of your other girls?"

"I pulled every girl I handle in there for this spot. All they wanted was this one. You turn on a camera, she gives you instant sex. I can't come up with anyone else like her. Damn it. You know what it costs when you're set to shoot tomorrow and you can't shoot tomorrow? You know what happens to you with all the union guys you got to deal with? Yeah, you know. You're a producer. Damn it. I'll never hear from that agency again."

"You need a real looker, huh?"

"Yeah. I need her in about two minutes."

165

"I know a girl might work."

"Yeah?"

"Such short notice, though. I doubt she's available."

"Can you call her?"

"Believe she's shooting something this morning, but I think I might be able to reach her. Would you mind if I used your phone?"

"Use it! Use it!"

She practically throws the thing at me. I dial.

"She's very busy, very in demand. Maybe I could get her over here to see you. Cross your fingers."

"You getting an answer?"

"One moment, Ellen. Just starting to ring."

The ringing stops. Someone picks up the phone.

"Stockton Film. Good morning," Claude says. "May I help you?"

65

By the time I get to my office I've already ripped off the pseudo club tie, mustache and beard. I'm Quinlan again.

The Singer's there. He remembers the twenty I promised him last night and doesn't want to give me a chance to forget about it.

I pay him and tell him a little of the Austin Bedloe story. He promises to keep his ears open, but considering the turn of events I figure he's lost his usefulness in this case.

A new girl answers the phone at Stockton Film. She tells me Claude's ill and will be gone all afternoon. Yeah, I know about that.

"Good afternoon," Mr. Stockton says. He sounds even worse than he did last night. "You got anything?"

"You know a guy named Austin Bedloe?"

"Bedloe? Nope."

"He's an actor."

"There's lots of actors in this city, Mr. Quinlan. Some I know. Most of them I don't, thank God."

"When they bury this one, he'll go into the ground looking a lot like your son."

"The man that got run over last night?"

"That's him. Wasn't doing so well as an actor. Looks like he decided to try another line. It didn't work out."

"Austin Bedloe. No, the name means nothing to me."

I hear the door to my outer office open.

"Hold the phone a minute, Mr. Stockton."

Maybe it's the Turtle paying me another visit. My hand goes to the wire cage under my desk and my fingers close around the Smith & Wesson.

I listen carefully. It's quiet. Then a sound. The sound of high heels moving across the floor.

"I'm in here," I say. "Come on in."

The high heels move in my direction. I hold the gun gently, out of sight. The door opens. It's Mrs. Stockton.

I put my finger against my lips and motion her to take a seat. Then I speak into the phone again.

"Just some kid selling magazine subscriptions," I say. "Listen, I want to know something about this particular individual we just talked about."

"You mean Bedloe?"

"Right. He ever been employed by you?"

"I'll have to get Miss Blitman to check the files."

"I'll hold on."

I smile at Mrs. Stockton. She sits there looking back at me without a smile. We wait.

"No record of employment for Austin Bedloe," Mr. Stockton says. "Anything else?"

"No. I'll talk to you."

66

"Good afternoon," she says. "How are you today?"

"The same's I always am. What's up?"

"You're all business."

"I don't get much business here, so I figure, whatever business I do get, I ought to get to it."

"I get the impression, from talking to Ethan, that you didn't tell him about our meeting the other day. Thank you for keeping it confidential."

"You're welcome. What do you want?"

"To the point, Mr. Quinlan. Always to the point."

"Lots of people try to get me off the point. I'm supposed to make sure they don't get away with it."

"What happened last night?"

"I don't know. What've you got in mind?"

"Ethan left the house late last evening. He didn't look well. When he came back he didn't look any better. He wouldn't tell me what it was about. Won't you tell me?"

"What makes you think I know?"

"It's something to do with you, Mr. Quinlan. I just don't know what it is."

Who the hell told you it had to do with me?

"You said Mr. Stockton wouldn't tell you what it was. But you're sure it's got to do with me."

"Yes."

I get the picture.

"Mr. Simson told you it had to do with me?"

"That could be."

"You're friends, you and Mr. Simson."

"I've known Mr. Simson for years. As long as I've known Ethan."

"Mr. Simson looks like a nice tough customer. Guess he makes a pretty good bodyguard."

"He's very loyal to Ethan."

"Is he loyal to you?"

"What are you getting at?"

"Nothing. I'm just curious. Mr. Simson looks pretty tough. Like maybe, someone got in his way, he might drive over someone in a car. Not even bother to look back or wave or anything. You think Mr. Simson's that tough?"

"Let's say, if you're planning to be rude to someone, don't be rude to Mr. Simson."

"What'd Mr. Simson tell you about last night?"

"He said they had to go out to meet you."

"He didn't tell you anything else?"

"No."

"When Mr. Simson speaks he doesn't say much."

"Not usually."

"Mrs. Stockton, I've got nothing to tell you."

"Something happened last night and it's got Ethan worried. I saw him this morning and he looked terrible. You're supposed to protect him."

Yeah. I know. I'm trying to figure out how to do that.

"I'm trying to protect him, lady. I care about him too. I don't know, maybe he had too much to drink last night."

"It's not liquor. It's something else."

She looks so sweet. I can't take any chances with her.

"Had a nice chat with your son-in-law."

"You talked with Howard?"

"Showed me some films. Quite a guy, your son-in-law."

"You didn't like him."

"His films didn't do too well, huh?"

"They weren't very successful. They weren't successful at all."

"So he made some movies and they didn't turn out. Your husband's got money, how come he doesn't bankroll Howard to another film? Howard might get lucky. It's happened before."

"Howard's scared. He wants to make another film. He's scared it won't be any good."

"So he just makes commercials. Met your daughter, too. Nice-looking woman. Takes after you in some ways."

"Yes. In some ways."

"You think she really loves her husband?"

"She loves Howard very much."

"Maybe, a guy like Howard, you either got to love him or you don't like him at all. That's not the way it is with Jamie. Nobody cares too much for Jamie. You all love Howard and nobody loves Jamie. Must be something about Howard I haven't seen."

"He has his problems."

"We all got problems. You say your husband's not looking so hot today. Why? He's worried about Jamie?"

"Ethan's afraid Jamie's going to end up on drugs again."

"Last time that happened, your husband threw Jamie into an asylum, they cleaned him up, put him back on the streets. So what's the problem? Jamie turns up on drugs, we can do it again."

"It wasn't just Jamie who went to a hospital, Mr. Quinlan. Ethan was sick for a while, too."

"You didn't tell me that part, the other day."

"That was three years ago. Three years makes a big difference at Ethan's age. If certain things happened now, I don't know how he'd take them. I don't want to see Ethan hurt."

"Maybe if you told me all you got to tell me, I could look after your husband a little better."

She doesn't say anything.

"Or maybe if you told me some things, it might get *you* into trouble. Maybe you want to help your husband, but you can't do it without making trouble for yourself."

The phone rings.

"Hello. Charlie Quinlan here."

"Quinlan? This's Sergeant Wayne. Lieutenant Barnes wants you down here."

"What a nice invitation."

"Ain't it. Barnes says get down here right away. Unless you want to lose your p.i. license."

"I wouldn't care much for that."

"That's what he said you'd say. You got fifteen minutes."

A nice little phone conversation to liven up the afternoon.

"Sorry, Mrs. Stockton," I say. "We'll have to finish this talk later."

"Why did my husband see you last night? What's going on?"

"I'll make a deal with you. If he *did* see me last night, I'll tell you what he saw me about. But first, I'm going to tell *him* you been coming to see *me*. You want me to do that?"

"No. I don't want him to know I've talked to you."

"Mrs. Stockton, you come to see me 'cause you want to tell me something. But you never tell me something, do you? Long's I know you're keeping something from me, I got to watch my step with you. That's how it goes. You got anything to tell me now?"

She doesn't say a thing.

67

He's balancing a foot on the edge of his wastebasket and snapping a rubber band against the back of his hand. He can't have anything on me. He's just fishing.

"Got your message, Jake."

"And you came?"

"Sure. What's up?"

"Always in a hurry, huh? How's your case? The case you don't have?"

Yeah. He's just fishing. I better not slip up.

"Which case?" I say.

"You got more'n one? You *better* have more'n one. Better be earnin' the green stuff pretty good these days if you're going to afford Le Brigand."

It's nothing. He's working on the hit-and-run at Le Brigand, so he made the connection. That's all he's got.

"Great food there, Jake. You ought to try it."

"What were you there for? Eatin' or gamblin'?"

"They got gambling at Le Brigand?"

"There's rumors to that effect."

"How come the cops don't close it down?"

"Don't talk to me. I'm homicide."

"Gambling's illegal. Ain't the cops interested?"

"Schmuck! Don't you think we'd like to close it down? It's

protected. You know that. Protected all the way up the line. Don't be a pain, huh?"

"What do you want, Jake?"

"Le Brigand. They got a busy parkin' lot. Tuesday night you got mugged by a bunch of kids. Wednesday night some guy's the victim of a hit-and-run. I'd call that a busy parkin' lot."

I look at him and show him nothing. How could he connect me to that hit-and-run? He can't. Not unless I slip up.

"Hit-and-run?" I say. "How's the guy doin'?"

"Aww, he's dead. We got lucky, though. Late last night someone calls us, gives us the number on the car that did it. Guy hung up without givin' his name. Too bad about that. Know anything about this?"

"No."

"This dead guy, splattered all over the parkin' lot. Austin Beckloe, or Bedloe, somethin' like that. Thought you might've run across him some place. Out-of-work actor."

"There's lots of out-of-work actors around town."

"This mornin' I talked to a guy he lived with. A real honey. Also talked to Austin Bedloe's agent. She's a sweetie too. They said Bedloe's supposed to be in Vegas."

"Too bad he wasn't. Maybe he'd still be alive."

"Could be. Anyway, the agent's named Ellen Bessie. You ever meet any Ellen Bessie?"

"I heard the name. All I know, she's an agent."

"Accordin' to the roommate and the agent, some guy's lookin' for Austin Bedloe, just this mornin'. Just before *I* was lookin'. Independent film producer. Ernest Gilmartin. What do you think?"

"Never heard of him. There's lots of independents around. Still, Gilmartin—it could be made up."

"I checked it out with the phone company. There's an Ernest Gilmartin livin' out in the valley. I went out and talked to him. Retired English professor. In his eighties. Lives in a wheelchair. It's a long trip to the valley for that kind of information. Got anything to say?"

Sorry, Jake. You don't have enough to catch me.

172

"No," I say.

"Son of a bitch."

"Jake?"

"Don't call me Jake!"

"What's the matter?"

"Jake's for when we're friends. Right now we ain't friends. Right now you're a schmuck. You call me Lieutenant Barnes."

He's running a bluff. I'm not going to break.

"Right. Lieutenant Barnes."

"Let me see your wallet."

This isn't the time to ask questions. I give him my wallet.

He flips through and takes out the photostat of my p.i. license. He throws the wallet back at me. He opens his desk drawer, drops in my license, closes the drawer.

"You're a sucker," he says. "It's all over, but you're a sucker and you don't know it yet."

68

I often wonder exactly what those things are which scare me.

There's lots of things I *should* be scared of. I can recover from a beating. I can heal from a gunshot. At least I have. And if someone's going to kill me—if it's really going to happen, it's going to happen. You can't spend your life fearing death. If you did that, the whole thing would be a waste.

But I know what scares me.

I can't do a thing without a license. I can't take a case, I can't do a thing. I need that license 'cause I need cases—like a goddamn junkie needs his goddamn dope, I need cases. To keep me going. It's my work. It's me.

That's how simple it is, damn it. Jake has me. He has my license and he has me. He knows it.

So what do *I* know? What do I figure?

I figure he's playing a hunch. I was at Le Brigand two nights ago. He figures maybe it's more than a coincidence. He figures I'm

173

Gilmartin. But he can't be sure. Not yet. He could pull in Ellen Bessie and have her try to identify me, but I haven't seen her around. Maybe he's just holding off, playing a hunch.

Maybe I should talk. If I talk, what'll it mean? Nothing. Right?

It'll mean I won't be giving any protection to the guy I'm working for. Protection is what I'm paid to give. I've got to sit here and keep my mouth shut.

Jake has nothing on me. He's playing a hunch. Running a bluff.

But he's got my license in his desk drawer.

"You called us last night with the number on that car," he says. "That much's okay. You should've left your name, but I can understand that part. But you also been playin' Ernest Gilmartin all mornin'. That means you know somethin'. Tell me about Bedloe."

"Sorry, Lieutenant. I can't help you."

"Schmuck."

"Far's the law goes I haven't done a thing. I know it and you know it. So what's the point?"

"The point is, I got your license."

He takes time for a cigarette. He rolls his own, and at times like this takes two days to do it.

"Quinlan, I got five homicides sittin' on my desk and some-one's sayin' I'm supposed to solve them. That someone's *me.* I'd like to solve them. What do I get this mornin'? I get Austin Bedloe. Supposed to be a clean hit-and-run, but some things're funny about it. I figure I'll spend a mornin' on it, follow up the obvious loose ends and close the case. Maybe if I write up a nice clean report they'll let me get back to the five homicides I care about. Followin' all this?"

"I got you." But I can't tell you anything, Jake. How can I tell you anything without screwing my client?

"So I go through the motions of findin' out who this Austin Bedloe is. I find someone's ahead of me. Ernest Gilmartin. But I figure that's a phony 'cause Ernest Gilmartin's a guy who lives in a wheelchair out in the valley. I figure this other Gilmartin, he's

174

you, Quinlan. And if a private investigator's lookin' into the case, that's bad, 'cause it means I got to look into the case too. So I call you down, I give you a chance to talk to me. Do you cooperate? No. Do you tell me what the fuck's goin' on? No. You waste my time. I don't need that."

How can I tell you anything without telling you everything?

"Lieutenant," I say, "you got me wrong."

"You been lookin' into Austin Bedloe. I don't think it, I know it. Think it over. You don't see it my way, I'm not going to be responsible."

You're bluffing. You don't have a thing on me.

"Jake, I don't know a thing."

"The hell with this," he says. "Get lost."

I pulled it off! He *was* just bluffing.

I stand up, stretching my legs. "Can I have my license back, please, Jake?"

"Fuck you, Charlie. Your license's dead. Go back to the movie business. You don't want to talk? Okay. The hell with it. Your license's dead."

You always have to know one thing. You have to know when it's time to fold your hand.

69

"I'll tell you what I can," I say. "I'm on a case, someone tells me this guy Bedloe, he may have some information. *May* have. Nothing definite. So I give it a try. Monday night, I locate Bedloe and try for a talk, but he gives me the slip. I find him again Tuesday, at Le Brigand, but I get roughed up by those kids and I lose him again."

"That part I know," Jake says. "Someone fittin' your description was seen walkin' Bedloe out of the restaurant Tuesday night. What happened in the parkin' lot? How come the kids mugged you but not him?"

"They just wanted my boots. They weren't interested in him."

"Okay, let it go for now. So you lost Bedloe two nights runnin'."

"Yeah. Last night I drop by Le Brigand, just in case he's there, and he's there. But before I get a chance to talk to him he's dead."

"Uh huh. And in the middle of the night you got a twinge of public spirit, so you phone in the license on the car which got him dead."

"Yeah."

"How come you waited so long before usin' the phone?"

I had to borrow a dime.

"I had some things to do first," I say..

"Maybe you thought your client was drivin' the car, and you needed time to check it out."

"It wasn't my client."

"So? What about this mornin'?"

"I still didn't know if Bedloe really did have any information for me. But he was dead, so I followed up wherever I could. Nothing turned up. Far's I'm concerned, it's a dead end."

"You sure of that?"

"No. But it looks that way."

"You're not sure of nothin'. What's your case?"

All right. We're going to find out just how scared I am.

"Sorry," I say. "It's confidential."

"The hell with you. With you, everythin's confidential. The kind of fuckin' toothpaste you use's confidential!"

Jake sucks in his breath. He sits quietly.

"Shit," he says. "Okay. You got any reason, any reason in the world to figure this accident last night wasn't an accident?"

Yeah. I got reasons.

"No," I say. "Pretty much the opposite. From what I can make out today, everyone'd like Austin Bedloe alive."

Jake sits there smoking his cigarette. He really lost control for a second. He sits there and lets it come back to him.

"Okay, Quinlan. This's the way I see things. I don't care much about Austin Bedloe. As for your story, I think you left out some parts, but I knew you'd do that. Waitin' half the night before tippin' us to the license-plate number, that don't sit too well, but

176

it ain't givin' me heartburn. Not yet. It was wrong, but you figured to get away with it, since we had no way to trace who made the anonymous call. However, I don't like the way you kept quiet when you came in here. You should've given me answers right away. And you're *still* holdin' back. Right?"

"That's what I'm paid to do. Look, I don't think anything I know affects your investigation. If I find out different, I'll let you know. If I talk about my cases, that'll be the end of my cases."

"That'd be a fuckin' shame. You'd have to go back to bein' a full-time actor."

"What do you want from me?"

"Charlie, I think you're nuts."

"That sound you hear's me going off the deep end."

"When you go, you won't even make a splash. What is it? Are all Hollywood actors neurotic?"

"I don't know, I was neurotic before I started acting. Maybe it's the sun. Out here everything gets a chance to grow, even the loonies. This city's a breeding ground, getting all of us ready for the loony bin."

"The sun? Pretty soon it'll give us all the big C. Aww, what the hell. At least we'll all have tans when we go. This Bedloe thing, you think it's an accident or a killing?"

That's how Jake works. He likes to sneak up on you. I do it the same way.

"I don't know," I say. "You're in homicide. *You* must think it's a killing."

"I think it's an accident. Like I said, I had to investigate. Too many funny things. This guy Bedloe, he's got dyed hair. Chemically dyed skin too. Too much dyein' for my taste."

"Probably too much dyin' for Bedloe's taste."

"I understand he was staggerin' drunk in that parkin' lot last night."

"He was a drinker."

"That's another funny thing. The autopsy says he's got two drinks in him, tops. He wasn't on pills or drugs, either. Maybe he just wanted people to think he was drunk."

Yeah. He wanted *me* to think it.

"Bedloe was an actor," I say. "Who knows why they act the way they do? You find the hit-and-run car?"

"You sure you phoned in the right number?"

"You got the number the way I saw it." I'm glad I'm not under oath.

"We're workin' on it. Traced the owner. Some electrician, he lives about a dozen blocks from Le Brigand. Says his car was stolen last night but he didn't report it till this mornin'. That's all he says. Could be he's tellin' the truth. Maybe we'll know somethin' if we turn up the car in one piece."

"Till then?"

"Till then I got five other homicides to look into, and the way I see things, they're all more legit'n Austin Bedloe."

"Then I guess you're not interested in this case. And I guess you don't want to keep my license. I guess you'll give it back, if I say please. Please?"

"You're a schmuck, Charlie. Who you workin' for?"

How much is that license worth to me? "It's confidential, Jake."

"Schmuck." He opens the drawer and throws the photostat at me. "Next time I'll keep it."

I almost make it out the door without asking the next question. My curiosity gets the better of me. It usually does. "Okay, Jake. You going to tell me?"

He's all grins, like a Sunday gambler ready to play his ace. "Tell you what, Charlie?"

"How come you're so sure it's me looking into Bedloe?"

"Schmuck. I know you're at the morgue last night, buyin' information on a hit-and-run victim."

"Allie talked?"

"That's women for you. They talk."

"Hell, I paid twenty for that information."

"You got your money's worth. You paid twenty for some information and that's what you got. You didn't pay the girl one cent for her to keep her mouth shut."

"I thought she was a friend."

"You don't have friends, Charlie. You're a p.i. P.i.s don't have

friends. Listen to me. I ain't got time to waste on this case. Like
I said, it don't look like my department. But you find out it wasn't
an accident, you talk to me. Right away. You don't want to make
me mad, Charlie."

Right. I don't want to make you mad.

I sure hope the Singer gave me the right number on that car.

70

It's four o'clock and I'm walking down the hall to my office. I don't
feel so hot. Nothing seems to be breaking in my favor.

Approaching me are two men deep in conversation. I better
say something or they'll walk right over me. No, they look up and
separate to let me pass between them. I do so and nod my thanks.
I realize immediately it's a mistake.

They each grab an arm and pin me against the wall so I can't
move.

I hear footsteps coming down the hall. I don't waste my time
hoping it's help. It isn't. It's what I think it is.

He steps in front of me and I see just a bit of the white bandage
on the back of his head.

"Returning my handcuffs?" I say.

"Mr. Quinlan," the Turtle says, "my boss still wants to see
you. Will you come with us, please?"

"Sure. I got the rest of the afternoon clear."

"You won't give me an argument today?"

"No. What the hell. Let's go."

"No argument?"

"Okay. I see what maybe you got in mind. You want to do
it, there's nothing I can do to stop you." I don't even care. You
want to hit me? Hit me. You might as well. I don't feel so hot
anyway. I feel disgusted. Maybe I'd just as soon you *did* hit me.
"Come on, Turtle. If you're going to do it, do it. Let's not stand
here all day."

He smiles. "Mr. Quinlan. Please. We don't want any trouble."

He's not going to hit me. I'm nuts. I want him to hit me. But he's not going to do it.

The two goons have me by the arms. I bring my feet up so they have to hold on tight to keep me from falling and I kick out into the Turtle's stomach. He goes straight back against the opposite wall.

The two goons brace me against the wall. I don't care. I had to kick out at something, so I did it. It was crazy. But it felt good.

The Turtle straightens up and comes toward me. I'm ready for him. I had my kick and now I'm ready for him.

He puts his hand along the side of my face. Then he takes it away and brings it back very quickly.

Everything goes black.

He doesn't bother to hit me again. He doesn't have to. The three of them put me in a car and we go for a ride. I recognize the lobby of the Beverly Wilshire Hotel as they drag me through it. A couple bellhops look us over but don't do anything about what they see.

We end up in a suite on the fourteenth floor.

The room's all blue velvet and carved white wood. Hotel-style pseudo-eighteenth-century. The furniture forces you to sit bolt upright. Floor-to-ceiling curtains and wall-to-wall carpet.

The Turtle takes the two goons into the adjoining room, leaving me sitting on a sofa. I could probably get up and walk out. I could probably get as far as the elevator if I ran all the way.

After a few minutes the door to the adjoining room opens and the boss comes in. Early thirties. Tall, with a muscular-looking body, well-conditioned. Black hair. Strong face.

I'm very interested to hear what this is going to be about. Very interested.

"Good afternoon, Mr. Quinlan," she says as she sits down. "Sorry about the inconvenient way you were brought here."

"No inconvenience," I say. She's a stunner. I'd try my David Niven on her but that didn't even work on Ellen Bessie, and what's sitting across from me now is really class stuff. "If you wanted me, you could've called me on the phone. Or sent along your picture."

"I guess you and Stanley didn't get along."

Stanley. A turtle named Stanley.

I've got this game pegged already, I think. Let's see what I can do with it.

"No," I say. "Stanley and me didn't get along. What're you doing for dinner, lady?"

She doesn't pay that any mind at all.

"Mr. Quinlan," she says, "I flew down to see you yesterday. You made me stay in town overnight."

"I had something I had to do yesterday evening. That's why Stanley came back empty-handed. But like I said, if he'd showed me your picture, maybe I would've come to see you anyway. But Stanley didn't do that, so it got a little rough. Maybe you don't care."

"I apologize for my method of contacting you. Stanley handled it wrong. Sometimes he doesn't understand his instructions properly."

"He said something about a job."

"Yes, Mr. Quinlan. There's something. It's worth some money to me."

"How much'd it be worth to me?"

"If you can do it, a thousand a week."

"I love ladies who're rich and beautiful. What's the job?"

"I'm a businesswoman, Mr. Quinlan. I have an associate here in Los Angeles. He makes collections for me. I think he's begun making collections for himself, too. I don't like that. Some of his collections should be my collections. You understand?"

Lady, I'm way ahead of you. I'm so far ahead, I'm going to try having a little fun with this.

"I'll whistle if I get lost," I say. "The way you look, I might whistle anyway."

"Mr. Quinlan, are you always this forward?"

"Often. You mind?"

"Not yet."

I didn't think you did.

"But first," she says, "let's talk business."

"I can't talk business from such a distance."

She comes over and sits on the sofa next to me.

181

"That's nice," I say. "I'm listening."

"If my associate's doing what I think he's doing, I don't like it. But my information could be wrong. So I want him followed for some time. I want him watched."

"Sounds too easy for a thousand a week. Must be something you left out."

"He's rather dangerous. That's what sets the price."

"Interesting. But it doesn't wash. You got a bagman who's pocketing too much of the take? Set Stanley on him. Stanley and those two goons who brought me here."

"A bagman pocketing the take?"

"You know what I mean. This thing's not on the up and up. The job's too simple and the pay's too good."

"Maybe it is. Do you care?"

Baby, what big eyes you have. Do you mind if I take your hand? You don't mind? Fine.

"I probably can't be trusted with this kind of work," I say. "Better use your own boys."

"I wish I could do that, Mr. Quinlan. But my associate, he knows them. The people I know, he knows. That's the problem. I'm in a position I don't like."

Lady, I'd like to put you in a position *I'd* like.

"I'm forced to use someone like you," she says.

"Someone legit."

"Let's say someone at least as legit as you."

"That's not too legit. When's the job start?"

"Immediately."

"Full time?"

"I'll need details on everything my associate does."

"In triplicate, no doubt. With all copies notarized." How far can I go with you, lady? Can I kiss you?

Yeah, I guess I can. But your heart's not in it. "Lady, you want to go out to dinner? I'd like to do that. I'd like to do more'n that, too, but I'm too much of a gentleman to mention that kind of thing. But this job? If I was you I'd send down one of my boys from San Francisco to take care of it."

"I didn't say I'm from San Francisco."

"You said you flew in."

"Not from San Francisco."

"That's right. Could be you flew in from Butte, Montana. Or maybe even Pittsburgh, or Paris, France. I say it's San Francisco."

"What makes you think that?"

Because you've got the greatest smile in the world.

71

"You're a hell of a good-looking lady," I say, "but you haven't sold me on any of this."

"What do you mean?"

"There's a guy named Victor Siletti. He runs a small piece of San Francisco. They say he's a nice little guy in his sixties. Used to work out of Chicago. I guess you work for him."

She takes her hand away from mine. "Mr. Quinlan," she says, "as it happens, I *am* from San Francisco, but I don't work for Victor Siletti."

"I'm on a case. You already know that. You're supposed to get me off the case. You make up this nice job for me, trailing some guy for nice money, and you figure I'm just a cheap private detective, I'll bite at your money."

"Are you serious?"

"Not often, but right now? Yes. I'm investigating a thing which may or may not involve a guy down here named Howard Banner. Banner, he makes TV commercials. Good ones. Three years ago he made some for a guy up in San Francisco, a guy named John Donhauser. Those commercials, they're so good they got Donhauser elected mayor. Did you vote for Donhauser?"

"No."

"The hell you didn't. See, Siletti, some years back he used to have a piece of San Francisco and he was doing pretty good. Then some things happened and for a while some *other* guys're doing pretty good. Then Donhauser got elected mayor and now Siletti's doing pretty good again. Probably a coincidence. Like it's a coinci-

183

dence your boy Stanley came to visit me last night when I was about to go out on a case.

"Anyway, long's Donhauser's been mayor, whenever there's a big investigation up in San Francisco, it never touches Victor Siletti. Only one trouble. Donhauser, he's got an election coming up, and he's the worst kind of politician. Not only is he dishonest, he's stupid. Too stupid to get himself reelected. For a politician, that's the worst thing. If he doesn't get reelected, he's no use to anybody. Not even Siletti."

"I really don't understand what you're getting at."

"ABC: Siletti wants Donhauser reelected. Siletti wants Howard Banner to make some commercials to *get* Donhauser reelected. I'm looking into something which may or may not involve Howard Banner. D: Get rid of me.

"I got Banner worried the other night, so he made some phone calls to some guys he knows in San Francisco. That means Banner must've been real worried, but we'll skip that. Anyway, Banner asked Siletti to send someone down here to pull me off. That's you. You figure maybe I'm so dumb, you'll do it without me realizing what's going on in front of my face. Or maybe you offer me enough money, even if I see the handwriting on the wall, I'll make believe I don't see it."

"Okay, Mr. Quinlan. Does that mean you accept the deal?"

"No. Stanley slapped me too hard. And yesterday he slapped a friend of mine. I didn't like that. I don't like this deal. You want to catch somebody, you're supposed to use honey, you know?"

She takes my hand again. Now I'll get some honey.

"Howard Banner isn't involved in anything which concerns you," she says. "You can take my word for it."

She kisses me. She does better than she did the first time.

"But whose word do *you* take?" I say. "Howard Banner's?"

"Yes, Mr. Quinlan."

"Call me Charlie. Another thing. I need a little more evidence'n just Howard Banner's word he's innocent. Can you give me any?"

She shrugs, then she kisses me again.

"I suppose we got a problem here," I say.

"Only if you pursue your case."

"That's what they pay me to do."

"That's too bad, Charlie. You have guts. But you don't have brains. Brains're better."

She puts both her hands into mine. She's all sugar now. "You shouldn't've said anything," she says. "Whatever you thought, you should've kept your mouth shut and accepted my offer."

"I'm not worried. Siletti doesn't like to kill civilians. That kind of stuff, he likes to keep it in the family. Siletti's smart. He knows Howard Banner's not worth the trouble a murder'd cause him."

"Charlie, you could be wrong."

"No. Besides, I got an ace in the hole. I'm going to do you a favor, lady. I got some information you don't know about, but I think you'll want to have it."

"I hope so," she says as she strokes my hand. "I do hope so."

"In the long run, Howard Banner ain't worth a thing to you. He ain't worth a dime."

"Charlie. Bluffing never works with me."

"No bluff. Donhauser faces reelection next year and Siletti figures he'll use Banner again to make some more commercials. But there won't be any commercials. Not this time around. Not from Howard Banner. Two nights ago Banner swore to me he'll never make another commercial for any politician. Ever. I believe him. Check around. If he told me, I'm sure he's told others. You might figure you could always force him to make commercials for Donhauser, but how do you force him to make *good* commercials—the kind you're going to need. You better find yourself a new candidate and a new advertising genuis. You're going to lose the election, lady. Banner and Donhauser, they're no use to you. Neither of them."

She takes her hands away from mine. Without another word she goes into the other room.

I think I've done pretty well so far. I don't know if that card was really an ace, but I played it like it was. With some people you have to play things like you know all the angles, or they'll blow you right out the window. Still, you have to be careful not to overdo it. I think I played it okay.

The two goons come out of the other room and sit down on either side of me. They don't say anything.

I feel okay now. I think I played it okay.

I find an Ethan Stockton cigar in my pocket and take it out. I light it. Nobody takes it away from me.

72

Time passes, but it doesn't bother me. I'm smoking an Ethan Stockton cigar and it's a damn fine cigar.

The Turtle opens the door for a moment to say something to one of the goons. I can see into the other room. The woman is sitting on the bed in there, talking on the phone. Then the Turtle closes the door and we wait some more.

A lot more time passes. I hear the phone ring in the other room.

Another five minutes. The Turtle comes in, stands by the door and looks at me.

The woman comes in. She sits in the chair by the door again. She's one hell of a good-looking lady. Last time she came in I got a couple kisses out of the deal. I wonder if I'll get any further.

Hell, I'm feeling okay now.

The Turtle comes over and rips Ethan Stockton's cigar out of my mouth.

I'm not feeling okay now.

"Think you told me something, Quinlan?" the woman says. "Think you gave me something, and now you're off the hook?"

"I don't know," I say. I think I played this wrong. "Guess it's up to you."

"Bet your ass it's up to me. The games're over. Got me? You think much of yourself right now?"

"No. Maybe I did, but right now I don't."

"Good. If you got some brains, you'll shut up. Maybe you'll know enough to shut up and listen to somebody else do the talking."

She stands up and comes toward me. She sits down next to me on the sofa, barely giving one of the goons enough time to make room for her.

"I been on the phone," she says. "I gave Dad your story."

"Dad?"

"Victor Siletti. You said you knew about Victor Siletti, right?"

"He's your father?"

"Shut up and listen. This guy Howard Banner, I don't like him. He's a pain in the ass. This past year, every time something goes wrong, Banner's on the phone to us to do something about it. He must figure all we got to do in the world's look after him. He needs a nursemaid, know what I mean?"

I nod my head.

"Okay, Quinlan. You sort of understand who you're talking to now?"

"Yeah, lady. I got you."

"Some people make mistakes. Take Stanley. He made a mistake. Getting into a fight with you yesterday. The fight wasn't a mistake. Losing it was the mistake. He knows I don't like mistakes, but usually Stanley, he uses his brains. How about you? You know how to use your brains?"

"I sure hope so."

"Okay. I think maybe you and me, we understand each other now. We'll go back to Howard Banner. Some guys, like Banner, they don't understand there's some things you can do and some things you can't do."

"You don't like Banner, do you?"

"What do you mean, Quinlan?"

"Banner. You and Banner. He calls you all the time? Whenever he gets in a mess? Okay, he's stupid that way and you don't like it. I understand what you're telling me. But there's something else here. You don't like Banner. There's some other reason."

"So what if there is? You figure you can get me to tell you why I don't like him, or you just want to get me in bed with you?"

"Lady, I'm not telling you a thing what to do. You're going to do whatever you want to do. I know that much."

187

"You better. The truth is, you're wrong about me and Banner. I like Banner. I really like Banner. You believe me?"

"I'll believe whatever you want me to believe."

"Bet your ass you will. I used to have a good, very nice-looking friend. Down here in Los Angeles. I like nice things. And nice people. Last New Year's I spent the night with my parents up in San Francisco. And this guy Banner, he decided to drive up to San Francisco. He's always driving up to San Francisco. He wants to do me a favor, so he calls my friend to come along for the ride. That was nice of him, huh? But on the drive up there's an accident. Now Banner, he doesn't get hurt. My friend, *she* got hurt. She had to have plastic surgery. I brought in the best fuckin' plastic surgeon I could find, but it didn't do any good. My friend, she doesn't look so nice any more. And I only like things that look nice. You might say I don't much like Howard Banner. He made me lose a nice friend."

I sure played this one wrong. All the way wrong.

"I'm going to check out your story," she says. "About Banner not wanting to give us any more help. If it turns out you're telling the truth, then we're finished with you. And we're finished with Banner, and I'd like that. But if I find out you been lying to me about Banner, that this's a story you made up to save your skin, that's going to be too bad. I'll have to arrange something for you. In my line you don't get ahead if you let people lie to you. That's what Dad told me on the phone, just now. So I hope you weren't lying about Banner. I'm sure you understand."

She drops her hand across my leg just above the knee and squeezes slowly to show me how strong she is. She's strong.

As soon as she's made her point she smiles and takes her hand away.

73

It's the doorbell.

I got four hours of sleep last night. After the Beverly Wilshire, I figured it was time to head home and get some more. My mind was going fuzzy and I didn't have any real leads to follow. Now the doorbell wakes me up.

I shake my head. Try to focus. The numbers on my watch come together, bounce back to their correct positions. Seven o'clock.

The doorbell again. I grab my bathrobe and move into the living room, stopping at Old Granddad long enough to get the Smith & Wesson and drop it into my pocket. It's been that kind of day.

I open the door. It's Claude.

"What happened?" she says. "You get mugged?"

"Several times. None of 'em worth talking about. Was I expecting you?"

"There's three Charlie Quinlans in the phone book and none of you're answering your phone tonight."

"Mine's off the hook. I was trying to sleep."

"I went to see one of the others first. Nice-looking guy. Single, too. I like you better. The third's in an office on Western. I didn't feel like snooping around an office." She pokes a bottle of wine at me. "Got a corkscrew?"

"If I don't, I'll borrow one. Come in."

"How come you told Ellen Bessie you're a movie producer named Ernest Gilmartin?"

"I'm an incurable liar whenever I talk to agents. I figure you got to meet them on their own level. I hope you didn't set her straight."

"No."

"What the hell you looking for?"

"I like to snoop. If I find anything interesting, I'll let you know."

She says something else I can't understand because it's coming to me over her back. She's out of the living room and into the kitchen. Then she's out of that and down the hall.

"That's the bathroom. They give you one with every apartment, no extra charge."

"Ellen Bessie thought I was taping a commercial at Stockton Film. I figured that's what you told her, let her think it. Right?"

"That's the door to the hall closet. You interested in closets?"

"You can tell a lot about a man from his closet. This agency, they got to shoot a commercial tomorrow, they can't use the girl they're supposed to use, she's sick or something. So they looked me over and I made sure they got something to look at. I'm going to do it. Out in Griffith Park. My first real job since I got here!"

"Congratulations. Can you sit somewhere? I'm getting dizzy watching you."

"I'm really up! Got to keep moving! Ellen Bessie wants to be my agent. The guy who's *supposed* to be my agent, he's more interested in going down to Mexico. From now on, Ellen Bessie's my agent. What do you think?"

"Good luck. Stop moving!"

"I got to pay her a commission. They get you a job, you got to pay them a commission."

"So I've heard."

"I'm not the kind of girl who just goes barging into the apartments of strange men, and if I do go barging in, it doesn't mean I'm looking for anything long-lasting. Right? I'm giving you the ground rules."

"I don't care about ground rules. What the hell're you looking for?"

She goes further down the hall and pushes open the door to my bedroom, goes in and flops across the bed.

"You found what you're looking for?"

"An actress gets a job, she's got to pay a commission."

"If this's a business transaction, forget it."

"You serious?"

"Afraid so. I never take payment in trade."

"Not even just once?"

Maybe. Just once.

74

The smell is fresh coffee and it wakes me up.

"You really conked out," Claude says.

"Yeah. Didn't conk out too soon, did I?"

"I'd say you conked out just about the right time."

"That's what I thought."

"Don't you remember?"

"I remember. Give me a refresher course sometime, I'll be sure to remember."

She still isn't wearing a thing. She's watering and pruning the house plants on my window sill.

"Domestic, too."

"Something wrong with being domestic?"

"No. I appreciate it. More'n I expected."

"What'd you expect? Why'd you give my name to Ellen Bessie?"

"She needed an actress. You needed a job. Seemed to make sense."

"You didn't just want me to owe you?"

"What? No."

"No? You accepted payment quick enough."

Brother. Now she's got guilt feelings.

"You came to me. I didn't come to you. You figure it was just a business deal, you can take off."

She doesn't say anything. She works on the plants.

"You ought to look after these things, Charlie. Plants need love and tender care."

"Don't we all."

"You're going to keep plants, you got to look after them."

"I used to have a gardener come in every other week, but I caught him stealing my razor blades. Now I got to look after them myself."

"Look, Charlie, I didn't think I had to come here. I just wanted to be sure, you know?"

"You didn't have to come here."

"Okay. I better put the steaks on."

"Sorry. I don't have any steaks."

"I know. All you got's fruit, eggs and bread. Don't you ever cook for yourself?"

"I'm pretty good at breakfasts."

"I went out and bought steaks. While you were asleep."

"I hope you got dressed before you went."

"I borrowed your raincoat."

"I'll be the scandal of the corner grocery."

Claude comes over and sits next to me. She puts her hand on my cheek. "Maybe you *did* do it just for a favor."

"Maybe I did."

She kisses me on the forehead. I think the steaks will have to wait.

The doorbell rings.

"You expecting a visitor?" I say.

"No."

"Neither am I."

75

I throw on my bathrobe and keep the gun in the pocket so Claude won't see it. I don't care who it is, I just don't want it to be the Turtle.

I open the door. It's not the Turtle. It's a hell of a lot worse than the Turtle. It's Carolyn.

I wonder if Claude's going to have enough sense not come out here.

I wonder if, before she comes out here, she's going to have enough sense to get dressed.

The breaks start going against you, they sure don't stop.

"What's the matter, Charlie? Aren't you going to let me in?"

She comes straight in and sits on the sofa. I really don't need this kind of thing tonight.

"Thought you'd be out looking for investors." Boy, do I sound stupid. "How much money you got left to raise?"

"What's the matter, Charlie? You look nervous."

"I'm on a case. I always look nervous."

"Hi," Carolyn says to something behind my back. "Claude?"

"Yeah. Who're you? Carolyn?"

I look at Claude. At least she got dressed first. In the top of my pajamas. I look at Carolyn.

Wait a minute. I look at Claude. I look at Carolyn.

"Excuse us, Carolyn." I pull Claude down the hall. "How'd you know her name's Carolyn?"

"I figured she must be the one who called before. You were asleep."

"She called? You talked to her? She knew you were here? You didn't tell me she called! Claude! Why didn't you tell me she called?"

"I forgot."

"You forgot? Some things you're not supposed to forget!"

I casually pop back into the living room.

"You called before. You knew she was here. You came over 'cause you knew she was here."

"You're pretty smart, Charlie. You ought to be a detective or something."

"I think I better get dressed."

"Yeah, Charlie. That'd be a good idea."

76

Claude's in the kitchen with Carolyn. Claude's working on the steaks. Carolyn's working on Claude. I sneak down the hall and try to hear something.

"The Shakespeare Festival in Colorado?" Carolyn's saying. "When were you up there?"

"About '72, '73."

"You know Jim Coates? He was up there around then."

Shop talk. Sure. Carolyn's saving the good stuff for me.

I try to figure how I'm going to approach this thing. I decide I don't have any ideas how I'm going to approach this thing. I go in.

"Carolyn? Staying for dinner?"

"I got to meet someone for dinner. What time's it?"

"Getting late. Almost nine-thirty."

"Oh, good. I can stay awhile."

Oh good.

"Carolyn told me she's a movie producer. She says she's got a movie starting production next week."

"Yeah, Charlie's one of my investors."

"Really?"

"Yeah. Putting in five thousand."

"Charlie? That right?"

I don't say anything.

"Carolyn says maybe she could use me in the movie."

"That's nice," I say.

"Claude was telling me she works for Ethan Stockton."

"Oh," I say.

"Ethan Stockton's supposed to be loaded. A guy knew Ethan Stockton pretty good, maybe that guy'd get Ethan Stockton to invest in my movie."

"Hmm," I say.

Claude brings over a plate. "Hope you like your steak rare. I should've asked. It's kind of rare."

"I like it rare."

"Charlie likes it rare," Carolyn says.

"That's good." Claude goes back to the stove.

Carolyn takes my knife and fork and cuts into the steak. The inside is red as a beet.

"Good-looking steak." Then Carolyn whispers to me, "I once saw a cow run over by a car. It was wounded worse'n this and still got up and walked away. But I'm sure you'll like it, Charlie."

"Bitch," I whisper, "that's a line from a Clifton Webb movie." I taste the steak. Rare. Very rare. "Steak tastes fine, Claude."

194

"Don't talk with your mouth full," Carolyn says. "I can never take Charlie out to eat with me. He always talks with his mouth full."

"Maybe I can cure him of that," Claude says.

"Maybe," Carolyn says.

I'm losing my appetite.

The doorbell rings. Whoever's out there, even if you're trouble, you've got to be an improvement over this.

I go to the door and open it. He looks like a movie star. Two movie stars. Dustin Hoffman's head on John Wayne's body.

"Quinlan?"

"Yeah."

"We got a mutual friend."

"Who's that?"

"A small guy who's kind of fat. You know who I mean?"

Oh brother. The Turtle's sent me another goon.

77

My gun's in my bathrobe pocket. My bathrobe's in the bedroom.

"My friend told me you like to give trouble, Quinlan. I don't want any trouble."

"Neither do I. Your friend's boss said she'd check out my story on Banner. I told her the truth. She checks, she'll see I told her the truth."

"You don't understand. I came for the goods."

"The goods?"

"The goods. The goods. To pick up the goods."

"What the hell're you talking about?"

"You give me any trouble, I'll have to take care of you. Shut up and give me the goddamn goods."

"I'll be glad to give you the goddamn goods! But I don't know what goddamn goods you're talking about!"

"Guess he's talking about me," Carolyn says.

"What?"

"Hi, Carolyn," the guy says. "Sorry. I got tied up in traffic."

"Your timing was fine."

"I did it the way you wanted it?"

"You did it fine."

"Carolyn!" I say. "You bitch!"

"Yeah," Carolyn says. "But it was fun."

"You bitch! You don't know what I been through today! You bitch!"

"Just keeping you on your toes, Charlie." She goes out to the hall and takes the guy's arm. "See you, Charlie. I'm going to go to dinner, now my date's here."

"You shouldn't've done this, Carolyn."

"Lots of people do lots of things they shouldn't do. When some of those people do it, they should be smart enough to leave the phone off the hook so nobody'll call while they're asleep."

"Bitch."

"Don't you love me any more?"

"Bitch."

"Same to you, Charlie."

She and the guy start walking down the hall. Then Carolyn comes back alone.

"All right. Where'd you get him?"

"Been saving him up for a special occasion. You aren't really mad at me, are you?"

"He tough's he looks?"

"Tougher. You still love me?"

"No. I never did."

Carolyn laughs. She disappears down the hall with the guy who looks like two movie stars.

I guess it was pretty funny now that it's over.

She's still a bitch.

78

By the time I get back to Claude's dinner I can't taste a thing.

"She was mad, huh?"

"It's nothing. We're just good friends."

"I guess she won't use me in her movie."

"She probably will. To show how liberal she is."

I let Claude do most of the talking during dinner. Regional theater in Seattle. Summer Shakespeare in Colorado. Heartbreak in Hollywood.

Hollywood is an old story and it doesn't change. Agents. Auditions. Lost parts. Strained hopes. Chasing after one good connection and a few bucks to put in the bank to keep you going. Running after a dream that's always a step and half ahead of you.

"You scared me the other morning. Asking if I'd be willing to kill to make it in the business. Telling me you knew guys who died 'cause they were in the business. I figured you were crazy."

"I'm crazy all right, but that was no story. My parents got divorced when I was fourteen. My mother starts going with an agent. He got me some extra work. TV. Films. I wasn't all that hot for it but the money was too good. He got me into some big stuff. *Ten Commandments. Ben Hur.*"

"Really? You know Charlton Heston? What's he like?"

"Big. Especially from the shoulders on up. I never got to talk to him. Worked with him three times, too."

"What was the third time?"

"A Welles picture. *Touch of Evil.* Welles was looking for extras to play Mexicans. I was standing there, he heard my name was Quinlan, he hired me. They slapped some makeup on me to make me look Mexican. I got five days' work out of being named Quinlan."

"What's that got to do with it?"

"Welles was playing a character named Quinlan. Must be he thought it'd be good luck having me around."

"You did a lot of acting?"

"Did a summer of *Damn Yankees.* A summer of *Funny Girl.*

Did *Funny Girl* in Vegas for eight weeks, too. Once did Nick in *Virginia Woolf*. Even did a bike picture, in the sixties."

"Why'd you quit?"

"Acting only works for me in small doses. Doesn't give me any long-lasting relief."

"What's that mean?"

"Doesn't fill me up. I need something thicker. Heavier action."

"So what do you do now?"

"Other things."

"You haven't told me the part about killing people."

"Yeah, I know. That agent I told you about, the one my mother went with. He wanted to make it big. He never did. One day he took sleeping pills. I always figured he was pretty well balanced. I guess he wasn't. You never know."

"That's terrible, Charlie. Was your mother still going with him when he did it?"

"It was the second time around for her. My father killed himself too. A year after they got divorced. But my mother got smart after the agent did it. She married an oilman and moved to San Francisco. You don't hear about too many oilmen killing themselves."

"Your father killed himself and you tell it like it's the normal thing to do!"

"Claude, that's exactly what I mean. Out here, I think maybe it *is* normal. My father used to be in the business and it helped things along for him, too. Anyway, it's part of it."

"I'm sorry I asked."

"It happened. These things happen. Maybe my mother had something to do with it. I don't think so. It was the business. Or maybe it was Los Angeles. It all played a part. You got to keep your eyes open. You chase dreams, sometimes they turn out to be nightmares. One day my father was working in the middle of the dream factory. Next thing he knew, it was all a nightmare. And he couldn't get back into the dream factory any more."

"I don't understand."

"Neither do I. I never did. It's a tough business. Don't fool

198

yourself. But maybe you'll beat it. You got a dream. Run after it That's the only way you can go at it. And today you got yourself a new agent. Maybe she'll bring you luck."

"I don't know. I figure Ellen Bessie's better'n my old agent, but I know a guy she handles, he says she's not doing so much for him."

I don't even have to ask. I already know. So I ask.

"Who's the guy?"

"An actor I know."

"What's his name?"

"Austin Bedloe."

79

"That's funny," I say. "Ellen Bessie was telling me about Austin Bedloe. He any good?"

"Talented and unemployed. Typical down-and-out Hollywood actor. Very talented, but he's the kind always just misses out on getting the job. But he's always up. Doesn't let it get to him. Every party I go to, Austin's there. Playing the clown. He likes to make himself up so nobody'll recognize him. He'll change his voice and make a pass at you, you won't even know it's him. Once he got me all the way to bed before I realized it's him. That was really funny. See, Austin's not the type to take girls to bed."

"He's gay?"

"Nothing wrong with that, but he is."

"You know him pretty well?"

"I guess so. I see him around."

I don't want to ask the next question. I'm afraid about what I'm going to hear.

"You ever try to get him some work at Stockton Film?"

"Yeah. He's got the worst luck in the world."

"Why?"

" 'Cause I did get him an interview and he almost got the job, but he didn't."

He got the job. It just wasn't the job he thought he was going to get.

"They kept calling him back for the lead in a very big commercial. Austin was sure they'd use him. Then they didn't."

"Who decides who they're going to cast at Stockton?"

"On all the big spots like that one, it's Howard Banner."

"Just Banner? Nobody else gets involved?"

"Hard to say. A lot of people sit in on the auditions. From what I see, it's really Mr. Banner's decision in the end."

"Lots of people get in on it? Like Jamie Stockton? Miss Blitman?"

"Jamie loves to watch auditions. Gives him a good excuse not to do any work. I don't think anyone asks for his opinion. Miss Blitman likes to watch when they're auditioning men."

"When an actor auditions for a commercial, doesn't he ever meet Mr. Stockton?"

"Mr. Stockton leaves auditions to Mr. Banner."

"So Mr. Stockton'd never meet Bedloe?"

"Oh, no, in a case like Austin he would. Austin was one of the final actors up for the spot. Mr. Stockton always sits in on all final auditions."

He told me he never met Austin Bedloe.

That's the way it is. You let yourself start liking someone and it comes back to haunt you.

Why didn't he tell me he knew Austin Bedloe!

"I called the office this afternoon. Mr. Stockton didn't sound too good. Voice sounded kind of weak."

"He looked pretty bad today."

"Drunk?"

"This wasn't a hangover. Something's bothering him. Probably his son."

"Jamie?"

"Yeah. Jamie's been gone awhile. Off on business, I guess. But I didn't think they'd trust him on any business. I don't know."

"You told me the company's got money problems. Maybe that's what's bothering Mr. Stockton."

"Could be."

I turn things over in my mind and decide to go back to something else which bothers me.

"I'm surprised Bedloe didn't get that part. I'd think Jamie Stockton'd try to get it for him."

"Why'd Jamie care if Austin got the part?"

"You said Bedloe's gay. I hear Jamie's gay. I'd figure he'd try to get Bedloe some work."

"Who told you Jamie's gay?"

"I heard he's not much with girls. I figured, what I heard, he's gay."

"I never heard anything about that."

"He ever try to make it with you?"

"No."

"So? Could be he's gay."

"Could be. I wouldn't know."

I wonder.

The phone rings. It's Mr. Simson. As usual his message is brief. "Mr. Stockton ask you come to house immediately, please. Very urgent business, Mr. Quinlan. We expect you how soon, please?"

80

The house is in the hills above Sunset Boulevard.

You come around a curve and there it is—a long, low house surrounded by a lot of land, flat and open in front and rising sharply in back. I suppose Ethan Stockton could've easily built an English castle up there, but a simple ranch house saved him the torture of climbing stairs with his weak legs and cane.

I get brought in without any fanfare and pretty soon I'm sitting across a desk from the old man in his book-lined study. He doesn't say anything at first. He sits behind his desk and he looks like hell. If you didn't know anything about him, if you didn't know the spirit he had inside him, you might wonder if he'd last the night.

Mr. Simson sits in the corner, ready to carry out any instructions the master might give. Mr. Simson looks like the completely loyal servant. And he looks worried.

I take a picture from an envelope and push it across the desk. "Friend of yours?" I say.

"I seen the face before." Mr. Stockton turns the picture over to read the information on the back. "So this's Austin Bedloe."

"That's him."

"I seen him before."

"I know. But when I talked to you on the phone this afternoon, you told me something different."

"I told you I didn't know the name. Now I see his picture, I know him. Met him a couple weeks ago, maybe a little longer. Up for a commercial we're making, but we decided to use another guy."

"If you'd told me that before, it might've been some help."

"Sorry, Mr. Quinlan. Now I see his picture, I recognize the guy. Don't think I ever knew his name, though. Think I'm lying to you?"

He looks pretty weak, but I can't let that stop me. You can't have too many feelings in this business or you'll never get the answers you need.

"Yeah, I think you're lying."

He pulls back deep inside himself, down into whatever it is gives him his spirit, and he gives me the look of a man who knows how to give other people looks. "You ought to believe me sometime, Mr. Quinlan. It could be dangerous for you, you don't believe me."

"I know. You give the nod to Mr. Simson, he'll do something pretty quick. But till that happens, tell me the truth. Are you lying?"

His look dissolves as easily as it formed, and he laughs. "Mr. Quinlan, you ever want to come into the advertising business, better let me make you the first offer, okay?"

"Maybe it's a deal. What about Bedloe?"

"The name Bedloe didn't mean a thing to me till you showed me this picture. I see a lot of actors without knowing their names."

202

"Why'd you want me here tonight?"

"I understand . . . You got called down to the cops today."

"Having me followed, Mr. Stockton?"

"No. A friend called me. What'd the cops want? Anything to do with me?"

"Your friend didn't tell you that much, huh?"

"Even *my* sources of information got their limitations."

"Glad to hear that. I was starting to wonder. The cops're investigating last night's hit-and-run. They want to make sure it's not a homicide."

"A homicide. So they think it's murder."

"Right now the cops don't know what to think. They'd like to think it's just an accident. That way they can write it off and forget all about it."

"You mean they're really not interested?"

"Cops're always interested. But cops're busy people. I can take a case and sit on it for a while, waiting for things to develop. Cops don't have that luxury. If something really looks like an accident, they hope it'll stay an accident. Makes life easier for everybody."

"You tell the cops this might concern my family?"

"I didn't mention you. I didn't mention any details of the case. All the cops know, they know I'm on a case and maybe the case had something to do with Austin Bedloe. That's all they know."

"Thank you, Mr. Quinlan. I appreciate it. Now, this hit-and-run, could it've been murder?"

It sure could.

"No," I say.

"You're sure?"

"I'm sure."

He gives me that look again. "No, Mr. Quinlan. It could've been murder. That's what you think. I don't look so good, do I? My age, you start to go, you go quickly. That's what you're thinking. Mr. Quinlan, I'm a tough old bastard and they ain't going to put me away that easy. You got something to tell me, you think you can't tell me 'cause of the way I look, forget that shit. Tell me what the hell you really think, damn it! Was it murder?"

"Could've been, but I hope it wasn't. If it was murder, who was supposed to get killed? Austin Bedloe or Jamie Stockton?"

I try to shoot a look at Mr. Simson without making it too obvious. If he's got any thoughts, he's keeping them to himself.

"Maybe someone thought they were killing Jamie, huh?" Mr. Stockton says. "I don't like that."

"I don't much care for it myself."

"What's your honest opinion?"

"I don't think it was murder." But I do. "You want to murder someone, this'd be a bad way to do it. Too easy to miss. Too much risk, all around. No, you want to kill someone, you pop your man off with a gun or a knife some place out of the way. Not in a parking lot. You know what I mean?"

"I'm afraid I *do* know what you mean."

"The odds point to an accident. The cops haven't found the car yet, but they know it belongs to some electrician who lives a dozen blocks or so from Le Brigand. Let's say this electrician, he went to Le Brigand last night. This being Los Angeles, he'd probably drive, not walk. Then he'd come out of the place a little later, or maybe a lot later, and he'd probably be a little drunk. Or maybe a lot drunk. It's a big parking lot they got there. I could see it happen. You'd get up some speed and you'd drive right over a guy before you even knew he's there. So let's say the electrician did that. Then panicked and took off. Later he starts to get worried. Maybe someone saw the accident. So next morning the electrician, he calls the cops and says his car's stolen during the night. It's plausible and it's logical. It might be something else, but I'd say the odds point to the electrician and a hit-and-run."

Mr. Stockton sits and thinks.

"That'd make sense," he says. "With what happened tonight, that'd make sense."

"I been waiting for you to tell me what happened tonight. So far, you could've handled it with a phone call. What'd you want me up here for?"

"Someone called me tonight. About two hours ago. You can listen to the conversation. Mr. Simson?"

Mr. Simson comes over to the desk and pushes down the button on a tape recorder.

On the tape a slightly familiar voice asks for Mr. Ethan Stockton, and when Mr. Stockton comes to the phone, the voice says, "I got your son. Now I'm supposed to kill him, but that wasn't part of my deal. Your son says you might pay to keep him alive. If you want him back, that's okay with me. But we gotta do it fast. It'll cost you twenty-five thousand dollars. I want it tonight."

81

As the tape continues to roll, I hear Mr. Stockton ask to speak to his son. Then Jamie gets to say a few words. He's all right and he thinks the man holding him will let him go if he gets the money without any trouble. Then the first voice, the one I know, comes back and gives instructions for the payoff.

He wants me to be the delivery boy. I'm supposed to leave the Stockton home precisely at midnight with the money in the front seat of my car. There's a list of ten places to stop, and at each spot I'm supposed to stay ten minutes with the motor running. End of instructions.

I'd say it's just about as sweet as it could possibly be.

"You always tape your phone conversations?" I say.

"Every call," Mr. Stockton says, "coming into or going out of this house gets taped."

"Why?"

"I like it that way. Sometimes comes in handy."

"He called two hours ago and he wants twenty-five grand by midnight. That's one hell of a request. How're you supposed to get it?"

"I got well over twenty-five thousand here, in the house. I got it in a wall safe."

"You're kidding. And our friend knows that? Mr. Stockton, you always keep that kind of money around the house?"

"Yeah. I was always living in foreign countries. Some of those places, I found it a lot safer to keep my money in my house'n in the local banks."

"You never lost the habit, huh?"

"Jamie knows I keep large amounts of money at home. If he had to bargain for his life, he wouldn't keep it a secret."

Yeah. I guess he wouldn't. It all sounds real neat and tidy. So much so, I'd like to go lie on a beach and develop a suntan.

But I'm still on the payroll. I'll go along.

"Mr. Stockton? You call the cops on this?"

"I decided to call you first. We only got a short time here and I'm not sure what to do. I don't know if I want the cops. You ever been involved in anything like this before?"

"Kidnap and ransom? Yeah. Once. The cops were called in."

"How'd it turn out?"

"Didn't turn out so well. But you can't compare cases. There's no rules in this sort of thing."

"I thought it over before you got here, Mr. Quinlan. I think I want to pay the money and hope for the best. I'd like to know what *you* think."

"Sure you'd like to know what I think. I'm the guy's supposed to make the payoff."

He doesn't say anything to that.

"Twenty-five thousand," I say. "There's been times I worked two years, I didn't make that much. But I don't think twenty-five grand means a hell of a lot to you. It's your choice, Mr. Stockton. It might do the trick, we'll never know unless we try. I recognized the voice of your caller. His name's Pastrano. He's a local thug. Lots of muscle but kind of short on brains. If he got told to kill someone and he saw a way to get out of it and make twenty-five grand at the same time, he might go for it. He might. I don't know. Could be a setup, too. If you want to take the chance this guy Pastrano's telling the truth, and he'll keep his word—and it's only a chance, you got to remember that—well, if you want to take that chance, I'll make the delivery. But there's no guarantee what'll happen, you got to understand that right now."

"Good. I was worried you might not want to take the money to him."

"I don't. I had a run-in with Pastrano the other night. I busted up his hand pretty good. That's why he wants to see me, he thinks he owes me something. And he does."

"I see. Then this could be a ruse, just to get at you."

"Could be just that."

"Don't take any chances, Mr. Quinlan. I don't want you hurt on my account, or my son's account."

"I sort of feel that way myself."

"You carrying a gun?"

"A gun? Why do you want to know?"

"I got some guns in the house. If you don't have one, I'll give you one."

"Sorry, Mr. Stockton. If you want Pastrano killed, you better find someone else. I'm not in the mood tonight. I'll deliver the money, but that's as far's it goes."

"No! That's not what I mean! You and I always seem to get off on the wrong foot, Mr. Quinlan. You're working for me. I feel some responsibility. I don't want you hurt because of my son or my problems. If this man Pastrano has it out for you, you better be ready for him."

"Just how ready you think I ought to be?"

"I've had certain experiences. Long ago. I know what I'm talking about. Guns can be persuasive. I think you ought to take one with you, just in case."

There's always a chance he means what he's saying. There's always a chance.

"Yeah," I say. "Guns can be persuasive. Sometimes the wrong way. Nope, no gun. It might help, and it might make things a lot worse, too. In any case, I take a gun up against Pastrano, I don't think it'd get your son back. That's what you want me to do, right? Get your son back?"

"Of course that's what I want. But I'm worried about you, too."

"I've gone up against Pastrano before. I'll take my chances. If he gets tough I'll put it on your bill. We'll forget about the gun."

82

A quarter to midnight. I'm sitting in my car in front of the house in the hills above Sunset. I don't like any of it.

Ransoms are bad. You never know if they'll work out or not. Most of the time you can't even be sure the guy you're paying the money for is still alive. I'm not convinced this *is* a ransom. Why? What am I trying to remember?

Why did the old man make that pitch for me to carry a gun? Did he want me going up against Pastrano with one of his guns in my hand? I don't know, so I didn't take the gun.

I sit behind the steering wheel and wait for midnight. I reach down under the front seat, pull open the flap and take out the Smith & Wesson, which looks as nice as the ones I keep behind Old Granddad and under the desk in my office. I put the gun back under the seat, leave the flap partly open and hope I can reach the thing in time when I need it. I'll need it.

On the seat beside me I've got a satchel of money and a thermos of hot coffee. It's going to be a long night. Pastrano's list will take me all over the city.

Still not midnight. I wish it was midnight. I turn on the car radio. My thoughts aren't adding up to much of anything. I'll try some music.

If I could save time in a bottle,
the first thing that I'd like to do,
is to save every day till eternity passes away,
just to spend them with you . . .

Croce. I'm already smiling. If he sings happy or sad, it doesn't matter. I always smile. It all comes out so easily when that guy sings. The way it sounds, he had to be the kind who knew where he was.

If I had a box just for wishes . . .

He died too young. So many of us die too young.

Some of us are stupid. We kill ourselves.

They killed themselves.

And dreams that had never come true . . .

I wonder which is worse. To have a dream that never comes true, or not to have any dream at all.

Twenty-five grand. To get the kid back. Yes? No? Some things have been set up. What's this? Another setup? The real thing? A dream?

My father had a dream and they took it away from him.

Enough. Get your mind off it. Listen to Croce. Take it easy. Things will be bad enough soon enough. Sit back. Listen to Croce.

Croce knew. I think he knew.

But maybe he didn't know, either. Maybe none of us knows. So we run.

Stop it, Charlie. Stop it. No dice. Settle down. Stop it.

Yeah.

Better.

Cool.

I can't afford to lose my mind tonight. I'll have to save it, maybe for tomorrow.

Croce's finished, replaced by the news headlines.

It's midnight. I've got work to do.

At least I know that much.

83

I drive along Sunset, take a left and go down the hill, and soon I'm parked across from an ice cream parlor in Westwood Village. I sit there with the engine running.

In the rear-view mirror I see a small black sports car pull up a block behind me. It keeps its lights on. I don't like the lights staying on. I watch it carefully, and I don't see Pastrano till he's already opened my car door. He gets in beside me. I say nothing about the large bandage covering his right hand.

He searches my body with his left.

"Whatsa matter?" he says. "You ain't got a gun."

"I don't believe in 'em."

"Bullshit. What've you got here, inna thermos?"

"Coffee."

"Coffee? We don't need coffee." He throws the thermos into the back seat. "Okay, Quinlan. This's it. You keep quiet. No talkin' at all, understand. Start drivin' to the next stop."

I pull out. The black sports car follows.

I drive along Wilshire and Pastrano gives me new directions. I turn corners, double back and soon we're in Westwood again. I look into the mirror and I don't see the black sports car.

We drive along the edge of the university, then further up into the hills where there are few houses and fewer lights.

Pastrano tells me to stop the car and leave the keys in the ignition. Now he's got a .45-caliber revolver in his hand. My Smith & Wesson is less than eighteen inches away from my right hand, but he keeps his eyes on me, and eighteen inches could be halfway to the moon for all the good it does me.

84

He orders me out of the car and comes out after me. He doesn't bring the money with him. That's bad. It means he plans to come back for it.

We walk into the woods. When we reach a moonlit clearing he tells me to stop.

"I'll leave your car where the cops'll spot it. Just tell 'em someone stole it, but you don't know who."

"That's what you did with the electrician's car? The car you stole to run down Austin Bedloe. You left it some place where the cops'll spot it."

"You think I ran down Bedloe?"

"Didn't you?"

"Bedloe and me was workin' together. I didn't have nothin' to do with that."

Keep him talking, Charlie. Keep him talking.

"I think you did, Pastrano. I think you killed him."

"I don't give a fuck what you think."

"Yeah. Guess you don't."

"You'll find the kid at the Park Motel, corner of Santa Monica and Lincoln. Room 6E. The kid's okay. All I want's the money."

Keep him going, Charlie.

"Very accommodating of you, Pastrano. He really there?"

"He's there. And he's okay. Listen, I was just in this thing for some money. Both me and Bedloe, we figured we could use the money. But now it's fallin' apart. I figure the old man's loaded, he ain't gonna miss twenty-five grand. So I'm keepin' my word onna kid. I figure, I keep my word, the old man'll write off the money and leave me alone."

Play for time. Time.

"I think you're right," I say. "You're getting smart."

"I was just followin' orders before. But now, with Bedloe dead in that accident—"

"You think it's an accident, huh?"

"Sure it's an accident! Whaddaya mean? Listen, now, I'm supposed to kill the kid. I ain't gonna kill the kid. Not for no lousy three grand."

"Not when you can make twenty-five instead."

"That's right. But there's one other thing, Quinlan."

Here it comes.

"You busted up my hand and I owe you. You know how it is."

This is going to be it, Charlie. You better say something, or do something. You better play for time and hope you have it figured right.

"You came at me with a gun and brass knuckles," I say. "What'd you expect me to do, just stand there and take it?"

"Yeah, you're right. But it don't make my hand feel any better."

"Pastrano, use your head. You kill me, who's going to find the kid?"

"I'm not gonna kill you. You want it inna right leg or the left? See, you're gonna remember me. Every time you walk."

"You're making a mistake. Think it over. Unless you want the cops after you."

"What? What's this about cops?"

"If you didn't kill Bedloe, and maybe I believe you on that, and if you're telling the truth about the kid being okay, I figure you're in the clear. Nobody'll come after you. But if you shoot me in the leg, you're in trouble. I'll go to the hospital to get the bullet out and they'll have to report it. The whole story'll break, and then the cops'll come after you."

"You better not tell the cops about me!"

"I'll have to. They'll grab my license and I'll have to tell 'em. So if you really want to shoot me, that's going to be the cost. You're going to have the cops after you."

He stands there. I don't know if I sold him on it. I need some more time and I don't have anything else to throw at him.

"The hell with you! I don't give a fuck! I don't give a fuck about the cops! You busted up my hand! The hell with you!"

Some people you can't reason with.

85

The shot, when it comes, misses my leg.

It comes from the woods behind me and catches Pastrano in the left hand. I see him drop the gun and his hand's full of blood.

Behind me, I hear someone coming forward. I turn in time to see the marksman raising his arm to shoot again.

"No!" I say. "He's dropped the gun. You don't have to kill him."

The marksman hesitates.

Pastrano doesn't wait to think things over. He turns and runs further back into the woods.

The marksman comes forward suddenly and his arm goes back up, but I step in front of him.

"Quick, Mr. Quinlan—he run away. We go catch him."

"No, Mr. Simson, we don't have to catch him. If we want him later on, we'll go after him then. He doesn't matter. Not now."

"Mr. Quinlan? You sure?"

"Yeah, I'm sure. Let him go. What kept you so long? I thought you weren't going to get here at all. I saw the car following me, I figured it was someone with Pastrano. Then I figured it must be you, but I was starting to think I lost you."

"You not lose me. Come, Mr. Quinlan. I think we go catch man in woods."

"We don't need him."

"But what about Mr. Jamie?"

"I know where Jamie is, the money's still in the car and I don't feel like spending the rest of the night searching the woods. You already did enough damage to that guy, we don't have to worry about him. Nice cannon you got there, Mr. Simson. Military Police .45, huh? That what you usually use, in circumstances like this?"

"First time I ever use."

"First time? Pretty good shot for the first time. Nothing but a little moonlight and you hit him straight in the hand. I assume it was his hand you aimed at?"

"I hit hand because hand where I aim."

"How come you didn't aim to kill? Would've been just's easy."

"I not kill."

"Yeah, but why didn't you? You could've, pretty easy."

"Mr. Quinlan. In old days my country you kill such man, that end of it. To kill man this country there is police. Questions. Many questions. Not worth it. Better this way."

"You calculate these things pretty well, Mr. Simson. What if he'd been pointing his gun at your boss, instead of at me? You think you might kill him then?"

He doesn't stop to think that one over.

"Mr. Quinlan. Any man point gun Mr. Ethan Stockton, I stop quick enough. Aim above nose. Between eyes. Pretty quick job. I stop quick enough. I blast him hell and gone."

"And you wouldn't care who asked questions later."

Mr. Simson turns around and starts toward the road.

I'm glad he wasn't shooting at me.

86

Mr. Simson follows me to the Park Motel.

The door to Room 6E is unlocked and we don't bother to knock.

Pastrano kept his word. Jamie Stockton's lying there on the bed, trussed up like a well-wrapped Christmas package. I take the gag from his mouth and the blindfold off his eyes.

He looks to be in bad physical condition, underfed and haggard, circles under his eyes. He looks a few years older than I expected, but other than that, Austin Bedloe performed a good makeup job.

Jamie blinks at me as his eyes adjust to the light. His first look at me is full of fear. He struggles back, away from my hands. Do I represent salvation or destruction? Have I come to save him or have I come for some other reason?

I move aside so he can see Mr. Simson standing behind me.

"Thank God," Jamie Stockton says. "Thank God."

87

It's the middle of the night but almost all of us are here. We sit around a massive wooden table under three Tiffany lamps.

Ethan Stockton looks weaker every time I see him.

Mrs. Stockton does a pretty good job of pretending she's never seen me before.

Amanda Banner looks at her brother and me, shifting her eyes first to him, then to me, then back to him. I think she likes him a good deal more than she likes me.

Jamie's busy eating a large bowl of soup.

Mr. Simson sits quietly in the corner. He watches Mr. Stockton and says nothing.

I keep my eyes on all of them.

"You've lost so much weight," Mrs. Stockton says to her son. "I can see it in your face. Did they feed you?"

"Cereal and milk in the mornings," Jamie says. "Later they'd bring in hamburgers or something. They gave me vitamins too. I feel okay."

Vitamins. That's a nice touch.

"If you saw them," Mr. Stockton says, "would you recognize them?"

"I never saw their faces," Jamie says. "They kept me blindfolded all the time, except at night they'd untie my hands and lock me in the bathroom, and I could take off the blindfold in there and wash up and shave and things. But then they'd tell me to turn off the bathroom light, and they'd open the door, but then they'd be wearing masks, so I couldn't see their faces."

"You must've seen someone," Ethan Stockton says. "When they kidnapped you—you must've seen someone!"

"Not their faces. They wore stockings over their heads. I came home from work, took a swim in the pool, and when I came back to the apartment they were in there. They grabbed me."

"How many of them grabbed you?" I say.

"First the big guy, he was pretty strong, he grabbed me from behind. And then this other guy, he gave me a shot of something in the arm. Knocked me out."

"You never saw their faces?" Ethan Stockton says again.

"I figure I didn't *want* to see their faces. You see their faces, then later on they're going to have to kill you so you can't identify them."

"Do you have any idea where they kept you?" Amanda Banner says.

"Must've been a house. Sometimes I'd hear kids playing outside, and there's always a lot of cars going by. Must've been near a freeway. The cars went by real fast."

"It wasn't till tonight," I say, "they took you to the motel?"

"Yeah. Tonight the big guy took me to that motel."

"A freeway?" Mrs. Stockton says. "Mr. Quinlan, would that help us find the house?"

"We'll never find the house," I say. "Even if we did, it'd be cleared out by now. Jamie, you figure there's just the two of them, or more?"

"Well, two guys grabbed me at my apartment. Far's I could make out, later, at the house, the big guy was staying with me. He kept getting phone calls. He always put me in another room so I couldn't hear what he was saying on the phone. Sometimes the big guy'd go out, but then he'd always lock me in the bathroom."

"Didn't the bathroom have a window?" I say.

"It was boarded up from the outside. I tried to push the boards off, but they were nailed on too good."

"So there's only the one guy with you," I say.

"Yeah, at first. But after a couple nights he leaves for a long time. A couple hours it had to be. When he came back there's someone with him. I heard 'em talking. The thing is, this other guy, his voice sounded like I heard it before somewhere."

"Someone you knew?" Ethan Stockton says. "Like a friend?"

I think I understand what's been bothering Mr. Stockton. He's got part of the idea I have, but he's only got part of it. And anyway, I've only got part of it myself. It still doesn't make sense to me.

"No, not a friend," Jamie says. "I just kept thinking I heard it before, but I couldn't place it."

"You heard it before," I say. "The voice belonged to an actor you met. Austin Bedloe. He auditioned for a commercial, that's how you knew the voice."

"Austin Bedloe? Wasn't he up for the Delvin commercial?"

"Yeah," Ethan Stockton says. "Austin Bedloe."

"I don't know. Could've been his voice. I wouldn't swear to it. If I hear it again, I might know."

"You won't hear it again," I say. "Bedloe's been impersonating you. He made himself up to look like you and he was gambling all over town."

"He was? Why?"

"Maybe we'll never know," I say. "Bedloe's dead. Got killed in a hit-and-run last night."

"Then it *was* Bedloe!"

"What makes you so sure?"

216

"Every night this other guy, it must be Bedloe, he'd come to the house and he'd go out with the big guy. But last night the big guy came back alone, and he was nervous. He kept saying something'd gone wrong. Then he made a phone call, long distance. I heard him talking to the operator and he gave her a number and I knew the area code, it was San Francisco. The big guy got so excited he forgot to put me in the other room, like he usually did when he talked on the phone.

"So he's talking on the phone, and he says there's been some kind of accident. The way he talked, I figured it must be the other guy who's been coming to the house got run over. So then, the way I made it out, whoever he was talking to on the phone told him to kill me. He told the guy he was talking to, if he wanted me dead he'd have to come back down to Los Angeles and do it himself. So when I heard—"

"Hold it," I say. "What'd he say? Exactly. The big guy. Did he say 'You got to come down here and kill him yourself' or'd he say 'You got to come *back* down here and kill him'?"

"Let me think. Yeah, the guy said 'If you want the kid dead, you better get back down here to Los Angeles and do it yourself.' "

"Jamie, you're sure of that?"

"That's what he said. Anyway, pretty close to it."

"Must've scared the hell out of you."

"I figured I was good's dead already when I heard that. I mean, up till then they never even hurt me, except for when they grabbed me. But when I heard the big guy talking that way on the phone, I got scared. I had to do something. I knew all the money you kept in the house, Dad. I didn't know what else to do. I figured maybe if you gave the big guy a lot of money, maybe he'd let me go. I mean, I could tell he didn't want to kill me, and I knew I had to do something quick, before this other guy got down from San Francisco."

"You knew your father had the money in the house all along," I say. "Why didn't you suggest a ransom before, soon's they grabbed you?"

"That's what I did! I asked them if they'd asked for a ransom.

And they said no, they weren't interested in that. So I couldn't figure out what they grabbed me for."

"But after this phone call you brought it up again, and now the big guy went for it?"

"Not at first. At first he said no. See, he's very nervous, 'cause of what happened to his friend. I mean Bedloe, I guess. But I could tell he didn't want to be part of murder. The way I understood it, the guy in San Francisco, he must've said he'd be down here in twenty-four hours. So I tried to talk the big guy into asking for money. It took me all day to talk him into it. He was real scared. But finally I convinced him. So he called Dad, and then he put me in a car and took me to that motel. Then he left me there. And I was scared. I mean, I didn't know what the hell was going to happen. But then you came, with Mr. Simson."

"All right, son," Mrs. Stockton says. "You're home now, and it's all right. You're safe. We'll take care of you."

"There's one more thing I want to know," I say.

"What's that?" Ethan Stockton says.

"I think Jamie's got something else to tell us. About the missing money. The money someone stole from the company."

88

Jamie goes white as paste when I say that. He looks at his father and says, "You know about the money?"

"We don't have to talk about this thing now," Ethan Stockton says.

"I think we do," I say. "Your father hired a new accountant and he found the discrepancies, Jamie. We know there's money missing."

"We can discuss this another time," Ethan Stockton says. "We don't have to go into this now. Jamie's home, that's the important thing!"

"If we're going to clear things up," I say, "we better get everything in the open—right now."

218

"I didn't take the money!" Jamie says. "Dad, I swear to you, I didn't take it!"

"If you didn't take it," I say, "how'd you know it's missing?"

"I knew this'd happen. I knew everyone'd think it's me. But I didn't do it! I didn't take the money!"

"Jamie," I say, "nobody's saying you did. Tell us what you know about it. Maybe it's got something to do with the kidnapping."

"But I hardly know anything about it."

"But you know there's money missing."

"Yeah, I know that. But it wasn't me! Dad, after I worked on that commercial, and you switched me to the new job, I didn't know what I was doing. I mean, I've never understood accounts and things like that. I was looking over the books, trying to see if I could get some idea what they're like. Some accounts, the running expenses for each commercial, they seemed high. I wasn't sure, so I checked them against accounts for a year ago. And even with inflation and everything, this year things seemed to cost a hell of a lot more. I figured something had to be wrong somewhere. But I was never good with figures, I thought it might've been my mistake."

"Okay," I say. "So you had to check with someone who *did* know the books. You checked with the accountant? Harry Spenser?"

"Yeah. That's what I did."

"What'd Spenser say?"

"I showed him what I found, and he said I was right. He said the accounts were being padded. Maybe fifty thousand or more."

"What'd Harry Spenser want to do about it?"

"He said he needed a couple days, to make sure he had all the facts. All the numbers. Then, he said, both of us'd go to Dad and make a full report. But we never did that. Before we could, Harry died in that car accident."

"Yeah, I figured something like that," I say. "But after Spenser's accident, how come you didn't go to your father with this?"

"I wanted to, but I was scared. I mean, Dad, without Harry

to back me up, I knew what you'd think. You'd think *I* stole the money."

"I wouldn't've thought that," Ethan Stockton says.

"Yes, you would've! Everyone would've! You think it now! You think's it's me!"

"Okay," I say. "That won't get us anywhere. So you were scared to talk to your father. So what'd you do?"

"Well, I had to talk to someone about it. I mean, sooner or later, someone else was going to find out what I found out, and then everyone'd figure it's me. I had to tell someone, and Howard, he understands that kind of thing, so I told Howard I had to talk to him about something important, but I didn't tell him what. We made an appointment to talk on Friday, but then we had to cancel that and we were going to get together on Monday. But Friday's the day they grabbed me."

We all sit and look at each other. Nobody seems much in a mood to talk.

Then Mrs. Stockton breaks the silence. "Mr. Quinlan? You think there's a connection between this missing money and Jamie being kidnapped?"

Okay. It's time to start poking into things a little deeper.

"I'll get to that in a minute," I say. "There's something you might's well know, Jamie. You're probably responsible for Harry Spenser's death."

"What?" Jamie says. "No, that's impossible! He died in an accident!"

"It may've been," I say. "How long was Spenser working for Stockton Film?"

"I don't know," Ethan Stockton says. "Five, six years."

Good.

"You remember looking very deep into his background?" I say. "Before you hired him?"

"We usually screen employees fairly well."

"You should've screened Spenser a little better. I checked with the cops, after I heard you had a dead accountant recently. Seems Spenser once spent some time in jail. Embezzling."

"I can't believe that!" Ethan Stockton says. "Harry Spenser?"

220

"It's a while back," I say. "He kept it pretty well buried, but I checked it out."

"You think it was Harry Spenser?" Amanda Banner says. "You think Harry Spenser stole the money?"

"Yeah. I think he was in on it. Jamie, you told the wrong guy about the missing money."

"You mean it was Harry?" Jamie says. "Harry stole the money? But if he did, how'd I have anything to do with his death?"

"Could've happened a couple ways. Spenser was a nervous driver, that's no secret. You told him about the missing money, and you got him a little more nervous. He didn't think anyone'd catch on so soon, he figured he'd plenty of time to cover his tracks. But you caught it and told him about it, and that must've really got him nervous. Too nervous to drive a car safely. So, could be he got into an accident. And he died. Except I think it happened a little different than that."

"I don't understand all this," Amanda Banner says. "You say Spenser took the money and then he had a car accident? But then, what'd that have to do with Jamie, and the kidnapping?"

"Yeah, Mrs. Banner. I know. But I'm not through. Spenser wasn't in this thing by himself. He had an accomplice."

89

"Spenser and an accomplice stole the money," I say. "Jamie found out there was money missing. Jamie told Spenser. Spenser told his accomplice. Spenser was probably nervous and wanted to run. The accomplice didn't want to run. The accomplice killed Spenser to keep him quiet. Then a new accountant got hired pretty quick, so the accomplice had to move fast, figuring the new accountant would discover the padded accounts just like Jamie did. The accomplice needed a fall guy to take the blame. The accomplice could've put it on Spenser but decided to go for Jamie instead. The accomplice arranged for Jamie to be snatched and hired Austin

221

Bedloe to impersonate Jamie to make it look like Jamie was still around town, gambling with a lot of money.

"Then the plan could've gone two ways. Austin Bedloe could stop the impersonation and they'd let Jamie go. What'd Jamie say? That he didn't take the money? That he'd been kidnapped? Who'd believe that? There wasn't any request for ransom. Everyone'd figure Jamie'd stolen the money, gambled it away all over town and now made up this story about a kidnapping. The only one who'd seen Bedloe doing his impersonation was me, and I'd turn up dead just like Spenser did.

"But they wouldn't necessarily have to kill *me.* They could kill Jamie. Then, if nobody ever saw Jamie again, we'd figure he ran off some place with whatever money he had left. That'd be the end of it."

"But then Austin Bedloe was run over," Ethan Stockton says.

"Right," I say. "That gave 'em a new problem. With Bedloe dead, and identified correctly, it was the end of the impersonation. The plan fell apart. But still, if the accomplice killed Jamie, if nobody ever saw Jamie again, we'd figure *he'd* arranged the impersonation so he'd have time to disappear. The trouble was, Pastrano didn't want to kill Jamie, especially when he figured he could make more money selling him back to us."

Ethan Stockton draws himself up straight in his chair. "The accomplice," he says. "It'd have to be someone who works for me."

I don't say anything.

"And besides that," he says, "the accomplice'd have to be in San Francisco last night."

I nod and let it go. I think I've come pretty close to the answers, more or less. Still, there's some things I can't quite put together yet, so I'll keep quiet. I'll just have to see what happens next. I need to set some kind of trap.

"No!" Amanda Banner says. "It's not Howard! You're wrong! It's not Howard!"

Ethan Stockton pulls all his strength together and rises stiffly, pushing against the floor with his cane. Mr. Simson is at his side immediately.

"Dad!" Amanda says. "It's not Howard! He'd never do this!"

"Sit down, Amanda," Ethan Stockton says. "We'll discuss this later. Among ourselves."

He tries to move away from his chair. Mr. Simson guides him. "Mr. Quinlan," he says. "Please come with me."

Mr. Simson has his arm around the old man. They go through a door and into the study. I follow.

I tried to get to the bottom of things here, but so far I haven't done it. I did what I could, but nobody broke. I'm still missing something, and the way I played it, somebody in this room figures they got me. Maybe they did.

I'm sorry about the lies I told about Harry Spenser, but Spenser's dead and lies can't hurt him now.

90

"I hired you to get Jamie back," Mr. Stockton says. "He's back. Three hundred a day and expenses, you said. You began Monday. Technically, this's Friday. Five days."

"No need to be so quick about it, Mr. Stockton. I'll figure my expenses and send you the bill. Anyway, I still got to clear a few things up."

"Things? What kind of things?"

"Things."

"All the way to the end you keep it to yourself, huh?"

"Yeah. You know me."

"No, I don't think I do. Mr. Quinlan, I'm going to pay you a bonus. You don't have to stretch your work into another day, just for some extra money."

"It's not the money, Mr. Stockton. Some loose ends I want to tie up. Take Harry Spenser. I was swinging kind of wild in there, could be I'm mistaken about Harry Spenser."

"Good God, man! The hell with Harry Spenser! He's dead!" He stops himself and lets the anger go. Then he speaks softly. "Look, if you're wrong about Harry Spenser, so what? Would it affect my son-in-law's involvement?"

"Probably not. I guess Banner could pad those accounts without Spenser's cooperation."

"Yeah, he could. So why look into it?"

"You don't want me to look into it."

"Let it go, Mr. Quinlan. Let it go. What do you want out of life?"

"I want to know some answers, for one thing."

"That's not what I mean. I mean your life. What do you want?"

"I don't know. Maybe I want to have the feeling, what I'm doing, maybe it does some good. I want to be able to look back at things and say to myself I did the best I could do."

"That's it?"

"There's a lot of crap in this world. I don't want to add to it. And I guess I'd like to say to myself there's a couple people I like, and maybe they like me. Maybe, I give it some thought, I might come up with a couple more things I want. I'd say that's about it, though."

"You got it pretty well straightened out for yourself."

"No. Tomorrow you ask me the same thing, I'll give you a different answer. Maybe tomorrow I'll want a Mercedes and a nice steak for dinner. I don't know."

"I'm a success, Mr. Quinlan. I got a lot of money, I live well, I do what I want. Mostly, I do. There's some things I've done, I'm not too proud of them, but at the time I did them I didn't see much else to do. I'm not some rich ass who gets to be old and starts feeling sorry about what he's done. I'm proud of what I've done, and whether other people think I'm a success or not, I figure I am.

"But that's not the end of it. You get to be old like me, you still got dreams. No matter what you got, no matter what life's like, no matter how old you are, you still got dreams. That's why I went into the business I got now. I wanted to get into films. The first time I ever saw my wife, I saw her in a film. Well, anyway, I got into this business, and I worked with commercials, and I did pretty good.

"Years ago I met Howard. I saw what he knew about film. Maybe I got to like him because of that. The movies he made, even the couple I paid for, they were crap. But the way he used film in commercials, he knew what he was doing. The things I wanted to do, he knew how to do them. And I always thought to myself, if only I could get Howard to do that kind of stuff in a film ... I mean, commercials, they're okay for what they are. But all they are, they're for selling things. A film, that can be something else.

"I knew I'd never be able to make a film. I haven't got the talent for it. But Howard, he's got the talent. If he'd just let it go. If he didn't let it scare him, I could make my film through Howard. *With* him, I mean. Do you understand? I've been working on it, I've been talking him into it, for over a year now. He's scared. He's made films and he knows they stink and he's scared to try again.

"I bought a book, it'll make a hell of a film if it's done right. I been working with Howard, writing the script. We're almost halfway through on the script. I got the money, I can produce the damn thing myself. He'll direct it. I figured that's as close's I'll ever come to the film I want to make, if I make it through him.

"There's something to Howard. Maybe you don't see it. You don't know him the way I do. There's something inside him trying to get out. So I thought I'd get it out. That talent in him. But now, with all this, I guess I won't."

"That's what's been bothering you," I say. "A couple days ago Banner told you I was giving him some trouble. He asked you to get rid of me, and you figured it meant he had something to hide."

"Howard told me you'd talked to him. He was scared of you. I couldn't figure it. It had to be he had something to do with this. He never got along with Jamie."

"Why'd you still want me to stick with the case? That's what I don't get."

"I wanted to know the truth. I thought I wanted to know."

"Yeah. Sometimes the truth ain't so hot."

"It sure isn't. Jamie's my flesh and blood, and I don't love him. I'm his father, I try to take some responsibility for looking after him, but that's about it. I suppose I'm a real bastard to say that kind of thing, but it's the truth. In the end, the truth's all you got left, even if you don't like it.

"You think I'm happy I got my son back? I'll tell you what

225

I think. I never should've hired you to look for Jamie. If I'd just let it all go, I'd be happier now. I don't know. Maybe we'd all be happier if we didn't know what's really going on around us."

"Mr. Stockton, I still think I should look into some things."

"Leave it alone, Mr. Quinlan. I don't care about the missing money and I don't care about Harry Spenser. None of that matters now. I still had some hope for Howard. I hoped I could get something out of him, if we could make that film. But we won't. Not now. The trouble is, a man can't live without hopes and dreams. I'm pretty old, and all I had was a dream tied to Howard. So now the dream's gone."

He writes me a check. Ten thousand dollars.

I guess he wants me off the case.

91

I head for the front door and catch Howard Banner coming in.

"What's going on?" he says.

"I don't know. What do you think's going on?"

"I just got home about an hour ago. My wife left me a note to come over here."

"Your brother-in-law's home."

"Yeah? You mean Jamie came back?"

"Something like that."

"He's here?"

I was right about Howard Banner straight from the first time I saw him.

"Big as life," I say, "and looking better'n you. You got a pretty good hangover, huh?"

"I always got a hangover. Wouldn't know what to do without one. God, I been driving all night. Straight through. Just stopped for gas a couple times. So Jamie's really here?"

"Yeah."

"I figured he'd show up, sooner or later."

"I bet you did. You going in to see him? You want to say hello, don't you?"

"Yeah. I guess so. Christ, I'm tired. Been driving all night. I like driving at night. You like it?"

"Not as much's you do. Go on. Go in and see your brother-in-law."

"Okay—let me alone! You don't have to push me. I'll act like a member of the family. Where are they?"

"Try the study first. I think Mr. Stockton wants to see you."

"Yeah. Okay. Okay. See you."

I continue on my way. I hate that punk.

"Mr. Quinlan," he says. "You don't like me much, do you?"

"I don't like you at all."

"Yeah. Did, uh . . . did some of my friends come to see you?"

"Sure, Mr. Banner. They saw me. Thanks for sending them by."

"They gave you a hard time, huh?"

"No. We got along fine. Had a few laughs, they shined my shoes, offered me coffee and cake. Sweet friends you got. Better watch it, though. You may not have 'em much longer."

"Look, Mr. Quinlan, you gave *me* a pretty hard time the other night. I didn't like it, so I called my friends, I asked them to get you off my back. Well, I guess you were just trying to do your job. Look, what I mean, I was wrong. If they hurt you, I'm sorry. Sometimes I do things like that, without really thinking about what I'm doing. I'll give them a call. I'll tell them not to bother you any more."

You'll give them a call? They might give you a call.

"Yeah," I say. "You do that. Give 'em a call."

"Yeah. I'll do that. Don't worry about it."

I watch him turn toward the study.

I don't know! I've got two million things going through my head at once. Some of them click into place and some don't. But my mind settles on a thought and I grab at it quickly. I've screwed up.

"Mr. Banner!" I say.

I'm too late. He doesn't hear me. He goes through the door and into the study.

I stand there, combing through my thoughts again.

A moment later the shouting begins.

By the time I reach the study Mrs. Stockton and Amanda have already come in, but their screams don't stop anything.

Mr. Simson could stop it but he just stands aside and watches.

Ethan Stockton's beating Banner with his cane and he's already opened a large cut on Banner's forehead.

As I rush forward the cane flies back and catches me on the side of the head, stunning me. Almost falling against the old man, I wrap my arms around him and hold on so he can't swing the cane. He fights hard against my grip. He's old and sick but he's still strong.

I hold on.

Suddenly his large body goes limp. He's heavy and I have trouble holding him up. He rests his head on my shoulder and begins to cry.

Banner doesn't waste any time. He gets out of the house as quick as he can.

So do I.

92

I gun my engine as fast as I dare and tear down the empty road. It's full of bends and turns, but no cars. Then I see the red Mercedes sports car below me. It's going at a moderate speed and taking the turns easily.

I hit the gas and pull alongside the Mercedes. Then I shoot forward, curving toward the side of the road, forcing him to nose in behind me. I do a pretty neat job of it and run him off without a collision.

I get out quickly and run over. Banner pushes open his car door and comes out swinging. I duck, pushing my hands forward and flat out so it won't hurt too much. I press stiffly against his belly and he goes off his feet, straight back against his car.

"Damn you!" he says. "I'll kill you!"

He comes at me again, both hands swinging. That's pretty stupid. I duck again, move forward and throw my right fist hard into him.

He doubles up and starts coughing. Then he sits on the ground.

"Want some more?" I say. " 'Cause if you want some more, I got a few things I can give you. Just tell me where you want it."

"Okay. You win. I'm no fighter."

"We both know that, don't we?"

I sit beside him, give him some time to catch his breath.

"That was stupid," I say. "Usually, people who know how to fight're smart enough not to get into fights. People who don't know how to fight ought to use the same tactics."

"I owe you something, Quinlan. You got me into something here and some day I'm going to pay you for it."

"Maybe you weren't paying attention back there. You almost got your head split open with that cane. I'm the guy who ran in and got you out of there. Remember?"

He doesn't say anything.

"Pretty sharp, Banner. I see why I never liked you. You just got worked over twice in less'n five minutes and you don't even ask why. Don't even care, huh?"

"You're going to tell me?"

"I might, but not if you're going to swing at me some more."

He doesn't say anything.

"Okay, Mr. Banner. I got a story for you. Stop me if you heard it before. Your brother-in-law's back. That surprise you?"

"I don't know."

"Want to hear the story?"

"I don't know."

"Jamie got snatched. Kidnapped. I been following around after some other guy who was *pretending* to be Jamie."

"Jamie was kidnapped?"

229

"What's the matter? Haven't you heard this story before? Yeah. Kidnapped. And almost killed, too."

"What the hell is this?"

"Some guy kidnapped Jamie, but this guy, he was working for someone else. So the other night they got into some trouble and the someone else who's sitting back, pulling the strings, he decided maybe the kidnapper ought to kill Jamie. This someone else, he talked to the kidnapper on the phone and said he thought Jamie ought to be killed. What do you think?"

"But you said Jamie's back."

"Yeah. I'm a pretty good detective. I never make mistakes. When I go out to find some kid who got kidnapped, I don't like to see the kid get killed. So I got Jamie back. No killing. Like the story?"

"I don't understand this."

"Just listen. The kidnapper had to call the guy who's pulling the strings, to get the orders to kill Jamie. But Jamie heard part of the phone call. Understand me now?"

"So? What'd Jamie hear?"

"Jamie heard the kidnapper make the call. Seems the guy who's pulling the strings was up in San Francisco the other night. And when the kidnapper didn't want to kill Jamie, this guy in San Francisco said he'd come back down here to Los Angeles and kill Jamie himself."

Banner doesn't say anything.

"Mr. Banner? You like the story? It got you caned pretty bad a few minutes ago. What do you think of that?"

He doesn't say anything.

"Come on, Mr. Banner. Let's hear it. Tell me this story's got nothing to do with you."

He doesn't say anything.

"No denials? No claims of innocence?"

"You son of a bitch!" he says. "You're behind this, Quinlan! What do you want from me?"

"I want you to tell me you didn't have anything to do with this!"

"The hell with you!"

230

We sit there for a while, quietly.
I can wait.

93

"This story's a lot of shit," Banner says. "I don't know what you're talking about."

"Yeah," I say. "You never know what's going on. The other day you told me, if you found the right story, you're going to make another film. But maybe you already found the right story. Maybe you been working on a script with Mr. Stockton. You think so?"

"Yeah. I guess so."

"You're scared to make the film Mr. Stockton wants you to make. You're scared you're going to fuck up."

"You think you know a lot, don't you, Quinlan?"

"No. I *want* to know a lot. I *always* want to know a lot. You think you got the guts to make that film?"

"I don't know."

"Come on, Banner. Show me something. Show me you're human, goddamn it! You want to make that film?"

"Yeah! Yeah! Yeah, damn it! I want to make that film! I'm a damn good ... Yeah, I want to make that film!"

"You punk. You're scared to make it."

"All right! I'm scared to make it. That what you want to hear? Yeah, I'm scared. I'm scared I'll screw it up again."

"Lots of people're scared. They're scared to do things. So they sit around and they don't do shit. You going to be like that? You going to be too scared to do what you want to do?"

He slumps back against the car. "I don't know. God, I don't know."

"The other night I thought your commercials looked pretty good. I didn't like what they said 'cause they sold something shouldn't've been sold. They sold a crook. But it looked to me like maybe you know something about your business. Maybe you could make a decent film, if you wanted. But not if you spend all your time feeling sorry for yourself."

"I know . . . I want to make that film. That's all I want to do. I want to make that film . . . I don't know."

"But you got caught up in this thing with Jamie and now you're all screwed up."

"I don't know."

"Get back in that car and drive up to San Francisco."

"What?"

"I don't want anyone to know where you are. Go back to San Francisco. Where you stay up there?"

"The Mark Hopkins. But I don't—"

"Shut up. Drive up there, check in at the Mark Hopkins, don't let anyone know where you've gone. Soon's you get there, give me a phone call. Here's my home number. You call me, I'll be home. No calls to anyone else. I'll give you eight hours to get there. Then I better get your call."

"I don't understand."

"I don't want you to understand. Do what I say."

"What're you going to do?"

"Whatever I do, I can't get you into any more trouble'n you already got."

"Yeah. Yeah, I guess so. I'll have to call my wife, though."

"The hell you will! You call your wife, you tell her where you are, she tells someone, someone tells someone, pretty soon we got half the city knowing you're up there. Only two people're going to know. You and me. Nobody else."

We sit there quietly a few more minutes. I probably should forget this whole thing. Just let it go. I can't do that.

"Why should I do what you say?" he says.

"Banner, I really don't care. I already been paid off, I'm finished with the whole thing. You don't want to do what I say? It's okay with me. I'll figure you're behind this thing, I'll go away somewhere and forget about it."

"You mean that? You don't think I'm behind this thing with Jamie? That's what you mean?"

"Let's say I haven't made up my mind. I'd like it to be you.

I got reasons to want it to be you. You don't do what I say, I'll figure it *is* you. But you do what I say, everything down to the letter, maybe I'll do some work and see if I can pull you out of this thing."

He looks at me like he's expecting me to say something more.

I get up and walk over to my car. "I don't know," I say. "Maybe I think you're behind it but I don't like the way it turns out if you're behind it. Too many people get hurt this way."

"I don't understand you."

"Yeah," I say. "Shut up and get up to San Francisco."

94

By the time I get home it's beginning to get light. I better make up for some of that sleep I've been missing out on all week. Before I go all the way nuts.

Maybe Carolyn's right. Maybe I ought to see a shrink.

No. It'd never work. I'd never trust a shrink. The trouble is, I never trust anyone. I'd rather stay nuts than put myself in the tentacles of a shrink. I'd probably end up worse off.

Things will work out. The pieces are beginning to fit together in my brain. It'll work out.

Hell, I don't know. What if they don't?

Sometimes things come to a boil pretty quickly. Too quickly. Then you have to let them simmer. You can't be too quick about it. You've got to be smart enough to know when to back off and wait. That's usually the hardest part—the waiting.

You have to wait and give them all a chance to forget you're there.

It's enough to drive you up the wall.

But I hold on till I get the answers. That's the job I do. Sometimes it's not easy.

But I'm not going to see a shrink. I know that much.

Hell, I don't know anything at all.

Come on, sleep. Let's get together. I need your help.

95

The phone's ringing. I don't look at the time. I know it's afternoon and I don't care to know more than that.

I pull the phone to my ear and settle back against the pillow.

"Quinlan," I say. "Ready, willing and sometimes able."

"Mr. Quinlan? It's me. Howard Banner."

"Where are you?"

"At the Mark Hopkins."

"Yeah? You sure you're not calling from Santa Monica?"

"No, I'm at the Mark Hopkins."

"What's your room number?"

"Six-twelve."

"Stay right where you are. I'll be back."

I hang up the phone and dial the operator.

"Good afternoon. Operator. May I help you?"

"Afternoon, Operator. I want to make a long-distance call to San Francisco. I want to speak to Mr. Howard Banner at the Mark Hopkins Hotel. Room 612."

"One moment, please."

Bing bing bong. Bong bong bing. Bing bing bing bing bong.

"Good afternoon. Mark Hopkins Hotel."

"Good afternoon. This is the Los Angeles operator. I have a long-distance call for Mr. Howard Banner in Room 612."

"One moment, please."

Ringgggggg.

"Hello?"

"Good afternoon. This is the Los Angeles operator. I have a long-distance call for Mr. Howard Banner."

"This's Mr. Banner."

"One moment, please. Sir, we have Mr. Banner on the line. You may go ahead now."

"Thanks, Operator. Mr. Banner? How you doing?"

"Mr. Quinlan?"

"You expecting someone else to call? Okay, guess you're at the Mark Hopkins. But you see how much I trust you, right?"

"You didn't believe me."

"Right. No calls to anyone?"

"I haven't called anyone. Just you."

"Keep it that way. If I get things worked out down here, I'll call you and you can come back. It'll take a few days. Okay?"

"I'll do what you say."

"Just in case you don't, I might call up there once in a while, just to make sure you're still there. I don't want you coming back down here before I'm ready for you."

"I understand."

"If I call up there, and you aren't there, I'll try again two hours later. But when I try the second time, you better be there. So if you go out, make sure you don't get more'n two hours away from your room. 'Cause if I call you twice and miss you both times, I'll say the hell with it. If you get bored, read a good book."

I still don't check the time. I just roll over and back to sleep.

96

The phone's ringing again. This time I check and it's almost six o'clock.

"Marlowe, Spade and Quinlan. This's Quinlan, the one who's nuts."

"How come you haven't been to the office all day?" Carolyn says.

"Been sleeping all day."

"Oh? With Claude, or someone I haven't met yet?"

"All by my lonesome."

"You okay? You don't sound good."

She's a goddamn mind reader.

"What's the matter, Charlie?"

"Nothing's the matter. What's my horoscope?"

"Hold on. Here it is. 'Everyone seems to arrive at nearly the same conclusion. Make good use of the occasion.' "

"That sounds okay. Must be I'm okay."

"Charlie, I got to meet some money guy later tonight. But not till later. You want to go to dinner first?"

"Not tonight. Got some things to think about tonight."

"You're sure?"

"I'm sure."

"You don't want to get together for dinner? I'll buy."

"Not today. I got to play it alone today. I got to work some stuff out. Sorry."

"You son of a bitch."

"Carolyn?"

"You're a goddamn son of a bitch, you're so fuckin' selfish."

"Carolyn, what the hell's got into you?"

"Some day I'm going to hit you, Charlie. When I get depressed I come and share it with you, don't I? I don't keep the fuckin' thing to myself. But you're such a selfish bastard you never share anything. Whenever you're down you run off by yourself and keep it in. When I need you I come to you! Don't you ever need me?"

Yeah. But I don't tell you about it. Something stops me. Maybe you're one up on me, Carolyn. Nothing stops you.

"Okay, Carolyn. I'm a creep, okay?"

"No. It's not okay. Some day you're going to want me to be there and I'm not going to be there."

"I know."

"No. You *don't* know. You never let me in on anything. You always got to keep things to yourself."

"Look, Carolyn, I can't help it. I know what you mean. You're right. I can't help it. I'm the way I am 'cause I'm the way I am. I wish I could change, but I can't."

"You don't want to change."

"I'll give you a call. Okay, Carolyn?"

"Don't bother."

97

I decide I better get out of the apartment. I drive down to Santa Monica, stop in some place I've never been before and have some dinner. I don't even pay attention to whatever the hell it is I'm eating.

I'm back home by eight, settled into a comfortable chair. On the bottom bookshelf I've got a line of books I've never read. I pull out *Mother Night.* I've been meaning to get to it for about a month. Vonnegut's one hell of a writer. At the start he says we have to be careful, because we are what we pretend we are. So we better be careful about what we pretend we are.

Thanks for the information, but it's come too late.

I read straight into the night.

It's somewhere around two o'clock when I finish.

I should go to bed and get some more sleep.

I don't do that. I just sit in my comfortable chair.

I'm going to crack this thing.

I'm going to crack this thing.

I sure hope I'm going to crack this thing.

98

Saturday morning. I fell asleep in the chair. It's early. Birds are singing. I feel a little better today. I don't know why. I just do.

There's something I'm trying to remember.

I know what my feelings tell me. I know what I think about this whole thing. It's not enough. I want to get going. But first I have to remember something. And I don't know what it is.

It's something someone told me. I'm sure of that. If I can only remember it, if it clicks in, maybe then I'll be sure which way to go. I want to be a little more sure before I move.

Do you understand what I mean? I've screwed things up a bit. I don't want to screw things up again.

I'll take it easy today. That's what I'll do. It'll come to me.

I read some magazines. Around nine o'clock I check the newspaper for stories about the Stocktons and the Banners. Nothing. If anything's happened during the past twenty-four, it isn't public yet. I've still got some time. When I move, I want to be sure.

What the hell is it? No, that won't get me anywhere. Must be calm. Cool. Collected. Must be calm.

I'm taking it easy. It'll come to me.

I call Carolyn around ten. She's not at the office, so I call her apartment.

"Hello," a man says.

If a man answers, hang up.

I don't feel like hanging up.

"Carolyn there?" I say.

"Hold on," he says.

"Who's there?" Carolyn says.

"Me," I say.

"The hell with you. I told you not to call."

"Have a good night?"

"What do you care?"

"Maybe I care."

"You okay today, Charlie?"

"A little better. How about you?"

"I'm on my way to eighty, maybe ninety thousand."

"Want to tell me about it tonight?"

"You're kidding."

"How about my place? Okay?"

"No, Charlie. First you'd have to make it up to me. For yesterday. You'd have to take me out to dinner."

"Any place in particular?"

"Some place expensive."

"Figures."

"You should've done it last night, but I'm glad you didn't. 'Cause I met a guy last night, he's the one's leading me to eighty thousand dollars."

"The guy who answered the phone?"

"No. He's an old friend, the guy who answered the phone."

238

"I'll take you to dinner, Carolyn. Some place expensive. But I want to come back here and take a look at a movie, later."

"What movie?"

"Something called *Bigtime*."

"What the hell's that? Something on TV?"

"No. You'll have to pick up a print for me. It's an oldie but goodie. From way back. In the thirties."

"Oh, I thought you meant something recent. Which studio made it?"

"I think it's Paramount, but I'm not sure."

"How the hell'm I going to find a print of something like that? It's Saturday."

"If you can find eighty thousand for your picture, you ought to be able to find a print of *Bigtime* on a Saturday."

"You sound better today. You really better? Or's this your idea of a joke?"

"I feel better."

"So you called me 'cause you want me to find a print of a movie for you."

"No, Carolyn. I called to say hello."

"Hello."

"Hello. Which expensive restaurant you got in mind?"

"As expensive as I can find. Pick me up around six."

99

I'm taking it easy today. I'm not letting it bother me. It'll come to me.

Late afternoon I hit the office to check my mail. Only one bill. A few circulars. A check for $240.00 from a client who's finally closed out the balance of an account I never thought would get closed out. The world's full of surprises.

I put Ethan Stockton's ten-thousand-dollar check into my office safe.

I call San Francisco. Howard Banner says hello. I say hello.
I say goodbye. Okay, that's covered.

I take out my harmonica and run through my repertoire.
I'm taking it easy today.

It'll come to me.

100

"He gave you a check for ten thousand?" Carolyn says. "So put
five thousand into my film and be my associate producer."

"It's not my money yet. When I've earned it, then I'll figure
out what I'm going to do with it."

I'm busy threading the 16mm print of *Bigtime* into my projector.

"Charlie. He signed the check. It's yours."

"Maybe. First something's got to come to me. And then I got
to do some things. After that, maybe the ten thousand'll be mine.
Tell me where you got your new eighty thousand."

"I lucked out with some guy last night. Ran into him at a place
on the Strip. He's a doctor—ear, nose and throat. He wants to get
into the movie business."

"You told him you'd do him a favor and let him invest."

"Gave him the whole spiel. First off, he wants to know if it's
really a tax shelter. That's all they can talk about these days, tax
shelters. So I told him no, it isn't a tax shelter. It's a delay of taxes."

"He must've loved that."

"Look, I'm honest. In my way."

"Ain't we all."

"Laid it out for him. I told him, right now a movie lives for
about seven years, and all that time it's depreciating. A film made
in 1965, today it's worth zilch. But the investors, they can acceler-
ate the depreciation and use the tax credit for further investment."

"Sounds cute. He understand what it meant?"

"Probably not. *I* don't understand it. But he liked the way it
sounded. I played fair with the guy. I kept telling him the whole

240

business's just a risk, a crap shoot. Hell, this guy just wants to tell everyone he owns a piece of a new film."

"When you going to start selling used cars?"

"He's getting a fair deal out of it, damn it! Besides, I really think this thing's going to make some money."

"I know. Through the roof. How does a guy working with ears, noses and throats come up with eighty thousand?"

"He doesn't. He comes up with twenty. But he's part of a group practice. Hell, they got a foot doctor, a gynecologist, they got everything, all they need in their group's an undertaker. Anyway, he set up a meeting, I met the whole bunch of 'em this afternoon. They all want to be in on this thing."

"You didn't show them any of your last film, I take it."

"Hell no."

"You're a wonder. Turn off the lights."

"Okay. What've you got in mind?"

"I got the film ready to roll."

"Oh. That's all, huh?"

I turn the switch and *Bigtime* plays across my wall. A very traditional picture. Cops and robbers, booze and broads. In various combinations, all of which have been used before and since. Some of the scenes are a little funny to watch now, but it's a film that still has some life to it. And every other minute my mind is wandering to something else.

Something else.

It'll come to me. Sooner or later.

Later I'm putting on the third reel and Carolyn's out in the kitchen.

"What kind of juice you want in your vodka?" she says.

"Tomato. I'm feeling red tonight."

"I like the sound of that."

It'll come to me. I will remember it.

Carolyn comes into the room with a glass in each hand.

She nestles into me and the sofa and gives me one of the drinks. "Remember, Charlie, when you pulled me down to that theater on Santa Monica to see you act in *South Pacific*?"

"That's a long time back. One of my milder wild oats."

"You should've stayed an actor, Charlie."

"Drink your drink, Carolyn."

It'll come to me!

We watch some more of *Bigtime*.

"That's the girl Ethan Stockton married, huh, Charlie?"

"That's the girl."

"Why'd she give up the movies?"

"She got married."

We watch the movie.

Years before I was born, Ethan Stockton saw a print of this movie and he came back to Los Angeles to marry Eve Carroll. As I watch her up on my wall I can understand what brought him back.

I wonder how the old man's doing tonight. I wonder if I can help him. I'll do what I can. It'll come to me.

"Carolyn, now you got me thinking about *South Pacific*."

"Yeah? What about it?"

"Bloody Mary. Remember her song?"

"Which one?"

"Where she says you've got to have a dream."

"That have something to do with something?"

"Yeah. Something Ethan Stockton told me. About dreams and how you got to have 'em even when you're rich and old."

"Maybe. But Rodgers and Hammerstein, they're sort of square these days. You know?"

"I didn't know. Someone forgot to tell me."

"Don't go soft, Charlie. This ain't a town for softies."

"Yeah. Nobody forgot to tell me that."

101

It's the end of the third reel, again.

After we watched *Bigtime* all the way to the end, I put it on for a second time. Carolyn had had it, so she disappeared into the bedroom. About half an hour later she came out and said, "Charlie, you already watched it once. You going to watch the whole thing again?"

"I'll be in later."

"You'd rather watch that movie than come to bed?"

"I'll be in."

"Yeah? Forget it. When you come in, don't wake me. I don't like playing second fiddle to a goddamn movie."

It's the end of the third reel now. I've seen enough. It did the trick. I switch off the machine, turn off all the lights and go into the bedroom.

Carolyn's sleeping on her side. I rub her shoulder softly till she wakes up.

"What's the matter?" she says. "What's wrong?"

"It came to me."

"What?"

"I been trying to remember something all day, Carolyn. For a couple days. It's been driving me nuts, 'cause I was sure I knew something but I wasn't sure why I knew it."

"What?"

"See, I want to get moving, but I wanted to remember something first. I figured if I could remember this thing, I'd feel better about what I'm going to do. And I know how I'm going to do it."

"You remembered something?"

"Someone told me something. It's the missing piece I been looking for. The piece that makes me think I got the other pieces. Now I think I got it figured out."

"You woke me up to tell me you remember something someone told you?"

"No, that's not why I woke you up."

"You woke me up 'cause you remembered something and now you feel like celebrating."

"Yeah. I think you got it."

"Charlie, this isn't the best way to run a relationship."

"Sorry. It's the best I can do."

"Either I must be crazy about you or I'm just crazy. When you're not on a case you're impossible and when you're on a case you're impossible."

"You're no bed of roses yourself."

"Charlie, you ain't the only one in the world with problems."

"What's the matter, Carolyn?"

"You been jumpy 'cause you wanted to get moving on some-thing, huh? *I* want to get moving, too. I start shooting a movie this Wednesday, but it isn't Wednesday yet. So all I can do right now, I can sit around getting nervous while I'm waiting for Wednesday to show up. Waiting ain't easy."

"I know. You want another drink?"

"And you. You ain't easy, either."

"You're terrific, Carolyn. I'm really glad I woke you up."

"Aww, Charlie, that's all I wanted to say. I wanted to tell you but I saw you had problems, so I didn't say anything. I'm finished talking now. You finished talking?"

"Yeah, Carolyn."

"Good."

102

I like Sundays. Most people are on schedules during the week, and on Saturdays they're running around trying to get done whatever it is they think they've got to get done. But Sundays are loose and unstructured. People let their defenses down. Generally a very useful day.

The Sunday paper carries no news for me, which I'm happy about.

I call San Francisco and check in with Howard Banner. He's still there. Then I start on breakfast.

"Want to know your horoscope?" Carolyn says.

"Not today," I say. "Today I'm out there all by myself. I don't care what the stars say."

Around four o'clock I make another phone call.

"This is Mr. Simson speaking. Who is calling, please."

"This's Mr. Quinlan. How's your boss doing?"

"Mr. Ethan Stockton not well. Resting in bed. It difficult here."

"He's pretty bad off, huh?"

He doesn't answer. Then, "Mr. Ethan Stockton ill."

"I'm sorry. I hope he feels better."

"Wait, please, Mr. Quinlan. Mrs. Stockton say inform her you call."

I wait. Not for long.

"Good afternoon, Mr. Quinlan. How are you?"

"I'm all right. How bad's your husband?"

That gets me some more silence. Then, "I called the doctor up here Friday, after you left. And he came back yesterday, and again a few hours ago."

"What's he say?"

"He says Ethan doesn't look good, he says it's not physical."

"So? What is it?"

"Ethan's in bed. He stays in bed. He's hardly eaten anything since Friday. The doctor says. . . he calls it a crisis of spirit."

"Nice phrase your doctor came up with."

"The doctor says, at Ethan's age a crisis of spirit can be a lot worse'n something physical."

If I'm going to do something, I guess I better do it.

"How's the rest of the family?" I say.

"Well, Jamie stayed here Friday. I insisted. Then he went back to his apartment yesterday. He was starting to look better. I think all he really needed was food. He's young, he'll be all right. Amanda stayed most of Friday, then she went home."

"What about Howard?"

"I don't know if anyone's seen Howard since Friday morning."

"Flew the coop, huh?"

"I don't know. I spoke to Amanda about an hour ago. She said she didn't know where he was."

"Mr. Simson said you wanted to speak to me."

"Me? No, I don't think so."

"Okay. You doing okay?"

"I'm a little tired. I've been with Ethan most of the time. He said he paid you. I hope he was generous. We know you did what you could."

"Your husband was a good deal more'n generous."

"I suppose you're already on another case."

"No. I won't take another case till I finish this one."

She's silent. Then, "I see," she says. More silence. "Mr. Quinlan, my husband loves to play with mechanical devices. I mean, for example, every phone in the house here is attached to a master tape recorder. I don't even know how it works. Isn't that something? Ethan, he loves to play with it. He's like a child with his first toy, sometimes."

"I heard about it. Look, Mrs. Stockton, I can't talk any longer now. There's some things I got to attend to, and I want to catch an early dinner. Five o'clock or so, Sundays, I like to catch an early dinner at Tulley's Bar, over on Highland. They got some pretty good chili there. Not like Chasens, but it's cheaper. Nice talking to you, Mrs. Stockton."

"Yes, it was. Goodbye, Mr. Quinlan."

At four forty-five I sit down in the last booth at Tulley's. When Mrs. Stockton comes in, Tulley brings her over.

103

"Margaritas?" I say.

"That sounds fine."

"I ran a print of *Bigtime* last night."

"You did? It's such an old film. Does it still hold up?"

"Most of it. You're lucky you never lost your looks. Most do. You ought to go back to acting."

"I still get offers occasionally. Usually television."

"You always turn the parts down?"

"I don't want to go back to that. I'm through with it."

I wish I could say the same.

"These days," I say, "you got to be pretty tough to get anywhere in the business. I figure, must've been the same back then."

246

"It was a little different then. Not necessarily better, but different. More 'devil-may-care.' Things seemed looser, people took chances. I think, now, everyone's running scared."

"You had the best scandals back then, too."

"We had fun in those days."

"I wonder what an actress had to do if she was up for a nice part and wanted to make sure she got it."

"You mean a part in something like *Bigtime*?"

"Yeah."

"Mr. Quinlan, you should be ashamed. I didn't have to do a thing."

"I figured you didn't."

"God, it's so long ago. I wanted to be a star. The things you do—when you're young and you want to be something, to get something. I think I would've done anything in the world to make sure I got that part in *Bigtime*. Fortunately, my memory's a little hazy on that subject. I don't know. Maybe I did do anything in the world."

"If you did, was it worth it? You never made another picture."

"I got lucky. I found being a movie star wasn't everything."

"What *was* everything?"

"For me, everything was Ethan. He was living in Argentina. He bought a print of *Bigtime*, he says he watched it every night till he came back to California to marry me. Whatever I had to do to get into that movie, it was worth it."

"That movie brought two men into your life. Ethan Stockton and his butler."

"Don't ever use the word butler in front of Mr. Simson. Or in front of my husband."

"You trust Mr. Simson?"

"It's hard to know him. He's a strange man. He'd lay down his life for Ethan. I'm not sure why he would, but he would."

"On a good night he might even kill for him."

"I think there've been occasions when Mr. Simson did just that."

"You mean, something the cops ought to know about?"

"I'm talking about years ago. The two of them came out of

Argentina very rich men. I suppose they'd have to do some hard things to get all that money."

"But that doesn't bother you."

"Occasionally it does. When you really love someone, you live with these things. Or maybe you just forget about them."

"Yeah. You love Howard Banner and you've learned to live with him."

"Yes."

"Your husband and your daughter learned to live with him, too."

"I wish you'd known Howard five years ago. He wasn't the same as now. He was very dynamic. Now it's different. Howard, he's got some talent, but not a lot. If he could accept that, if he'd just do what he can do, maybe he'd be all right. I mean, he's good enough for commercials—"

"But he wants to be better'n that."

"That's what hurts him."

"There's lots of people who want to work in this business, and when something stops them from doing it, they go a little nuts. Sometimes they go off the deep end, and it's all over for them."

"You understand what I'm talking about. Yes. This city's filled with that kind. When Howard began to make films he was a real go-getter. But when his films turned out failures, *he* became a failure. Then he had that awful car accident. Now I don't know him any more. He goes one way, then another. One minute I think I'm seeing the old Howard and the next he's a total stranger."

"Sometimes a guy wants to work in the business and they won't let him."

"What?"

"Nothing. Just thinking about a guy I once knew."

Leave it, Charlie. Stick to business. Tonight it's business.

"Mrs. Stockton, you came to see me the other day, you wanted to get me off the case. You thought Howard was behind Jamie's disappearance."

"I didn't know. I thought, but I didn't know."

"What're you saying? You weren't sure it was Howard, or you *were* sure?"

"He's become so unpredictable. Self-destructive. This thing with Jamie, I couldn't be sure Howard was involved. I did know about the missing money, of course. It was just—Howard's done such crazy things this past year."

"You came to me and told me Jamie used to take things. You really hoped Jamie'd taken the money."

"Isn't that awful? I hoped it was Jamie. If it was Jamie, well, we're used to Jamie stealing things. Ethan would've understood that. You see, when I came to you, I knew wherever it led, whatever you found out, it'd only hurt Ethan in the end. One way or another. And it has, hasn't it? Perhaps you were right the other day. Perhaps, sometimes, someone has to be hurt. And there's no way to stop it."

"That's one of those things I wish I wasn't right about."

"It's not your fault."

"Some of this *is* my fault. I'm supposed to be objective, but I wasn't. I wanted to get Howard and I wanted to get him good."

"What?"

"You came to get me to leave Howard alone. You didn't mean to do it, but you told me something which made sure I'd go after Howard. Guilty or innocent, you got me on Howard's track so I wouldn't let him loose."

"How did I do that? What did I tell you?"

"You told me he made those commercials for John Donhauser."

104

"We've all got problems, Mrs. Stockton," I say. "Part of my problem has to do with politicians. When you told me Howard made those Donhauser commercials, you set me up to nail him."

"I don't understand. Donhauser did something to you?"

"Not a thing. I never met the man, but he's a politician. He's a crooked politician, but even if he was honest, it wouldn't've made a difference. I'm against politicians and I'm against people who build fake publicity for politicians."

"What are you telling me?"

"This town got buried once. By an epidemic. And there wasn't any serum to cure that epidemic. I knew someone who used to be a screenwriter. He wrote nice meaningless film comedies that didn't do a thing but give people a little entertainment. He wasn't a big talent, like some were, but he could turn out a decent film script. But one day he got caught up in the epidemic, and once he had the bug, everyone around him got scared of him. They wouldn't let him work any more. They kicked him out, along with a lot of other people. Some of the others, they had a lot of talent, so later on some of them got to work again. But my father didn't have that much talent, so once he caught that disease he was sunk."

"You mean he was blacklisted?"

"He wasn't a Communist. He didn't know a thing about Communists. Or politics. He was in the wrong place at the wrong time and he got named. Once you got named, that was it."

"He never worked in films again?"

"Some of his friends sold scripts under other guys' names. My father couldn't get away with that. He couldn't get a job in this town. My mother tried to get him to move away from Hollywood, but he wouldn't do it. He had to stay here 'cause he figured this's where the action was. He figured the day'd come he'd get back into films. Drove my mother crazy, so she finally had to divorce him."

"I'm sorry. Is your father still alive?"

"He gave it up a long time ago. Your doctor said it. A crisis of spirit. He never understood what'd happened to him. He didn't understand politics, he didn't understand any of it. He died without ever understanding. I don't understand it, either. I guess there must've been a few of those politicians they figured they were saving the country from something terrible. But what were they saving the country from? My father and his movie comedies? It doesn't make sense. The only sense I can make—some of those politicians must've known what they were doing, but they didn't care. They were out to make marks for themselves. If some people got ruined along the way, that's just part of politics. So I don't think much of politicians, and when you told me about Howard making those commercials, I didn't think much of him."

"You wanted to hurt Howard."

"I wanted to kill him."

"I see," she says. "You must have a reason for telling me this. Why? Do you think Howard *wasn't* behind this thing?"

"I didn't say that. But I was looking too carefully at Howard and not carefully enough at some others. You ready to tell me why Jamie disappeared years ago?"

"I'm sorry, Mr. Quinlan. I can't talk about that."

"You're always afraid to tell me the things you want to tell me."

"It's Ethan I'm worried about. If there was something I could do to get Howard out of this, I think I'd do it for Ethan's sake."

"Even if you knew it was wrong?"

"I don't know. Mr. Quinlan, I'm scared about this whole thing."

"If you want to go home, it's all right. I already know what I'm going to do."

"What?"

"Maybe I figured out what it is you don't want to tell me. Some things've got to be done. I can't just let things lie."

"Ethan's sick. He's very sick."

"I know. I don't want to see him hurt."

She reaches across the table and touches my hand. "I've told you nothing," she says.

"You didn't have to. Look, I don't do anything now, it'll just get worse sometime later. Things don't go away, they either get better or worse."

"I haven't told you anything, have I? I was afraid to come here, but I felt I had to see you. Can I trust you, Mr. Quinlan?"

"You can trust that I'll do whatever I think's best for your husband."

"I have to trust you, don't I?"

"I know he's sick. I want to see him better. I'm going to see what I can do. You didn't tell me anything. You were right to come here. If things work out, I'll be speaking to you. And your husband. I'll try to make it soon."

I hold up my glass with my free hand. "To better times, Mrs. Stockton. To *Bigtime* and Eve Carroll. The kind of woman worth a trip from South America."

105

As soon as she's gone, I phone Lieutenant Jake Barnes.

"Been expectin' a call from you," he says. "What've you got?"

"Maybe I got nothing. I got two questions. You find the car that killed Austin Bedloe?"

"The electrician's car? We found it. All the fingerprints belonged to the owner. The steering wheel's wiped clean's a whistle. Could be the owner did that himself—to make us think someone stole his car."

"You feel like telling me the rest?"

"What makes you think there's more to tell?"

"I don't. I'm guessing."

"Um hmmm. Charlie, when this thing's over, I'm expectin' you to turn up on my side, or you're in plenty of trouble."

"I understand."

"We found the car parked three blocks away from the electrician's house."

"What do you make of that?"

"Pretty neat. But if I was an electrician, and I ran over a guy with my car, if I decided to run off and later report my car stolen, I'd park the damn thing in some back alley on the other side of town, I sure's hell wouldn't park the mother three blocks away from my own house."

"But if someone stole the car, they might have to drive back to pick up their own car, if that's where they parked it."

"Got any suggestions who that someone might be?"

"No. I got another question. You got a list of Bedloe's personal effects. Was he carrying any car keys?"

252

"I can tell you this much. He wasn't carryin' a wallet. Or else someone lifted it."

"All I want to know about's the car keys."

"You lift the wallet, Charlie?"

"I don't lift wallets from dead men. Any car keys?"

"I'll have to check and call you back."

"Okay, I'm eating dinner at Tulley's."

I'm in the middle of my chili and Jake comes in and sits down across from me. He doesn't say a thing. Tulley brings him a bowl of chili and we sit there eating like two strangers. I wait for him to finish. He orders dessert. I order dessert. Then he goes into his cigarette-rolling trick. I give him all the time he wants.

"Okay," he says. "So Austin Bedloe wasn't carryin' car keys. So what'll that prove?"

"I followed Austin Bedloe for two nights running. He was driving a blue Buick LeSabre both nights. But the night he got killed, I didn't see the Buick in the parking lot at Le Brigand. You say Bedloe wasn't carrying car keys, so how's Bedloe getting around that night? He went out to the parking lot. What's he going to do out there? Wait for a taxi?"

"Maybe a friend was drivin' the Buick."

"Yeah, I think that's what Bedloe thought. But the friend'd switched the Buick for another car he'd just stolen from this electrician. That way, Bedloe was looking for the Buick and he didn't see his friend coming to run him over till it was too late."

"Some friend. That'd make it homicide, Charlie."

"You're ahead of me on that. You always were. I was too busy hoping it was an accident. I thought it made more sense that way. Now it makes more sense this way. You figured it for a homicide all along."

"Maybe. Okay, we got ourselves a homicide."

"Two homicides."

"You're ahead of me for once. What do you know I don't know?"

"Too soon, Jake. I got to check some stuff out. I'll give you this. You know a guy named Pastrano? Local boy. I think maybe his first name's Louie."

"I know a couple Pastranos. One of 'em's on the force."

"Not this one. My guy's pretty thick, but big and strong."

"I know a Joey Pastrano. Heavy-set, slow. Does a lot of jobs for guys. Jobs nobody wants to do, so they give 'em to him. He comes cheap. Dark hair, eyebrows runnin' together in the middle of his face, always needs a shave."

"That's the guy. He's in it. If I'm you, I'd get a line on him."

"He going to be tricky?"

"He's pretty bad off. He's got a hand crushed in a doorway, all bandaged up now. I helped him on that. Last time I saw him the other hand was full of blood, so I don't think he's in too good condition. If you find where he is, you could probably send a couple babies to pull him in without too much trouble."

"What'd I want him for? He do the homicides? I pull in a guy, I got to have a little proof. From what I hear about Joey Pastrano, he likes to swing his fists, but I don't think he's got it, it comes to homicide. You got proof?"

"I didn't say he killed anyone. Matter of fact, I don't think he did. Not directly. But it's a whole big mess and he's in it."

"Doesn't sound like I got much cause to pull him in."

"I'm not telling you to pull him in. Locate him, if you can. He might come in handy. Just see where he is and have someone watch after him till you need him."

"How come I'm going to need him?"

"Pastrano's pretty dumb, but he won't go behind bars if he's got something to sing about. I think he's got plenty to sing about."

"Pastrano's pretty flaky. Won't make much of a witness."

"He'll do okay for you if I get the stuff to back him up."

"If this's homicide, I'm going to want a nice neat package."

"I haven't got it all figured yet. Maybe I can come up with something. If I do and I give you a call, you might want to have Pastrano somewheres you can tap him on the shoulder and pull him in for a talk."

"How much time you plannin' to take on this?"

"I'm doing what I can."

"Get somethin' done pretty quick, Charlie, or I'll have to pull *you* in and run some things I got. And don't fuck up. Okay?"

254

Jake takes off.

Now I have my hooks baited and in the water. Time to start reeling in and see what I catch.

First I phone the Mark Hopkins in San Francisco.

Room 612 doesn't answer.

Okay. Maybe he's out to dinner. Or a movie. I could sit around for a while and keep calling till he gets back.

I don't feel like sitting around. So he isn't in his room? I'm ready to move and I don't care if he's in his room or not.

If Howard Banner's being a bad boy, I'll know it soon enough.

106

It'd be a good night for a drive to Malibu even if I didn't have a reason to go there.

I find the house and park in the driveway. Nobody answers when I ring the bell, but I'm patient. On the fourth ring I get results. The door opens and Amanda Banner stands there in a white caftan which drapes to the floor. She belongs to a drinking family and she's keeping up her end of it.

"What do *you* want?" she says.

"I'm looking for your husband. Is he here?"

"No. I don't know where Howard is."

"That's too bad."

I take her in my arms and kiss her. She tastes like Scotch.

"What's going on?" she says. "You were different at your office. I thought you weren't interested."

"Then, I wasn't. I was working for your father, and I figured it'd be a conflict of interest. Now he's paid me off and I'm ready to negotiate a new deal."

She steps back and I have to reach out to grab her before she falls over.

She laughs. "I feel a little wobbly. I better go in and sit down."

"Sounds okay to me. Am I coming in with you?"

"Come in. What the hell."

She leads me into the living room. It's too large and too white. Expensively modern. Lots of objects in here, and still it's bare. Art objects. And enough furniture to do the job.

"You like a drink, Mr. Quinlan?"

"You said something about money the other day."

"Oh? Money? Money. Money money money. Wonderful stuff."

"Wonderful when you got it. Not so wonderful when you haven't."

"I thought my father paid you. I heard he paid you a lot."

"It was a start."

"Now you want to pick up some more."

"You got it. I'd like to hear an offer, if you still want to make me an offer."

"Certainly, Mr. Quinlan. Lots of money. All the money you want. You know why I want to give you money? Because of what you've done for my husband." -

She tries coming at me in a straight line, but curves over to the right and ends up on the sofa.

"You stupid bastard!" she says. "You must be crazy. I wish Howard was here—he'd show you. He'd kill you! I asked you to leave him alone. Look what you've done!"

"You figure this mess's my fault, huh?"

"I told you to leave Howard alone!"

"Mrs. Banner, the reason I came here, I think I can fix things up."

"You already fixed things up. Where's Howard? Where's my husband?"

"He's in San Francisco. I sent him up there."

"What?"

"Friday morning. After what happened at the house, I figured I better get him out of the way."

"What? Why the hell'd you do that?"

"If you want him back, I'll get him back. I can make everything all right for Howard, and I'll do it, if the price is right. If the price isn't right, I won't do it. It's too tricky unless I can get some cash for it."

256

"You're insane."

"No. I got the story all set. This's how we'll put it together. Your brother Jamie stole the money along with Harry Spenser. When Spenser died in that car accident, Jamie panicked. He figured he'd be caught, so he faked his own kidnapping. You can see how that'd work out."

"What? I don't understand."

Listen to me, lady. Get your head out of the bottle and listen!

"Jamie threw the blame onto your husband," I say. "But the truth is, Howard's innocent. He didn't have a thing to do with it."

She's too drunk. She doesn't understand.

No. Wait. I think she does understand.

"My God," she says. "My God! Is that true?"

"No, it isn't true. Of course it isn't true, but it sounds true, doesn't it?"

Now she looks confused again.

"Mrs. Banner, I know my business. I can make it look true. That's all I got to do, make it *look* true. Your mother came to me this afternoon. You know what she wants? She wants to believe Jamie's the guilty one. And the thing is, your father told me pretty much the same thing on Friday. They don't care what *really* happened. They'd like to believe Howard isn't involved in this thing. That'd make them happy. Your father's real sick 'cause of this thing. I like your father and I want to help him. If I can show him it wasn't Howard, that it's Jamie who's behind this, that'd make your father feel pretty good. He'd feel bad about Jamie, but he'd feel good about Howard. I think he'd be okay then."

"Why're you telling me this?"

"Your mother and father wouldn't go for this. I'd never get any money out of them for this kind of thing. But I figure you'll pay to get your husband back. See, I'm all for happiness, as long's it pays. I sent Howard up to San Francisco, but I called him up there a little while ago and he wasn't there. No answer. So maybe he's back down here. If he's here, I'll talk to him. I'll make the deal with him. But you say he's not here. Okay, maybe he's still up in San Francisco. If he's not here, I'll have to deal with you, Mrs. Banner."

She's still too foggy for what I'm telling her.

"Mrs. Banner, it's simple. You pay me enough, you and your husband, I'll get your husband back. We'll make a lot of people happy."

I think I got through to her. She's turning the whole thing over in her mind, but it's a mind soaked in liquor and it's taking her a few minutes.

"Mr. Quinlan, you mean you can really do that? You can put Howard in the clear? Just like that?"

"Not just like that. It'll take some work, but I can do it. Howard was smart the other morning at the house. He took quite a beating with that cane and everything, but he kept his mouth shut and got out of there. If he'd said something, there might be trouble. But he didn't. I know how to fix it all up. Your parents trust me, so I can do it."

"You mean you can make it look like Howard's innocent?"

"That's right. I don't know if I should, but I will."

"The only way you can do it," she says, "you've got to make it look like Jamie did it? Like Jamie stole the money?"

"I'll say the right things, your parents'll believe me 'cause they'll *want* to believe me. Jamie can say he's innocent from now to doomsday, your parents won't believe him. I got some things covered on my own. If Jamie goes to the cops, the way I'll handle it, the cops won't believe him, either."

"You'll put all the blame on Jamie."

"Get it straight, lady. I won't do this just out of kindness. I figure Howard stole that money from the company, and I want some of it. I got a friend who needs some money, and I'm expecting you to get that money for me. You understand me?"

"But you say Jamie's really innocent. You're willing to do this to him?"

"Okay, I don't like it either. But I don't know Jamie. Jamie's nothing to me. I'll do it. For some money I'll do it. Christ, it's the best thing for your father, that's why I'll do it."

I put my head in my hands and sit there.

"It's all so simple?" she says.

"Yeah. Just that simple. I don't care about Jamie, I care about the way things come out for your father. The way they've come out so far, I don't like it. So I'll change things around."

"If you're paid to change things."

"Damn right. *Only* if I'm paid. Now you got it."

She sits frozen still. She probably thinks I'm a bastard. Okay, I'm a bastard. I'm going to settle this thing.

"How can I let you do it?" she says. "Jamie's my brother."

"The hell with that. To do this, we need a fall guy. Jamie's going to have to be it. That's part of the price for saving your husband."

"It'll never work. You're out of your mind."

"It'll work. Mrs. Banner, it'll work. I'll *make* it work. All I want to know, I want to know how much you'll pay me to do it."

"I won't pay you anything. Get out of here, Mr. Quinlan. I won't go along with this. I won't let you do this to Jamie!"

I finally let my body relax against the back of the chair. "I know, Mrs. Banner. I know you won't."

"What?"

"Lady, you played it all wrong just now. I was almost home, but I needed something. You gave me the last answer I needed."

"What?"

"You're really something, Mrs. Banner. I always thought it was you and your husband behind this thing. Even coming over here, I still thought it might be that way. Guess I was wrong."

"What?"

"It wasn't you and your husband. It was just you. Your husband didn't have a thing to do with it."

107

She blinks at me and shakes her head to clear it. She's already too late.

"You should've told me how much you love your husband," I say. "How you'd do anything for him, even sell out your brother. That kind of stuff."

"What do you mean? What'm I supposed to say?"

"Nothing, Mrs. Banner. No more lies. Especially about how much you love your husband."

"I *do* love him!"

"I already heard that part at my office, remember? You told me to leave your husband alone. It sounded nice and made me more suspicious. You wanted me to suspect your husband. The whole thing was an act. You wanted me to be sure your husband was up to something, but you said something that bothered me. You knew about the missing money. You said your father told you about it. That sounded sort of funny, 'cause I already asked your father and he said he hadn't told you. I figured if you knew about the money, it had to be because you knew who stole it."

"You're right. Howard told me about it."

"Howard told you about the money and Howard's behind Jamie's disappearance, huh? The kidnapping, I mean. I considered that for a while. I could go for Howard grabbing Jamie and hiring Austin Bedloe to impersonate him, but I couldn't figure out why Howard'd hire a stupid hood like Pastrano. I mean, Howard's got connections. He'd get top talent from his friends in San Francisco. But Howard's got some screws loose and sometimes he doesn't put things together so well, so I let that part go, but it bothered me. Anyway, I figured you and your husband were probably into this thing together.

"But Friday morning at your father's house, I started to wonder. Howard came in and I told him I found Jamie. That should've been pretty bad news to Howard. It should've meant his whole world was falling apart. So what'd he do? He stopped to apologize to me for setting his friends from San Francisco on my trail. Then I looked at this thing from another angle. Maybe Howard didn't have anything to do with this thing at all. So when I came here tonight and you didn't know where Howard was, that was a good sign. I mean, if you *really* didn't know. I pushed you along to see if you'd pay me off to clear your husband. You wouldn't. You can't. You want Howard to look guilty. You always wanted that. I think you hate him, Mrs. Banner. I'm not sure why yet, but I can make enough guesses. Anyway, the way I see it now, Howard was never involved in any of this."

I take a picture from my pocket and put it in front of her. "Nice picture, Mrs. Banner. Not too recent. How long ago? When he was in college?"

"It's part of a family picture. It was taken when Jamie first joined my father's business."

"Your father wanted to hire a detective, then he didn't, then he did. You figured he'd probably hire one sooner or later, so you told him it'd be a good idea. You pushed it 'cause you figured that way you'd have a little control over things. You got some stuff together. Like this picture. Jamie looks a little older now, not like he did when this picture was taken, but the picture, it's a dead ringer for Austin Bedloe made up to look like Jamie. Bedloe could dye his hair, he could darken his skin, but the trouble was, he still looked too young. He looked like Jamie looked about ten years ago. So I was given a ten-year-old picture of Jamie, so I'd follow Bedloe and think he was Jamie. When you were sure that part'd worked, you had Bedloe killed so it'd look like an accident. Maybe you used Pastrano for that, to run a car over Bedloe. You figured if we thought Bedloe died in an accident, we'd also think Howard'd kidnapped Jamie and now he had to kill him. But Howard didn't kidnap Jamie. It was all your idea."

"You think *I* kidnapped Jamie?"

"No, I don't think that. I had this feeling Jamie hadn't been kidnapped, but I couldn't figure out why I felt that way. It's been bothering me for days. Then, last night, I remembered and everything came together. See, when I checked out Jamie's apartment, I found out he sells marijuana on the side. I met one of his customers, a cute little girl with a baby on her hip. She told me something. Before Jamie disappeared, he told this girl he'd be gone for about two weeks. Funny, huh? How'd Jamie know he was going to be kidnapped before he got kidnapped? Lady, your brother was never kidnapped."

She stiffens her back to put up a fight.

"This is preposterous. Get out of here. Immediately!"

"Good, you're starting to sober up a little. I'll give you some earlier stuff I put together. New Year's Eve. Howard had that car accident and after that he couldn't work. Your father put Jamie in charge of Howard's commercial. Jamie screwed that up, so your father gave him another job, probably little more'n a title. Jamie didn't like that. He wanted to get back at lots of people, so he started padding the accounts and stealing funds. He got away with it for a couple months, but around the time he went over the fifty-thousand level Harry Spenser caught him at it. Spenser must've said he'd tell Mr. Stockton."

"This is crazy! You said Spenser was an embezzler. You said *he* stole the money."

"Lady, I only know two things about Harry Spenser. He used to be an accountant—and now he's dead."

"You said he'd been in jail. You said you checked with the police about him."

"I made up all that crap. I needed a story, Friday morning, to see if I could crack the story Jamie was telling. Jamie told that thing like he'd rehearsed it a hundred times, so I threw him a curve. I threw him a lie—that Spenser had a jail record. It almost worked. Jamie almost broke when I said he was involved in Spenser's death. I guess Jamie *was* involved in it."

"Harry Spenser died in a car accident. Everyone knows he was a terrible driver."

"It's too convenient, you know? It's got to be murder. Maybe Jamie did it, but I don't think so. Jamie looks too weak. I figure, when Spenser discovered what Jamie was up to, and Jamie knew he found out, Jamie came to you and told you he was stealing the money. *You* probably made the decision to shut Spenser's mouth. It could be you hired Pastrano to do it, but Pastrano's a thug and he knows what homicide means, I don't think he'd go that far. No, this was done by someone who didn't understand what murder means. Probably you. And later you killed Austin Bedloe the same way.

"As for killing Spenser, you knew it'd only be a temporary solution. You knew your father'd hire a new accountant, who'd also discover the missing money. And Jamie, he's a kleptomaniac in good standing from way back. Your father'd figure it was Jamie,

262

so you had to act quickly. You tried to save Jamie by making it look like Howard was the thief. You arranged it all, lady. Jamie's disappearance, the impersonation, Bedloe's accidental death, a kidnap plot which suddenly fell apart—the whole shooting match."

"No, I didn't! I didn't do these things!"

"Yeah, lady. You did it. See, once you start off, once you kill someone like Harry Spenser, it never stops there. It keeps on going. You can't control it."

"You think I did all these things? These terrible things? You think I did all this to make it look like it was Howard?"

"You had to pin it on someone. With Howard, people could believe it might be him 'cause everyone figures he's nuts."

"I love Howard!"

"Lady, I saw the two of you in the screening room the other night. I think you're jealous. Jealous of a movie screen. Nothing you do'll pull him away from that screening room and his old films. And they're pretty rotten films. I guess, whenever he comes home, he's probably just on his way to San Francisco. It's been hard on you, I'll give you that much. Maybe a lot harder'n I know. When Jamie told you what he'd done, stolen that money, you saw a way to turn it against Howard. I think you wanted revenge."

"You're wrong! I wouldn't hurt Howard!"

"There's more to this, too."

"What?"

"You know what I mean. There's something else. You cared about something else."

"What the hell're you talking about?"

"Let's just say you wanted to protect your brother. You thought your father'd kick him out of the business, maybe disinherit him, maybe even call the cops, when he discovered what Jamie'd done. But why'd you care, Mrs. Banner? Why'd anyone care about Jamie? He's a hopeless case. He's no use to anyone. Not to himself, not to anyone."

"Jamie's a good boy."

"He's a goddamn coward. He won't even come out and fight for his sister, with me here yelling at her."

That does the trick. Jamie comes running in from another room behind me.

But he's too quick. Before I'm out of the chair he gets his fingers into my hair and yanks my head back for all he's worth. He has me pretty bad. I reach back to grab his sleeve, but it's no good. He isn't wearing a shirt. He isn't wearing any clothes at all.

He keeps his pull on my hair, and pain ripples through my head.

Bracing my feet on the floor, I quick-jerk my body out of the chair and backward against his chest. I put all the force I have into it. He loses his grip as we fall to the floor.

We both lie there, me on top of him and both of us on our backs. I roll off, balance on my knees and give him a hard punch in the stomach. Just the one punch, but it's hard and sufficient. He starts coughing violently as he tries to catch his breath.

I want to hit him again. I want to hit him hard. Harder. I want him to get up and take a swing at me. I want to hit him in the stomach again. I want to break his nose. I want him to give me an excuse. I want to hit him again.

He coughs. He sits there and coughs. It's no good.

I get to my feet and rub the sides of my head. It's clear enough, but the pain's there to stay for a while. I pump air in and out through my mouth. Jamie continues coughing on the floor.

Okay. The hell with him. It's over. It's all over.

108

It's not over.

Amanda's coming out of the kitchen. She's screaming.

She's got a knife. The blade's about a foot long.

A sober woman could do a lot of damage with a knife like that. God knows what a drunk might do.

She comes straight at me. I keep my eyes on the blade. I step aside and she stumbles past, waving the knife. She doesn't come close.

264

She tangles up in Jamie's feet and falls, dropping the knife into her brother's leg.

It slashes straight down and cuts deep. About six inches above the knee.

She stops screaming. He's too full of shock to make any noise. All either of them can do now is look at the damn wooden handle sticking straight up into the air.

Neither of them has the presence of mind to remove it from his leg.

I have to do that.

The thing is, I still want to hit him. And now I can't.

109

"Where you keep the bandages?" I say. "This's pretty bad."

Sitting silently on the floor, they look at the gash in Jamie's leg, watch the blood drip into the off-white carpet. I try again.

"You got any bandages in the house?"

I can't get anything out of them. The sight of real blood has turned them both to stone. I go through closets looking for things I can use. Some silk scarves work for a bandage and stop the flow of blood. I wrap them in layers around the cut and tie the ends together. It's really a bad cut, I hate to look at it.

As I work, Amanda nestles her brother's head against her shoulder to comfort him. I know one thing. It's not the first time tonight they've been in each other's arms.

"That'll have to do for now," I say. "It's a bad cut. You want me to call an ambulance?"

"No," she says. "I'll take care of my brother. Everything'll be all right."

"Sure, Mrs. Banner. You make Jamie believe that, and you try to believe it yourself. When that doesn't work, you better call a doctor."

I stand and look down at them, huddled together.

"This's why your mother's been afraid of me. Why she really

265

wanted me off the case. She was afraid I'd find out about this and tell Mr. Stockton."

"How'd you know?" Amanda says. "If my mother didn't tell you, how'd you know?"

"I'm not sure. Maybe I didn't know. Jamie didn't have any girls and everyone told me he wasn't gay. I figured he had someone. The odds pointed to you. The way I had it, when you were sixteen your mother found out something was going on, so she sent you East. She didn't tell your father, she kept it secret. She didn't know how to stop it, so she sent you to school in the East and vacations in Europe. She didn't want to let you near each other. When you did come back, when she couldn't keep you away any longer, it all seemed to work out. You met Howard and fell in love with him, and married him. That must've been tough on Jamie. He hadn't found anyone else. When you married Howard, Jamie was scared. He thought he'd lost you. That's probably why he disappeared years ago and turned to drugs. Yeah, that'd work out right. Howard told me he didn't know anything about Jamie's first disappearance 'cause he was in Europe then, and the only time Howard was in Europe was during your honeymoon."

"Go away, Mr. Quinlan. I don't want you here. Leave us alone."

"You came home and you found Jamie was missing. Neither of your parents seemed to care where he was."

"Nobody ever looked after Jamie. Only me."

"I figured Jamie had to have someone. And you, you didn't seem to get anywhere with your husband, so I figured maybe you had to have someone, too. It fit together that way."

"Nobody ever cared about Jamie. I always had to look after him."

"He came to you for protection when Spenser caught him stealing the money. You're the only person he could turn to."

"Howard stole the money. Jamie used to steal things. Long ago. He *used* to steal things. Not now. He's stopped doing it. You've got it all wrong, Mr. Quinlan."

"Yeah. Sober up and write me a letter telling me how it really was. I got to go. I got another appointment to keep."

"You'll call the police?"

"Not yet. I got to talk to your father first. But after that, I'm going to have to call the cops."

"It's all Howard's fault. I didn't do anything—Howard did. He stole the money. You can't prove anything different!"

"I'm afraid I can."

"You're going to tell my father? About this? About Jamie and me?"

"I don't know. I think I'm going to leave that part out, if I can. I'm not sure I can."

"Nobody'll believe your story. That's all it is. A story. You can't prove anything."

"Mrs. Banner, if you really care about your brother, you better get him a doctor. His leg's pretty bad. You better call a lawyer, too."

"You don't understand about Howard and me! It's Howard's fault!"

If there's anything else to know, right now, right at this moment, I don't want to know it.

I walk out of the house and close the front door behind me.

The night air's crisp and sharp. It does wonders for my head. I turn my car key in the ignition and reach forward to shift gears, but I hear something.

She's standing in the front doorway. She's yelling something. I can't make out her words over the sound of my car's motor. Her eyes have gone wild, I can see that much.

I turn off the motor, but now she's going back into the house. She's nuts. I don't know what she wants. I sit, looking at the house. Now she comes back out. She's got the kitchen knife in her hand again. I feel like taking the thing away from her and giving her a spanking.

She comes out of the house, down the steps, but not toward me. She sees me watching her but doesn't say a thing. She's still got the knife.

The hell with her. I'm getting out of here.

She's walking over to the side of the house. Is she looking for something?

267

She's still over to the side of the house. She's got the knife at waist level. She looks at me. She looks away. She's gone crazy, I guess. The hell with her.

My God!

110

I'm not going to let this happen! It's happened too many times already!

I'm out of my car and running toward her.

She turns with her back to me. I reach out at her.

She swings around and the knife's high. I go forward beneath it.

The knife swings back across the air and I reach for her arm. I've got it, but she still struggles against me with the knife.

She fights at me with her free hand. I don't try to block her fist. I hold her other arm and move my hand toward the knife.

She's very strong now. We struggle back and forth. She's got energy and determination. She tries to swing the knife.

I've still got her arm. I close my hand around hers. We've both got the knife now.

She swings at me. Again and again. I hold on. I force her grip and she almost loses the knife. I reach for it.

I've got my hand on part of the handle. She's got part of it too. The blade's going to cut into my palm.

I swing with my other hand, keeping it open, flat, not making a fist. I can't make a fist. A fist could kill her.

I swing my open hand against the side of her face. It's a hard slap, hard enough to send her straight back. She's lost her grip on the knife.

I've got the knife in my hand. She comes at me. I swing my open hand against her once more. Hard.

She goes down to the ground and stays there.

111

Jamie's still sitting on the floor, over in the corner now. I leave him alone.

I call Jake Barnes.

"It's me," I say. "I'm down in Malibu. You better come."

"Why? You got things in a nice little package for me?"

"I don't know, Jake. I got a story for you. It's involved, but I got most of it."

"What've you got?"

"I don't know. I got what I got. Come on—get out here!"

"Okay, Charlie. Settle down. You going to be there when I get there?"

"I'll be here. I got to be here. I almost left too soon, Jake. I got a girl down here, she almost pulled a suicide on me."

"What'd she do? Pop some pills?"

"She tried to open her wrists with a knife. I had to slap her a couple times to get the thing away from her."

"Knife? Sounds serious."

"She made sure I got a good look at what she had in mind before she tried anything."

"One of those, huh?"

"Come on, Jake. Get down here fast. She needs watching."

112

She's sitting on the grass. I sit down next to her. She doesn't look at me at first.

"That was stupid," she says. "What just happened, I mean."

I should do something. What?

"Yeah," I say.

"You went inside. What'd you do? Did you call my parents?"

"No. I don't want to talk to them yet."

"You said you wouldn't call the police. Not yet."

"Yeah, but then you got stupid, so I had to call them."

"I understand. I'm sorry if I scared you."

"Mrs. Banner? You want to go inside?"

"No. I'd like to sit out here. Will you sit with me?"

"Yeah, I'll sit with you."

The air's very clear. It's getting cooler. I'm trying to find something to say.

"I really love Howard," she says. "He loved me when we got married. You should've seen the honeymoon we had. I showed him things in Europe he'd never known they existed. You ever been to Europe, Mr. Quinlan?"

"Nope, not yet."

"Europe's wonderful. How can I describe it to you? It's just ... it's like real life. You can really live over there. All those vacations I had in Europe, I knew everything there was to know. I showed all of it to Howard. It was wonderful. I wanted to stay over there forever. He wanted to come back. He wanted to make another film. Then, when he made it, it was so bad he became a laughingstock in this city. He was never the same again, and I guess that was just about the end of things."

"You didn't love him any more?"

"I still love him. I've always loved him. It was him. He was never the same again. No, once he was. Once he was the same. You know when it was? Last New Year's Eve. I don't know what got into him. He came home and we made love and he was himself again. He was the same man he used to be for one whole hour. That's all it lasted, one hour. Then he left me and went off to San Francisco with some tramp, some girl he liked better than he liked me. But they didn't make it, did they? No, they didn't make it. I'll tell you what I wish. Howard and that tramp, I wish the two of them'd died in that car. How could he do it to me? You know what the papers said? 'First Accident of the Year. Film Director Howard Banner and Unidentified Woman.' Check it out, that's exactly what it said. Word for word. You don't believe me, check it out."

"Mrs. Banner, that girl he picked up, she—"

"It was slightly humiliating, Mr. Quinlan. Slightly humiliating! A nice way to start off the year, your husband's name all over

270

the papers! 'Unidentified Woman!' I wish they'd both died in that car!"

"Mrs. Banner, that girl had nothing to do with your husband. She belonged to someone else. Howard just picked her up as a favor to someone he knew who lived in San Francisco."

"You know what happened? That tramp's face got messed up a little. It should've been worse! It should've been a lot worse! Everything, it's all Howard's fault!"

She stops talking for a while and we sit there. I want to say something, but it won't make any difference. So we sit and wait for the cops.

"I don't really know how it happened," she says. "I really don't. Jamie came to me. I couldn't let that accountant talk to Dad. I tried to talk the accountant out of it, but I couldn't get anywhere with him. I had to kill him. I had to look after Jamie. Things just got out of hand. You called the police, huh?"

"Yeah."

"Do you have to tell them? Couldn't you make up something?"

"Spenser's dead. And Bedloe's dead. There's some things, you do them, you got to be ready to answer for them. Once you go over that line, one way or another you got to pay up. That's the way it is."

"But I don't want to pay."

"None of us wants to pay."

"Do my parents have to know? Will you tell my father?"

"Mrs. Banner, you saw your father. You saw what this's been doing to him. It's been killing him. Didn't you care?"

"Please don't call me Mrs. Banner. Call me Amanda."

"All right. Amanda."

"Of course I cared. He's my father. You think I wanted to hurt my father?"

"You *did* hurt him."

"But I didn't mean to. I just didn't know what else to do."

She snuggles close to me, her head against my shoulder.

"Where's my husband tonight, Mr. Quinlan? Is he in San

Francisco? Why isn't he home with me? He's my husband. Isn't he *supposed* to be home with me?"

"I'll call him, Amanda. If you want me to."

"He's *never* home. He's gone. He's *always* gone. Here, there, he's always gone. He's never here with me. He's always somewhere else. I love him. I really love him. I need him here, at home, with me."

"I'll call him, I'll get him back down here."

She doesn't say anything. Then she says, "Well, maybe I shouldn't've done the things I did. But I did them. Now, I guess, Howard'll know I'm here. He'll *have* to know I'm here, won't he?"

A few minutes later the cops drive up. Their headlights pick us out, sitting in front of the house. She has her head close to mine. I have my arm around her.

I'd like to do something for her.

But I don't know what to do.

113

"It's a funny thing," Jake Barnes says.

"Good. I could use a joke."

"Well, Charlie, it's not *that* funny. But it's funny enough. Your guy Pastrano, I didn't have to look far for him."

"You got him already?"

"Already had him. Pastrano's been locked up since yesterday."

"How come?"

"Schmuck tried to hold up a gas station. You had it right, about his hands. They're both in pretty bad shape. The other night he tried to hold up a gas station, belonged to two brothers. Both the brothers're there, it's early in the morning, they're just opening up, this guy Pastrano tries to knock 'em over. Well, he had his hands all chewed up and bandaged, I don't know what he had in mind, all he's got, he's got this knife. He figured he's going to hold up the place with a knife. These two brothers, they got a couple guns. So they showed him their guns, then they knocked the shit out of him. After they finished that, they called us. Time some cops got there, they could've scooped the schmuck up with a spoon. Tryin' to hold up a gas station with a fuckin' knife. No brains at all."

"He needed money. He figured he had to get some money real quick and get out of town."

"He sure picked the wrong gas station."

One of the other cops brings Jamie from the house and puts him in the back of the car with his sister.

"Don't look too happy," Jake says. "Neither of them."

"They don't even know what they done."

"Yeah, Charlie? You think so, huh?"

"I don't know about the kid. Maybe he knows. But her, she's got it all screwed up. I don't think she understands any of it."

"Doesn't matter. Doesn't matter if you understand what you're doin' or not. If you do it, you answer for it."

"That's what they say."

"No, Charlie. That's what we say. Someone's got to say it, so we say it."

"Yeah. Way I see it, she's ready to spill the whole story to you. Right now."

"Yeah, she looks ready to talk."

"But you won't make her talk. You'll take her downtown, but you won't try to get the stuff out of her. Not till we get a nice high-priced lawyer to sit across the table from her and look after her."

"Come on, Charlie. What's this crap? I know the rules. You get the lawyer down there, we'll be waitin'. What the hell? You think I'm some schmuck, I don't know how the game gets played? What the fuck you think I am?"

"I didn't mean anything. It's been a long night. I got a lot of things on my mind."

"Okay. Don't worry, we'll wait for the lawyer. When we get her talkin' we'll make sure the lawyer's there to hold her hand. What's the matter? You don't want to see this thing come out?"

"I want it out. I'm with you. I tipped you to Pastrano, right?"

"Okay. We're both edgy. I don't like suicides, either. You sure you don't want me to talk to her folks? I got enough of the story now, I can talk to them."

"It's my business, Jake. They got to know and I got to tell it to them. I want them to hear it from me. Just do me a favor and play it cool. Wait till we send you a lawyer."

"Okay. Charlie? You going to be okay?"

"Just keep an eye on her for me."

114

Did you ever have that feeling that you wanted to go?
And still you have that feeling that you wanted to stay?

I've got that feeling. I've been walking around this house for fifteen minutes. I want to get out of this place, but I can't. I'm just sort of stuck here. No reason to it. I'm just not ready to leave. I don't know why.

I take the phone and call San Francisco. The Mark Hopkins. This time he's there.

"There's a midnight flight," I say. "You got plenty of time to make it. I'll pick you up at the airport when you get here."

"You mean everything's okay now?" Howard Banner says.

"Everything's okay. I'll tell you about it when you get here."

"Well, I'll drive down, in that case."

"No. You'll catch the midnight flight. I want you down here fast. I'll meet you at the airport."

"Okay, Mr. Quinlan. You're sure it's safe to come back?"

"You've been gone long enough, Mr. Banner. It's time to come home now. Your wife's expecting you."

Okay. I got one thing done. But that was the easy part. I'm not quite ready for the rest of it.

I don't know. I don't know what to do. I'm just sitting here, looking at some blood on the carpet, and all I hear is Jimmy Durante's song.

Did you ever have that feeling that you wanted to go?
And still you have that feeling that you wanted to stay?

115

I start driving toward the city, but I'm not ready to go there yet.

I stop at a bar near the beach. I've been here a couple times before. It's quiet for a Sunday night. There's a small group at the end of the bar and some more people at the tables. There's a woman standing alone at the far end of the bar.

Her legs are too thin and her nose is too long but I guess she has something. The bartender seems to think so. He's down at that end with her. She's got a face as plain as the sidewalk. I wonder if a guy like me could pick her up.

I go down to where they're talking.

"I'll take some vodka on the rocks," I say, "and whatever the lady's drinking, you can bring her another."

"No thanks," she says. "I'm just waiting for someone."

The bartender brings me mine and then he's called to the other end of the bar. The lady and I are on our own.

"You busy tonight?" I say.

"You got terrible technique."

"I know. You busy tonight?"

"Yeah. I got to go to a cocktail party in Bel Air."

"Bel Air's a long ways off."

"Yeah. I'm waiting for a friend to come in."

"Hope he gets here."

"When he gets here, I hope he looks a lot better'n you."

"I look that bad?"

"You look like hell."

"Been having a tough night."

"So? We all have tough nights."

"Do we?"

"Yeah, buddy. We all have tough nights."

"I almost saw a girl commit suicide tonight."

"Almost?"

"Yeah. Almost."

"Well, then it could've been worse, right?"

"Could've been a lot worse."

"And you feel like hell, huh?"

"I don't know. I feel up and down, I don't know how I feel."

"Sounds like you got postcoital depression."

"Maybe so."

"You're not much fun to stand at a bar with."

"Sorry."

"I hope when the guy I'm waiting for comes in, I hope he's in better shape'n you."

"I hope so, too."

"You going to snap out of it?"

"I don't know."

"You look like the kind of guy who hates his business."

"Yeah. I hate my business. And I love my business. I don't know what the hell I feel."

"You sure are screwed up."

"It's a screwed-up world."

"Things didn't work out for you the way you think they should?"

"I don't know."

"I'd sure as hell never want to go out with a guy like you."

"That's okay, lady. I probably wouldn't be interested in a lady like you, either."

"You sure's hell aren't going to pick me up with a line like that."

"I'm not in shape to pick anyone up tonight."

"That's okay with me. I've got to go to a cocktail party in Bel Air. I got business there."

"Yeah? *You* in a business you like?"

"I don't know. I spent all last year putting together a film. I lost my shirt on that film. I didn't make a cent on it. But I didn't go around crying afterward. I jumped back in, and now I'm ready to go with another film. You ought to learn to be like me. You ought to learn to snap the hell out of these things."

"I'm trying. I had it all figured right. But I wasn't ready for the girl to try a suicide."

"But you stopped her."

"Yeah. I was just in time."

"You want to come to Bel Air with me?"

"No. I got things to do. I got to see the old man. And later on I got to pick up a guy at the airport."

"But you're going to be all right?"

"I'll be all right. In a while."

"Look, you want me to stay with you?"

"I'll be all right. Better go up to Bel Air and hook some sugar daddies."

"If you want me to stay with you, I'll stay."

"I know. Thanks for waiting for me. I'll be all right."

"Don't look for too much, huh? You always look for too much. Save what you can. You can't ask for more'n that. The only thing you can do, you can save what you can."

"Okay, Carolyn. That's what I'll do."

"Give me a call later. I ought to be in by two or so."

She walks out and nobody turns to watch her.

Except me.

116

I drink my vodka and sit staring into the glass. I've got my mind on too many things, so I just sit and look at what's left in the glass.

The bartender comes over. "Didn't make it with the broad, huh?" he says.

"I wasn't her type."

"No great loss. She wasn't much to look at. Stick around, we'll get some better lookers in pretty soon."

"No you won't."

"Having one of those nights, huh? Want a refill?"

"I'm looking at something in the glass here."

"What's the matter? It's clean."

"You got me wrong." I hold up the glass and we both look into it. "See what's in there? Ice."

"Hey—you on downers or something?"

"The ice looks nice and hard. But you leave it alone, sitting here in the glass for a while, pretty soon it's all melted. Pretty soon it ain't so hard any more."

"You need another drink. I'll get the vodka."

"Don't bother. I feel better now. I never understand how these things work. I feel better now."

"You do, huh?"

"Ice melts. First it's hard and cold. Then it's nothing. It melts and it's nothing at all."

"Better let me get the vodka."

"No. I got things to do and people to see."

"What's the matter? You don't want to see 'em? I know the feeling."

"A minute ago I didn't want to see them. Now I do. When things're trying to get us down, we can't let them do it, right? We got to fight back."

"Sure, buddy. Whatever you say."

"You're not with me?"

"Sure, I'm with you. But I don't understand you."

"Maybe *you* need a drink."

"*I* need more customers."

I put some money on the bar.

"Thanks," he says, "but that's a little too much—unless you're buyin' another drink."

"Buying one for you, friend. On me."

"Okay. Thanks. Sure you won't join me?"

"I don't need another. Not now. I'm okay now."

"You are?"

"Yeah. I still got to go see someone, but what I'm going to do, I'm going to figure to myself I'll save what I can."

"Good luck."

"The way I'll look at it," I say, "someone lost a dream. And maybe now I can give it back to him."

278

About the Author

BRAD SOLOMON was born in Syracuse, New York, and attended Brandeis University and UCLA. His background is in teaching and the theater. He and his wife live on Long Island in New York. *The Gone Man* is his first novel.